P9-APH-492

Lilac Moon

Shelly Frome

ISBN 0-9719496-5-4

Library of Congress Control Number:
2002106910

Published by
Shangri-La Publications
#3 Coburn Hill Road
Warren Center PA
18851-0065 USA

shangrila@egypt.net
http://shangri-la.0catch.com
570-395-3423

Library of Congress Cataloging-in-Publication Data

Frome, Shelly, 1935-
Lilac moon / by Shelly Frome.
p. cm.
ISBN 0-9719496-5-4 (alk. paper)
1. Women journalists--Fiction. 2. New England--Fiction. I. Title.
PS3606.R585 L45 2002
813'.6--dc21

2002007584

For Susan
and the magic hour

ꕥ ✧ ꕥ

Barbara Allen

Trad - Child 084

'Twas in the merry month of May
When green buds all were swelling
Sweet William on his death-bed lay
For the love of Barbara Allen

He sent his servant to the town
To the place where she was dwelling
Saying, You must come to my master dear
If your name be Barbara Allen

So slowly slowly she got up
And slowly she drew nigh him
And the only words to him did say
She said, Young man, I think you're dying

He turned his face onto the wall
And death was in him welling
God bless, God bless to my friends all
Be good to Barbara Allen

When he was dead and laid in grave
She heard the death-bells knelling
And every stroke to her did say
Cold-hearted Barbara Allen

O mother o mother, go dig my grave
Make it both long and narrow
Sweet William died of love for me
And I will die of sorrow

Barbara Allen was buried in the old churchyard
Sweet William was buried beside her
Out of Sweet William's heart grew a red red rose
Out of Barbara Allen's a briar

They grew and grew in the old churchyard
Till they could grow no higher
At the end they formed a true lovers' knot
And the rose grew round the briar

Lilac Moon

by

Shelly Frome

One

The damp May wind was weaving a tangle of black clouds when Katie first screamed. Her cry was aimed at everyone and everything including God.

Slipping onto the spanning back porch of the rambling colonial, she cheered on the rain. It was fine that there was no pink twilight. Fine and fitting. At least the sky might weep a little, as if something mattered.

She started to raise her fists, but then let them drop to her side. Like everything else about her, her fists were small and ingenuous, totally non-threatening. Still and all, it was pretty brazen of her. She'd never dared yell at God before. Maybe now, at long last, He would answer. Let her know what was on his mind.

Katie cut herself off. She was in dangerous territory here. Best to run hard, run past it. Fly so fast that she would leave this grungy existence. Dash past the torments to some other zone--way beyond the meanness and confusion. And finally get a moment's peace.

But the fear that had no name crept in and became the old familiar quiver. Was God really still punishing her for the boating accident? But that was so many years ago. And good things had happened since. Yet here she was, up in the Litchfield Hills lured by the same play, the same part of Barbara Allen. Haunted by and drawn to the same old Scottish ballad.

"Good grief," Katie muttered to herself. "I must be nuts . . . caught in a stupid circle with no end."

What was it Sarah always said? 'Get a grip, Alice. Don't overload the circuit.' Yes, she would do that. Take her customary nightly jog to her summer theater and rehearse the opening scene, the moment when Barbara Allen and the Witch Boy first met. Jog and rehearse. Stick to her guns, stick to the routine and let nothing stop her.

The silver disc glinted behind the clouds for one brief second, paled, glinted again and then dissolved into the gunmetal gray of the sky. Setting out into the curtain of moist, pulsing darkness, she wished she wasn't so totally alone. She pressed on. Imperceptibly, the mist began to change to drizzle as she circled the old, weathered, red barn.

She ignored the croaks and squeals and all the sounds of spring, letting the rainwater pelt her cheeks and trickle down her face. Breaking into a lope, she continued to do her darnedest to sprint past her troubles and focus only on the task at hand. Soon smidgens of hope flickered into the corners of her mind. It would be so great to have some company--Sarah, the one person left in the world who would listen to a person even if that person was spooked and made absolutely no sense. Sarah, her old childhood chum, would have to reply to her letters, come out of the woodwork, wend her way up from the Connecticut shore and give her some overdue support. Straighten out her head so she could just live her life.

Katie picked up the pace, cutting through the dripping pods and weeds that smothered the one-time formal gardens. She telescoped her jaunt into a single record-shattering run: through the stand of vineyard stakes, past the pond, by the costume shack and the scene shop, up the wooden steps to the backstage entrance, onto the stage, into the limelight.

The squeals grew louder, more insistent, joining the mix of scudding gray sky, croaking, splattering rain and a new whisking sound darting through the laurels and sprays of lilac. She was panting now, loping harder, when the whisking sound skittered behind her and in and out of the blips of the raindrops. Traces of grapevines and wooden stakes slipped into view like a skewered trawling net. The squeals faded to a whimper.

The rain beat down harder, hissed and dribbled. The wind kicked up, sending a shiver through her ribs. If only she wasn't so petite. If only she had enough size to stand up to things and make certain people take notice.

Something long and tubular jutted out from a trellis dead ahead. She flinched, noting the glowing forked end of a divining rod pointing to a brace of sawhorses marked with red strips of cloth. To the left of the sawhorses was a dark mound. Between the mound and the sawhorses was a neat, tamped-down aisle.

Breaking into full stride, she took the aisle and dashed through. The second she hit the gap between the mound and the warning flags, she stumbled. In that same second, a hand smacked her from behind and the ground gave way. The back of her head struck first, her pelvis twisting and scraping as she spiraled down, screaming and grasping onto shards of canvas and sticks that hurled more mud and gravel on top of her, driving her lower, mixing with the well of mortar and stones that enveloped her as she slid lower still, choking her, packing her in until her fall was finally broken by a pool of stagnant water.

An airless hush filled the cavity as suddenly as her fall. She waited for the bad dream to end, for the sickening filth and pain to dissolve, for the sky to clear, for a voice to tell her to wake up. She curled up, groping for her pillow, wondering why the bed was as damp as clay. Above, the rasping bite of a shovel cut into the lull and then faded into the raw blackness.

It was an imperfect murder. Katie was not dead. She was also not alive. She was somewhere between. Something or someone had pulled her out of the well. Someone or something had sucked the dirt out of her throat. No one or nothing had eased the stabbing pain at the back of her head and the throbbing that circled her waist.

There had been flashing lights, a litter, a sensation of being strapped down and covered. There had been glimmers of green and white linen and words that filtered in and out: "... bleeding . . . fracture . . . easy, easy . . . what do you think? . . . who knows? . . ."

The words became jumbled and blended in with the drone of a motor and bumps and swerves. The drone grew louder, the bumps and pain struck at her harder and faster and a shadow figure constantly checked her eyelids and questioned her again and again. "Can you open them? . . . that's it, that's good . . . What happened? . . . how did you get there? . . . What hurts? . . . how much? . . . What's your name? . . . what's today's date? . . . who's the president? . . . " Katie's lips had moved but the sounds hadn't come out right, not like they were supposed to. She may have answered. She didn't know.

Then there was a circus of lights and noises. Shuffling feet traipsing in and out. New words were spoken: ". . . ER . . . trauma team . . . call Doctor So-and-so . . . code three . . . cranial bleed . . . go to the O.R., evacuate the fluid . . . unless it resolves or reabsorbs . . . And the pelvis? . . . Stick to the head. Why fix an axle if the motor's shot? . . . "

Blurs of blue linen with different voices, poked at her, touched her, taking turns, looking in her eyes, constantly working on her eyes. A lot more talk, a lot more touching. And someone always muttering about vital signs. Bad dialogue. Repetitive. Boring. Same stage business, same lines over and over. But she wasn't on stage.

At some time the circus cut off. What took its place was unreal, perhaps in some other world, another planet. It was made of green glass. Panels of it that sometimes slid off in the distance and to her side. It certainly wasn't earthly glass; it had no glare.

The gaggle of human sounds was replaced by beeps, whistles, bells… and an eerie hush. A few low murmurs seeped into the abyss from time to time. So did a few passing shapes and a nearby whoosh and hiss.

The closest she came to real life was a tube that seemed to have been thrust straight down her throat and had taken over her breathing. Some kind of collar clamped her neck and ropes and pulleys rose above her. Occasionally, a male or female whisper drifted down from a mile away, asking her to squeeze her hands and blink her eyes. Her arms were locked but she wasn't sure where. Just when she thought she had located them, there was a pin prick of a needle that sent her off to a darkening limbo.

Sometimes new words invaded the darkness and hung there suspended: ". . . airway . . . I.C.U. . . . EKG . . . one blown pupil . . . inappropriate response . . ." Sometimes other words came from the darkness, moved into the lull and passed back into the pitch black: ". . . move your feet . . . wiggle your toes . . . start an I.V. . . X-ray the skull . . . what did the CAT scan show? . . . will the cranial bleed reabsorb? . . ."

And sometimes in the muted stretch of space and time, the words became totally incomprehensible: ". . . mannitol . . . neuro-vascular . . . pneumo-fluid . . . nasal canula, stat . . . "

There were also periods of nothingness--no darkening and no moving shadows--in which Katie sensed that she and other creatures were lined up in identical bays, preserved for another millennium when the sun would shine, skies would turn blue and she and the other former earthlings would again become animated.

And once in a great while, when the piercing pain broke through at the back of her head and her lips quivered wildly over the tracheal tube, she cried, "Why?"

Now, bracing herself for another onslaught, sensing that all but a few creatures like herself remained, she half-wished and half-prayed. Her only hope lay hidden somewhere . If there was a forwarding address, and if the letters she wrote truly did arrive before whoever had tried to do her in slipped into this void to finish the job. If there was time, Sarah could be her sentry. Her champion. Maybe even erase the stain of guilt for something awful she must have done to deserve this. So she, Katie, could return to earth and keep looking for the spirit of the moment, even if it always had to be make believe . . .

Unless someone else would, or could, take up the gauntlet.

No, there was no one else. It was Sarah or nothing.

Two

ith the scent of salt air in her nostrils, Sarah Bucklin ambled by the pitched roof of the bed-and-breakfast where she was staying. The break in the road beckoned to her--marshes to her left, marina to her right, the rickety bridge leading to the Guilford Point dead ahead.

She glanced over at the clusters of fishing craft that clogged the inlet: weathered lobster and clam boats, bulky one-man draggers, gleaming rows of power cruisers, their tapered bows pointing toward Montauk at the easternmost tip of Long Island only thirteen miles away. It was time for yet another pointless stroll.

Soon the flagstone restaurant was behind her, as were the pike-like pilings that flanked the tiny bridge, the asphalt and marsh grass that splayed out beyond, and the hauled rocks and slabs of pink granite that kept cars from tumbling into the Sound.

A short time later, her bare legs dangling in the water, peering into the baby-blue sky, she located the reef rocks that were called Inner White Top and Outer White Top and caught a glimpse of Chatfinch Island. Straining her eyes a bit more, she half-saw and mostly imagined her escape route sweeping inextricably back to the Connecticut River and Essex--the pristine stomping grounds where she and Katie had grown up.

What was she doing? Vegetating. Adrift. Killing time. Words like that. Why couldn't she make up her mind? Either stay a features reporter and keep interviewing colorful characters or take the job as editor of the *Today's Woman* section--one or the other. At first she had put her ambivalence down to the uncertain times: the threat of terrorism in the air, on the streets, in the mail. And then there was the uncertainty about her boyfriend. But he was always saying goodbye at this time, always off doing research. Other motives came to mind but no amount of reasoning made even a dent. She was ambivalent and listless and that was that.

She had been on this vapid, coin-flipping hiatus now for three days; it was Friday morning, the eighth of May, and still the ambivalence went on. Putting the issue on hold, she continued to gaze into the shimmering span of horizon line until the now familiar, short jerky shadow fluttered behind her. She twisted slowly around and caught a glimpse of the scrunched-up face and lumberjack hands that passed for her landlady. At this point Sarah was firmly convinced that the woman was a troll.

"Excuse me, dear," said the troll, perched gingerly on the crags a few feet above Sarah's head.

Sarah mumbled, "Uh-huh," wondering about the creased manila envelopes clutched in the blotchy paws.

"Well, hon, this came for you. Hand delivered you might say. But he was disappointed that he'd missed you." As usual the blinking nearsighted eyes were straining for bits of unusual news she could spread about the harbor. Any little indiscretion would do.

"Uh-huh," Sarah mumbled again, waiting for the kicker.

"It was only an hour or so ago. And when I saw you flit by the house without a glance back, I thought I'd better--" The troll paused, the pouches in her face working away as if she were reciting and had forgotten her lines. "He had gray hair, the neatest pin-stripe suit you ever saw . . . crisp lapels, shiny shoes and very polite speech."

"Dad."

"Come again?"

"Never mind." Sarah could picture the whole scenario--her resourceful banker father barging into her apartment building next to the Yale Co-op, leafing through the pile of mail in, around and under her box, assuming she'd been keeping company with her latest or God knows who, then coming across the receipt from the troll and voila! This was the price of not checking in with your folks at least once a week.

"Of course if you're in hiding, dear, and don't want this mail . . ."

Before the troll could continue her fishing expedition, Sarah scrambled up the slabs of granite and snatched the envelopes. The mail was postmarked six days ago, four days ago and two days ago from Lakeville. It came from Katie.

"Okay, Katie pooh," Sarah muttered to herself, "what's up?"

Still straining and blinking her eyes, the troll grew anxious as Sarah sorted through the contents. "Well?" said the troll. "Bad news? How much longer will you be staying with us, I mean?"

"Like I told you, I'll let you know."

The troll opened her beady little eyes even wider and spread her bow legs on the craggy rocks to gain greater purchase.

"All right?" Sarah said. "Okay?"

"Shortly?"

"Shortly. You bet. Uh-huh." Sarah was mumbling by rote now. She riffled through pamphlets on the history of Katie's mythical Waybury, the summer theater, a dog-eared real estate brochure, and three cryptic letters. The syntax was so unlike Katie's usual musings and daydreams that Sarah didn't hear the troll commenting on Sarah's sensible cotton top and casual denim slacks that went with her sensible, casual attitude. She also didn't hear the final sigh of resignation or catch the troll's shuffling gait as she headed back toward the connecting bridge and the dock.

The first letter was a jumble, something about her stepbrother Russell dropping in out of nowhere with his "guilt machine," bringing up the old so-called association between the play Katie was fixated on and "Mom and Dad's drowning." The letter ended with a plea for some kind of reassurance.

The second letter started on the same note and indicated that things were getting worse:

Okay, you're on secret assignment, have gone incognito and can't check your phone or e- mail messages. Fine. Just fax me a reply and we'll call it quits. In your newspaper lingo, this is the story of Katie, and by extension Sarah, because Sarah pushed it until Katie finally went back to deal. However, somebody swipes her keys and check book plus things like the theater road has now been made impassable and Tommy, the total non-threat brand new hubby, getting murky on me are happening.

Get the picture? Katie, you're a victim of wrong thinking and misinformation, you used to say. Well guess what? That's right, you got it. Right thinking and right information

are unavailable. Wasn't there an old movie about driving a gullible, child-woman bonkers to get her out of the way?

Got your attention now? Call me with a sharp reporter's slant. I need a friend.

That means you.

Katie

Still not comprehending what exactly was going on, Sarah scanned the final letter and paused at the last two paragraphs:

Now it's clear over the edge. Arthur was poisoned, I know it. Arthur, my wedding present from you, my puppy St. Bernard. But the veterinarian, Dr. Dudley, says—never mind. The point is, nobody or nothing will back me up. And I've been so crazy mad at everybody. Just a few minutes ago, to make it even worse, just as I'm passing the overhang of the barn . . . Oh forget it. It's too disgusting. And good ol' stepbrother Russell keeps hinting that I brought it all on myself. Like before. Well I couldn't live with that.

What would it take to get you up here? That's right, I'm calling in my marker. I need something. If nothing else, that Oh-give-me-a-break, will you? attitude would really help a lot around about now. I mean, I am really starting to lose it.

Katie

P.S. I just reread this note. I sound hysterical. If nothing else give me a call and tell me to get some therapy. Okay?

Mulling all of this over, Sarah covered the distance from the cove and the bed and breakfast in quick time. Her thought pattern followed suit. The puppy? Somebody poisoned that cuddly gift Sarah had put her heart and soul into? The last time on record that Sarah had put her heart and soul into anything.

Moving into the tiny hallway of the saltbox cottage, still deep in thought, she bumped into the troll.

"Oh dear," said the troll, hopping to one side.

"Sorry," said Sarah, scurrying past her up the carpeted stairs.

"Wait a second, hon."

Sarah paused at the landing and glanced down. "Yes?"

"Well, my dear, you did say . . . "

"What?"

"About leaving. You see I have this young couple from Cheshire and if you are departing today or thereabouts . . . I mean, I would really appreciate it, if it's not too much trouble that is, if you would be more definite."

"Do you mind? Give me a minute, will you?"

Sarah paused. She had been short with the troll. She didn't usually act that way with strangers. Or with anyone, matter of fact. She usually took it all in stride, amused at everyone and their foibles. She was no longer amused.

"Sorry," said Sarah glancing back over her shoulder. Undaunted, the troll kept staring up at her with the same scrunched-up smile, wringing her oversized hands.

"Just have to make a few calls," Sarah added, unlocking her door at the top of the landing, barging in and slapping the mail onto the quilted comforter that encased the queen sized bed. The sunlight etched Sarah's shadow on the white paneled wall, reminding her of Katie's pronouncement long ago. "Listen, Sarah, just 'cause a person has a roundish face and kind'a wide hips, doesn't mean that person isn't a winner in all other departments and another person's best friend." Reaching for the phone, Sarah mumbled, "Some winner. Some best friend."

Sarah hesitated. She'd forgotten what Katie's married name was. In typical Katie fashion, there was no return address on the envelopes. A call to the Waybury Playhouse produced nothing. No answer. The clerk at the town hall, however, did manage to come up with the fact that a Thomas and Kathleen Haddam had recently been included on the grand list. The clerk started to go on about something but Sarah cut her off. The information operator revealed that at the customer's request, the phone number was now unlisted.

A call back to the town clerk eked out some reluctant hearsay. "Not sure, mind you," the dry crackly voice said, "none of my business. But if you're a friend . . ."

"Yes?"

"It's just that we haven't heard from her and rumor has it--but I could be wrong. She said she would come in Monday and make arrangements about her taxes. Today is Friday, you see."

"Wait a second," Sarah said. The dry crackly voice was chattering so fast that Sarah was having trouble following her. "What aren't you sure of? What rumor?"

"I beg your pardon?"

"The thing you're not sure of."

"Oh, you mean the accident."

"What accident?"

"I said I wasn't sure."

"Is she all right?"

"Don't know that either."

"Where is she?"

There was a pause as the clerk was either catching her breath or trying to remember. "Sharon," the clerk finally said.

"Sharon?"

"Where the hospital is located . . . Well, I'd better hang up. It's strictly business--the taxes, that is... small tiny hamlet like this... summer people flitting in and out. What can you do?"

A call to the hospital made things worse. No, the person at the desk said, the hospital can't give out that information. Interested parties have to get in touch with the family. Yes, if her condition was stable, the hospital could acknowledge it. No, if a caller was not a member of the family, the caller could not be switched to the nurses' station.

Sarah should have lied. That's why she had been relegated to features. She was good with amenable people but lousy at hard news and tactics. Rehashing her failed hospital call in her mind, she flinched as the phone jangled, recovered and snatched up the receiver after the third ring.

"Sarah?" said the affected voice that belonged to her mother. "What is the meaning of this?"

"Oh great," Sarah said, trying to think of some way to cut her mother short without hurting her feelings.

"Yes, isn't it?" Mother went on. "The real question is, how is it possible that one's own daughter breaks off contact, is actually only a scant thirty minutes away and--"

"Oh come on, Mother, please?"

"Well, pardon me."

"I'm a little pressed, okay? It's about Katie."

"Katie--now there's another case in point. She called here about six times asking for you. You couple that with shunning your parents and you have to conclude something is remiss."

"Mother," Sarah said, "for your information, for the three-millionth time, I don't shun you. Second of all, I had no idea about Katie, and third of all, the last thing I need right now is your patronizing tone."

There was a long pause. Finally Mother said, "You are being curt and rude."

"I know."

"Very curt and very rude."

"Yes."

"Which must mean you're upset or on some difficult assignment, engaged in some activity much more important than us."

"I'm not working at the moment."

"Don't tell me that. Hot and cold, Sarah, that's how you run. Let's finally face it."

"Let's not. Let's call time out and get off the line."

"I am trying, Sarah. Are you?"

"No."

"Precisely."

Sarah tried placating her but it did no good. She asked her Mom to give her the benefit of the doubt, hung up on the next series of clipped consonants and sighs and left the receiver off its cradle.

Second thoughts. If she had gotten in touch with ever-disappointed Mom, she would have connected with Katie. And if she had connected, maybe she could have intervened. Battling the second thoughts and sudden hunger pangs, Sarah's brain continued to rev. Who would deny a perky thirty-something a chance to try her hand and finally get a life? Who would kill her puppy and wish her harm?

No answer came to mind. Not a clue.

Sarah hurried down the narrow flight of stairs, flitted into the tiny kitchen and plucked one of her peaches out of the refrigerator. One of these days one of these diets would do her in. She no sooner bit into the pulp, the juice running down her chin, when the troll reappeared.

"Well?" the scrunched-up face inquired, the mannish hands lathering an invisible bar of soap. "What's the verdict, dear? Staying or leaving?"

"Leaving," Sarah said, taking another juicy bite. "Definitely leaving."

The troll chuckled and skipped out of view.

Three

Taking Route 9 north, Sarah thought of turning off to Essex: the easy-way-out with its perfectly measured white picket fences outlining its perfectly appointed sea-captains' homes. Totally reassuring--the flower boxes just so, each sailing vessel anchored in its designated slot on the Connecticut River, streets going only one way to avoid any unpleasant friction, every shop positioned according to scale, every resident and tourist knowing his or her place; the Griswold Inn, in turn, fulfilling every visitor's dream of a quaint nautical hostelry and tavern. And high on a little knoll winding down to the square's cobblestone streets lay Sarah's sparkling white saltbox home-sweet-home with its essential matching shutters and glazed front door.

In less than five minutes, she could slip into the driveway, sink into the white leather sofa and listen to her Dad telling her that anything would make more sense than racing her beat-up Honda Accord into some remote section of the state to consider yet another one of Katie's follies. Sarah could simply send flowers and attach a note. No other action was warranted or prescribed.

Almost immediately, a childhood memory crossed Sarah's mind. The first image: two closed caskets. The second: a painted angel high up on a stained glass window. The figure appeared to be far above it all, gazing off and away from the bodies of Katie's drowned parents. Like the figure, Sarah shed no tears. Instead, she made a vow that she too would keep her distance and do her level best to stay out of deep water.

In contrast, Katie kept skirting the edge. Constantly humming the Joan Baez rendition of the ballad of Barbara Allen. Claiming that any person who stood on the sidelines, who didn't reach out and take some risks had no real blood flowing through their veins.

Sarah passed the Essex exit, gunned the motor and skewered into the fast lane, headed north toward the Middletown exchange. It was now three-thirty p.m.

Had she, Sarah, really remained detached all these years? Yes, pretty much if you thought about it. Always the counterfeit sailor, testing the shoals, bars and reefs but just barely; and always within sight of land, ready to beach the boat and cut her losses. Even now, she was going into a hospital, sure, and she might have to look a little pain and suffering in the eye. But, at the same time, she was taking yet another hiatus within the span of a few days. Deflecting. Drifting off course.

Veering back into the slow lane, she loosened her grip on the wheel and came to terms. She would look into Katie's predicament and take it from there. As for her career move, she would put it on the back burner for the time being: End of discussion.

To put her mind to more productive use, she mentally catalogued and sifted through the material in Katie's pamphlets. After a time she formed a thumbnail sketch of the backwater Katie felt compelled to return to in order to break the spell.

Waybury was a ghost town with a distinct past and no future. Situated high up in the northwest section of the state, it once boasted an endless supply of ore and the Great Falls, flourishing gristmills, sawmills, and foundries--the blast furnace supplying chains and anchors for Old Ironsides. But after the Berkshire Power Plant came along and damned the Housatonic, the Great Falls and Waybury went bone dry.

Except for the playhouse. Built in the late thirties, relying on the train from New York and the tourist trade trickling down from Tanglewood and the nearby resorts, it featured slick summer fare with the usual famous-name attractions. But that was all in the past. Katie's pipe dreams notwithstanding,

Waybury was now but a memory. The resorts had long since closed down, the train service was nonexistent, and a fledgling summer stock company was bound to lose its shirt.

So why not give Katie enough rope and let the enterprise die of natural causes? Why go to all the trouble of tormenting her and do God knows what that landed her in intensive care? … unless the whole thing was a sham. And what had happened was just as the hospital intimated: an accident; the result of chance and the way things go when you don't watch your step.

No way, thought Sarah. We're talking about Katie. Lithe and limber. Dancer material. As agile as they come.

Three hours after she'd left Guilford the terrain began to climb, adding to Sarah's impressions of this little corner of the world. The sky was choked off by narrow buckling roads, hemmed in by stands of maples. Past Mohawk Mountain, the maples were joined by cathedral pines, the ragged thick trunks of the maples rising thirty feet until overcome by the straining, spindly pines which rose hundreds of feet higher until they finally touched daylight with their crowns of spiky green.

Approaching Cornwall, the Litchfield Hills began to prevail, stretching out like a clan of sleeping giants, some with enormous bellies and mammoth jutting chins; others with sharp knees jerking up, cordoning off the rolling road. When the Hills surged even higher and the maples and pines resumed their pitched battle, it was obvious why Katie's stepbrother Russell had parked himself on Katie's lawn. He had found new raw territory, a perfect linchpin for his mellow-preacher long-suffering medicine show. In some backwater, away from those who were highly informed and responsive to breaking news and the day's events.

Sarah cut off this line of thought. Fabricating tales about stepbrother Russell was getting way ahead of the story and a total waste of time. Overloading the circuit.

It was twenty after six when Sarah geared-down, approaching the relief from the agitated terrain that was Sharon, Connecticut. Green rolling lawns dotted with lazy spreading white oaks fronted the spacious colonials that lay hidden along the relatively flat main street. The sky was now faded and inky, the air a bit cool. No one was out walking, a few cars tooled by amid the long shadows.

She parked on a green verge, stretched her aching calves, slipped on a pair of moccasins and then looked around for some passerby who might give her directions. Presently, a white-haired lady, driving ever so slowly in her beige Mercedes, came to an easy stop and, with a casual flourish of her index finger, pointed Sarah two blocks north and one meandering block to the left.

A minute or so later, Sarah pulled into the visitors' parking area and was slightly thrown off guard. Hospitals were supposed to jut out or up, like Yale-New Haven, not contract into a cluster of white cubes, slots and rectangles with dwarf ceilings. At any rate, this was it: her immediate destination. She would see it for what it was and take it from there.

Inside the white brick structure were more cubes and rectangles. The woman at the desk nonchalantly guided Sarah down a narrow corridor to the I.C.U. It was all so casual, unlike the grief Sarah had been given over the phone. The receptionist didn't even ask who Sarah was.

Moments later Sarah slipped into a silent, motionless vacuum. Two lifeless forms lay in a series of bays to her left. A nurse's station stood to the right behind a sliding glass window, men in white coats scribbled noiselessly on clipboards beyond. The light was a pastel green; there were no odors, no murmurs or conversations. The only sounds were muffled beeps, blips and drones. No one questioned Sarah's presence; no one even noticed that she was there.

Padding in a bit further, Sarah noticed something definitely out of place. The slim figure was of medium height, a long shank of coarse brown hair fell over the collar of his rumpled denim jacket. His face was gaunt, his eyes pale and sunken. In the half-light he had the look of those super-sensitive young men who are always cast as Jesus or the rookie cop who has no idea of the corruption that awaits him on the mean streets of New York.

The thin wrist and tapered fingers inched forward. In that same moment, Sarah recognized the broken-doll figure with the pixie face. Her eyes were closed, her tiny stomach barely rising and falling.

The second the tapered fingers touched the tube that was running into Katie's body, Sarah half-whispered half-shouted, "Hey." The "Hey" cut through the silence. The lanky form pivoted and whisked by her, throwing her off balance, generating another half-whisper half-shout.

She hurried back into the corridor. As the figure dissolved into the whiteness, Sarah's memory bank clicked-in and came up with the answer. This was Kevin, the one who had played Jimmy in *The Rainmaker* in Katie's shoreline production just a few months back--the guy who had slipped on and off stage like a wary lynx. The one who kept eyeing Katie, not like the goofy kid brother from the play but more like a lovesick teen.

After a few more furtive glances here and there, she gave up the chase. She turned back just in time to meet the oval face that went with the square shoulders and white uniform.

"Sorry," Sarah said to the nurse. "About raising my voice back there, I mean."

"Look," the nurse said, "relatives are nice. And rescuers are too. In their place, under the proper restrictions."

"Uh-huh."

"This is an I.C.U. Surely you realize that."

"Sure . . . of course." Sarah looked down and away, feeling like a kid who had just been caught running down the hall in the second grade.

"Well I trust you will compose yourself ."

"You bet. Whoa, hold on," said Sarah, traipsing after the retreating square shape. "Fill me in, will you? I'm her best friend."

"Friend?" said the nurse, swiveling on her white heels. The plastic badge with the colored snapshot declared that this was the patient care manager, Pat Reed.

"Look, can we cut the tap dance? Do you mind?"

The square face bristled, the full lips hardened.

"I'm sorry," Sarah said. "Once again, I'm sorry. It's just that I've gotten these letters, tried calling, raced up here, and the first thing I see is this guy Kevin reaching over her. So naturally I had to react."

The square face tightened even harder.

"Sorry," Sarah said for the sixth time. "Forget that. You see, when you used the word 'rescuer'--look, humor me, okay? I know I sound a little rattled but--"

Rolling her eyes, Sarah made another stab at it. "If you would try to believe that there's a lot of concern here and I'm usually very articulate, we can get through this in a flash. Please?"

The square face softened, paused for moment and finally said, "The EMS coordinator called him that. 'Her rescuer', he said."

"EMS?"

"Emergency Medical Service. It seems this Kevin fellow dug her out of her predicament."

"Dug her out?"

"Listen, you'll have to excuse me. I was starting my break and only came over to apprize you of the rules."

Pat Reed spelled out the strict procedures. Then, as an afterthought or moment of weakness, she hastily divulged that Katie had fallen into a cistern the other night in the pouring rain. Shortly thereafter--owing to Kevin's intervention--the paramedics had arrived, kept Katie's condition from deteriorating and rushed her to the E.R.

"What are her chances?"

"Touch and go, especially with the cranial bleed. We're monitoring. Doing our best to keep her alive."

"Can you operate?"

"Not with a cranial bleed."

A long pause and then Sarah added, "Can I just stand beside her bed? Very quietly?"

After a longer pause Pat Reed said, "Just for a moment."

"Thanks."

"No talk. No agitating gestures. No disturbance."

"Absolutely."

"All right then." Pat Reed strode away like a drill sergeant who had, at long last, gotten the last raw recruit in line.

Sarah tiptoed over and braced herself. There would be no flinching. No staring at the tubes running into Katie's body, no glances at the apparatus inserted down her throat. No reaction to the bleeps, clicks, hisses and whistles. And especially no sniveling at the sight of Katie's bruised little arms strapped to her side.

For an instant Katie's eyes fluttered, her left hand reached for something that wasn't there. Her lips seemed to form the words "Sarah?" and "Have you come to . . . ?" It was impossible to be sure. In that same second, the frail left hand found Sarah's fingers and squeezed hard.

In response, Sarah squeezed back. Tears welled-up in her eyes and she felt the catch in her throat. But it was okay. The silence hadn't been broken. Nothing had jarred whatever thread Katie was hanging by.

Squeezing back was a promise. It didn't spell out exactly what Sarah would do or how far she would go. But it was binding all the same.

Four

y the time Sarah had checked into a motel in Lakeville, it was seven-thirty and pitch dark. She was bone tired and ravenous once again.

She had chosen Lakeville because it was exactly halfway between the hospital and Waybury: back to Katie in case there was any threat of someone trying to finish the job; up to Waybury to make sure that the police were actively zeroing in on the perpetrator.

On the other hand, common sense told her that she was letting Katie's letters get the best of her. There was no evidence that warranted suspicion of foul play as they say in the movies. Just the fact that Katie was in critical condition and, thanks to the pseudo-actor sometimes-set-painter Kevin, she had been rescued from a near-fatal fall. That was it as far as Sarah knew. That was all. Let it ride for now, she told herself. Keep playing it as it lays.

Sarah winced as she glanced at her image in the bathroom mirror. There were bags under her eyes. Her no-nonsense bobbed hairdo was limp and frayed, matching her naïve behavior at the hospital. Even after showering and donning one of her business outfits--navy blue blazer, man-tailored blouse, matching long skirt, thick reading glasses—-her image hadn't improved. She now probably came across like a bank examiner who had spent too many nights going over the books or a jaded agent for the I.R.S. And, at the same time, someone who was out of her league. But what difference did it make? Her appearance at this moment was beside the point. She left the motel room and slipped back behind the wheel.

The drive took her out of Lakeville, rolling higher, confronted once more by the surging timber. This time, in the web of darkness, the battle was being waged by the hardwoods against the softwoods: beach maple and oak going against pines and basswood on both sides of the road, hovering and tangling in the balmy stillness. Her only goal was to get a bite to eat at the inn in Waybury, which she learned was still serving till nine, get a closer glimpse of the lay of the land, return to the motel and sleep.

After twenty minutes of holding her own with the shadowy ribbon of road, she came to a blue sign embossed with white letters. Under the glare of her headlights the weathered marker declared that a sawmill and gristmill had been erected in this vicinity in 1741, an ironworks in 1743, and a fulling mill in 1747. Nothing else was noted. 1747 apparently was Waybury's last year of any note.

Cruising into the deserted village, it was easy to see why the marker and the hamlet were dissipating. It was as if a hodgepodge of architectural shapes had been randomly strewn across one long block and allowed to tumble around the corner. Then, due to lack of interest, the project had been abandoned. The scattering began with the library, a Queen Anne style dusty brick gingerbread house, and continued across the way with a squashed white structure fronted by a belfry and steeple butting against a squat little hall with columns and a lopsided peaked roof. Further down, back on the left side, lay a brace of four-story towers made of crumbling gray shingles, their cathedral windows all boarded up. At the far corner, a series of buckling steps led up to a flat building crowned by three rounded gables. In the center section the words "Town Hall" floated above the cornice. Sarah surmised that the constable, or whatever he was, would be stationed here. She made a mental note. Tomorrow, first order of business.

Turning left past the hall, she spotted the inn. One more random design--Italianesque with a flat roof and square sides. It was constructed of clapboard, painted yellow and featured a long sagging front porch enveloped by a wooden railing. Green shutters were tacked on here and there as an afterthought.

Diagonally across the street was a junkyard of rotting cars from the thirties and forties. Butting against the wrecks stood a low brick garage christened "Benjamin's." Between the wrecks and the sign, a scrawny girl in a white T-shirt was pulling a second T-shirt over her rumpled jeans as Sarah was doing a U-turn. The T-shirt asked "My Place or Yours?" in Day-Glo red.

Pulling in front of the inn, the garage directly behind her, Sarah wondered about the village's actual population. In the brochure Katie had sent, there were supposed to be "800 thriving residents." From where Sarah stood, the center contained at most a handful; the outskirts possibly a hundred or so more, plus an iffy number of tourists who might happen to drop in between Memorial and Labor Day. What threat could the opening of a playhouse pose to anyone in this ghost town? Why did the person or persons unknown go to all this trouble?

What trouble? countered Sarah's better half, realizing that unfounded assumptions were seeping back into her weary brain.

Before Sarah could climb the warped front steps of the inn, the scrawny girl in the T-shirt was on top of her.

"Hi, I'm Alice. What's your game? What do you do?"

"Later, okay? Some other time."

The nasty retort surprised Sarah as much as it did Alice. "Sorry," Sarah said. "Been a long day." At last count, this was the tenth time she'd said "sorry" in the past three hours. Surely a personal record.

"Long day, sure," said Alice. "Gonna eat, right? Head into the lobby, make a sharp left and there you are. Can't miss it. It's all full of glass, like a greenhouse."

Sarah followed Alice's directions with Alice hard on her heels. Presently, she was seated by a youngish waitress with straw-like hair sprouting in three directions. Sarah ordered filet of sole, the only non-lethal item on the menu, and found herself confronted by Alice's glistening black eyes. There were no other diners. It was just Sarah, Alice directly across from her, and twelve empty sets of white tablecloths, maroon place settings and ice cream parlor chairs.

Gazing past Alice's constant stare, Sarah noted the wicker baskets hovering overhead stuffed with artificial blue and red petunias. She also noted the wall of tiny rectangular panes of glass set in twelve-over-twelve panels running the length of the long side porch. She was indeed in another world.

"That country western music you hear is from the bar," Alice said, trying to draw Sarah's attention back. "It's on the other side of the lobby down back. Doreen is tendin' it. Want me to get her to get you a drink?"

"No thanks." At this point, all Sarah wanted was to wolf down some food and collapse.

"So why are you here and when are you goin'?"

"That's cute, kid. I take it back about being sorry."

"Or are you just visitin'? And if so, who?"

"Look, don't you have something to do?"

"No way. A girl's got to protect her territory. Besides, tomorrow is Saturday."

"No school."

"You got it. So, as I was sayin', nobody new comes in unless it's about that stupid summer theater. Well, it's not exactly stupid if we're talkin' about Kevin. But if we're talkin' about that producer-actress or whatchamacallit, and you're here to not leave well enough alone. What I mean is, I got a right to know just what exactly is goin' on?"

The words kept spurting out of Alice's mouth, forming incoherent sentences spinning off from one fuzzy topic to another. Except for the mention of Kevin, and Sarah's recent memory of his slight frame hovering over Katie in the ICU.

"So, how about it?" Alice said, her little beady eyes squinting. "Just the cards on the table. Before Benjamin, my sleaze of a dad busts in, that is. I mean, I got enough on my mind, you know?"

On the one hand, Sarah wanted the girl to get permanently lost. On the other, Sarah was getting curious about what vague tie Alice had with Katie and what she meant by "Are you here to not leave well enough alone?"

"So?" Alice pressed on. "Another fact is, nobody comes here after nine except to drink. So, since you're not drinkin', you must be up to somethin'."

"Do you always spout off like this to a total stranger?"

"No. It's the hormones, which you must know, if it's any of your business. My body changin' and all. And when you're dealin' with an older dude and you do stuff and you got absolutely nobody to talk to. I mean, what can you expect?"

"Do stuff?" Sarah said, nibbling on the bland dish of seafood and rice which had just slid unobtrusively onto her place setting.

"Hey, man, who's askin' the questions here? All I wanna know is your angle."

"Because of Kevin?," Sarah said almost absentmindedly as she made short work of the entrée.

"Yeah, if you must know. He keeps hittin' on me while I help him with his lines. With the witch play, I mean.

"'Dark of the Moon'?"

"You got it. Jeez, I didn't know anybody ever heard of it, it's so old. Must have been written before anybody was born. Anyways, what I'm saying is, I got a whatchamacallit."

Sarah looked up from her plate. "Vested interest? Investment?"

"Yeah."

All of a sudden Alice clammed up, as if realizing she had almost tipped her hand. Lowering her eyes, trying to look nonchalant, she tried her level best to slow her delivery down to about thirty-three-and-a-third R.P.M.'s. "So what do you do? Are you connected with that Katie or Kevin or what?"

"Katie."

"Oh yeah?" Alice looked around, pursed her almost non-existent lips and then planted her bony elbows squarely on the table. "Well I'm not sorry. Not sorry one bit. She uses her little girl act to turn guys on. Which causes a whatchamacallit--love triangle and stuff. But never mind. What do you do, man, and, like I'm gettin' tired of askin' what you're after."

Sarah sipped her mineral water, still not knowing what to make of this. Shivering a bit as the clammy air seeped through the panes of glass, Sarah reminded herself that she was in the presence of a hyper kid, twelve going on thirteen from the looks of her.

As Alice kept it up, intermittently prodding Sarah and blurting out imagined assaults to her puberty, Sarah heard the voices of distant editors: "where did you get this? . . . if you can't corroborate it, don't waste my time . . . you're useless without a bullshit detector . . ." Sarah tore into a an orange slice and told herself to take anything this kid said with the proverbial grain of salt.

"Hey," Alice said, pushing her sliver of a face forward. "Are you listenin' to me?"

"What? . . . Oh, sure."

Sipping the last of her mineral water as Alice went into the story of the girl who had just been molested in the Pennsylvania woods, Sarah practiced being a sieve, letting the drivel pass through her, only half-listening to keep herself awake. Occasionally, however, curiosity crept back in and little probes sputtered out of Sarah's drowsy lips.

"Tell me," Sarah cut in, "what do you really know about Katie?"

"I knew you weren't listenin'. I knew it. And you still ain't leveled with me."

"Have you been hanging around her house, is that it?"

"No."

"The playhouse?"

"Just when when ol' Benjamin did the wirin' and stuff."

"Benjamin?"

"My ol' man."

"But why do you call him--?

"To get his goat, to drive him up a tree." Alice pulled her elbows off the tablecloth and sat up ramrod straight. "Say, what are you tryin' to pull?"

"The wiring, you say? You were at the playhouse when--"

"Benjamin--the garage in back of your head—when he was . . . Hey, who cares? What's this got to do with my sex life? I don't get you, man. First you snap, then you fade, then you start in on the playhouse and ol' sweetie pie Katie. I don't wanna talk about her."

"Then why did you bring it up?"

Alice began to squirm, twisting a knot of her scraggy hair, pulling the clip in and out of her ponytail. "What is this? She send you to tell me to lay off Kevin? And now you're pissed 'cause it's too late. 'Cause she has had it."

"Drop it," Sarah said, doing all she could to keep from throttling her.

"Tell me," said Alice, leaping up, her skeleton frame breaking into a spastic dance. "How's she doin'? Is the playhouse gonna run or not? Is Kevin gonna stay?"

Before Alice could press on, a beefy figure lumbered into the room, jostling two tables, jerking Alice away like a twig. "What did I tell you, huh? Huh?"

"It's okay," Sarah said, rising. "We were just getting acquainted."

"I'll bet."

"Besides, tomorrow's Saturday," said Alice, rubbing her arm.

"Quiet, you," said the man who was obviously ol' Benjamin, Alice's father. "It's too late for you to be hanging out as you damn well know, and I never want you botherin' nobody, as I told you over and over."

"I wasn't bothering. We was just talkin'. Woman stuff and all. I mean, since Mom split, whudduyou expect?"

Crinkling up his red forehead, Benjamin glared at Alice. Alice cowered. "Get your butt outta here, please," Benjamin said, the words rasping from somewhere in the back of his throat.

Alice glanced back at Sarah, started to leave and then looked back again. "Next time we talk fair. Tit for tat." Another slow burn from Benjamin and Alice was gone.

"Gotta sit on her," Benjamin said, forcing a strained smile. "She's like a fox terrier. You give her an inch and she lights out for whatever catches her eye."

To cover an awkward pause, Benjamin swiped his sweaty face with the back of his hand and hollered back in the direction of the bar, "Ain't that right, Doreen? Ain't that Alice to a T?" Swiveling his thick neck back in Sarah's direction, Benjamin nodded, answering his own question, made his apologies again and barged out of the glassy porch as quickly as he had barreled in.

As the waitress cleared the table, the object of Benjamin's bellow slipped into view. Doreen was a sight. Her wrinkled face was framed by dyed black hair, chopped short with bangs and triangular sideburns. Huge gold starfish earrings were clipped to her pointy ears; a thick puff of white cotton taped onto her left eye. Her metallic blue sack dress clung to every bulge in her body, front and rear. Sarah felt sorry for her, even as the waitress whispered in Sarah's ear to pay her no mind. It seems Doreen had been on the sauce again and smacked her eyeball stepping on a rake.

"Couldn't help but overhear," Doreen said, focusing her good eye, moving toward Sarah, parking a few inches in front of her table. "You and Alice, I mean. Only snatches mind, but I figured I better give you the skinny on her. In case, by some mistake, she got hold of your ear."

Doreen cocked her head and beckoned Sarah to step into the dark-paneled lobby. Sarah shrugged, left a tip and followed her in.

Leaning against the chipped mahogany counter of the front desk, Doreen cocked her head again, this time in the direction of Benjamin's garage across the street. Ignoring the shouts for service that came from the back room, Doreen nodded her lacquered head and said, "You are just passin' through, right?"

"Is this how you always greet strangers? You and Alice?"

"Come again, hon?"

"Intercept them and pry into their personal affairs."

Doreen grew quiet, obviously thinking it over. She smiled, hummed an obscure little tune and then started in again as nonchalant as she could be. "Now about Alice . . ."

"Some other time. Okay?"

"Needs a mother is all I was gonna say. She's at that stage, know what I mean? And everything she says should be--"

"I get it. I got it, I know."

"Feisty, huh? I like that."

"Sometimes. Right now, mostly just tired."

Doreen looked down at the frayed maroon rug, then up at the flaked ceiling, then circled behind the mahogany counter. "Let's you and me start over. Just shoot the breeze, okay?"

"Look, is there something else on your mind? Otherwise ..."

Doreen didn't answer. Fishing out a mug and a flask, she sloughed it all off with the old "medicine for my cold" ploy, hummed another tune and then muttered, "Summer theaters . . . vineyards . . . give me a break. Don't know piddle about pruning back in winter . . . knock the darn fruit buds off, needs a whole new trellis system anyways . . . "

"Look, lady--"

"Doreen, hon. Just make it Doreen."

Draining the contents of her mug, Doreen broke into a forced grin and circled back to Sarah's side. "I do that sometimes. Mumble about nothin'. Ask questions about nothin' at all. Just love a new face."

"Right. If you'll excuse me . . ."

"Ah, on your way back then?"

"To the motel."

"Oh." Doreen fingered her chopped bangs and peered back up to the flaked ceiling with her good eye. "Got some further plans?"

"Not tonight."

"Hold your business close to the vest, huh? Well, let's just say you didn't drive all the way up here just to hang out."

"That's right. I hold my business close to the vest."

"Sure . . . sure. Just wonderin' is all. In case somethin' comes up."

"Tell you what. You draw me directions to Katie's house. In return, I'll admit that Katie's my friend. Then we can end this tap dance. Deal?"

"Katie's house?"

"Estate, whatever."

"What for?"

"General information."

The glazed eye flicked up to the ceiling yet again. In the interim, Sarah had a half-formed notion of checking in with Russell, the evangelical stepbrother. At least he was someone Sarah knew, someone Katie had mentioned in her letters. And then, of course, there was Tommy the bridegroom; the one Sarah had met a few weeks ago at the wedding in Westport -- pleasant, nondescript Tommy, who had never worked a day in his life. He too was doubtless on the estate. Sarah very well might want to confer with either or both: after first touching base with the town constable.

These were thoughts, very drowsy thoughts. If nothing else, they helped counterbalance the quirky static inflicted by Alice and Doreen.

Grunting, Doreen plucked out a pen and scrawled away on the inn stationary. Handing Sarah the cursory map, she winked and lowered her voice as if divulging some secret information. “Place has gone to seed. Nothin’ to see, if that’s your pleasure.”

“Thanks,” said Sarah, easing out past one of the heavy paneled front doors.

“You bet,” Doreen said, scurrying down the steps after her. “Use me or sell me short. Your loss or your gain.”

“Gotcha.”

“You’ll see, you’ll see. By the way, how’s she doin’? You seen her?”

Sarah nodded, averting the bulging eye and lumpy body, and slid behind the wheel.

“What shape would you say she was in?”

“Who?” Sarah said, gunning the motor.

“Cute,” Doreen hollered over the revving idle. “Real cute.”

The last thing Sarah saw as she backed out was Doreen’s fluttering purple fingernails. “Any time, hon,” Doreen called out, cupping her hands. “I’ll be here.”

Sarah shook her head. It seemed that everywhere you went there was always a Doreen. In Stony Creek she called herself Tugboat Annie, took tourists for a cruise around the Thimble Islands and recounted scandals about the inhabitants. And there was Faye at the beauty shop in Branford; New Haven Rachel, who strolled up and down Elm and Chapel, offering you anything illicit your heart desired; and Eunice who ran the hot dog stand and astrology booth on Hammonasset Beach--spinsters all with juicy tales to tell, always looking for ways to jazz up their empty lives.

Casting thoughts of the Doreens of this world aside, Sarah headed back up the winding black-timbered road, seeking the clarity of the Lakeville streetlamps and a clean, quiet place to rest her overworked brain.

Fifteen minutes later, she pulled into her parking slot at the motel and modified her sleep allotment. She was no longer on a break mulling over her quasi career. Somehow or other--even though it may not make much sense--she now had a life on her hands.

Five

arah was up at the crack of dawn. It was Saturday, May 8th. The light filtering through the motel blinds told her it was going to be a clear crisp day. The imagined voice of her features editor burbling in her brain told her that she had until tomorrow to decide about running the *Today's Woman* section or remaining on the same old stand. The bubbly voice quickly faded, replaced by thoughts of the most expedient agenda on Katie's behalf.

A cup of black coffee and some juice in the nearby diner at seven-fifteen didn't help. Sarah still wasn't sure where to begin. A quick check with the bleary-eyed girl mopping the diner counter had dispelled one assumption. There was no constable in Waybury who would be up and about by eight. In point of fact, there was no constable in Waybury, no state trooper, only a go-between: First Selectman Will Gibble, formerly of the state barracks in Canaan. He would saunter into the town hall no earlier than nine-thirty.

After a second glass of reconstituted grapefruit juice, Sarah turned again to the bleary-eyed girl and said, "How do you know all this about Gibble and Waybury?"

"My ex is from there."

"Uh-huh. But suppose I go to someone here, in Lakeville, I mean?"

"Is it Waybury business?"

"Is what Waybury business?"

"Whatever you need a trooper for."

"I guess."

"Then you're stuck with Will Gibble. You can ask. You can waste your time. You can even ride over to the barracks in Canaan. They'll just send you back to Will. That's the deal."

"And you know because--"

"My ex tried it. Tried to get some action on his stolen pickup. Wound up right back with Will."

Sarah slid off the stool, caught a reflection of herself in the front window and rolled her eyes. Her face seemed even rounder than usual, the eyes more sunken than the night before, and the blue blazer was wrinkled. Turning back, Sarah said, "How about the vet?"

"Huh?" said the girl, mopping the rest of the counter for no apparent reason. "Oh, you mean Dr. Dudley, you mean the animal hospital."

"Whatever. Wouldn't he be up and about?"

"How did you know I'd know?"

"Just a hunch."

"Good guess. You see, I know, cause my ex--"

"Had a dog and used Dudley all the time."

"That's right. How did you know?"

"Another hunch," said Sarah teasing.

Sarah decided that looking into the alleged poisoning of Katie's St. Bernard puppy was as good a tack as any till Selectman Will Gibble deigned to open his doors. Besides, Sarah had kept the puppy for two weeks before turning him over at the wedding reception. The little fellow's demise was starting to get to her, making inroads on her consciousness like Katie's condition. Adding to her uncharacteristic irksomeness.

The girl said, "Dudley's over in a big white salt-box right between here and Waybury. You could see him and then catch Will Gibble. That way you wouldn't have to hang around here. Good idea, huh?"

"Not bad."

"Just had a hunch."

Sarah let her have that one as she flipped out a pad and started her notes.

The girl said, "Hey, are you some kinda reporter? I mean, the way you talk, jerk out a pen real quick and all. Are you?"

"Sort of."

"Major crimes and stuff?"

"Features."

"What's that?"

"Human interest."

"Like?"

"Why does the bag lady hang around the Sterling Library?"

Shaking her head and pursing her lips, the girl said, "I don't get it?"

"It's okay."

"No, no," said the girl squeezing her yellow sponge, passing it from hand to hand. "I'm interested, I swear."

"It's the big library at Yale."

"So?"

"So it turns out that she was a one-time scholar and wanted to be closer to the rare books. Even snuck in and slept there."

"Cool. Awesome."

"Uh-huh."

"No, honest. I still don't get it but I want to hear more."

Sarah edged away. “Later maybe. We’ll see.”

“Hope you dig up some local stuff,” the girl added. “I love that. Then we could talk. Hope you do good.”

Sarah eased out the door hoping she could indeed do some good and whisk back to Katie with something to report.

✧

“I told her,” the veterinarian said, pushing the overweight golden retriever onto the aluminum scale. “There are a thousand tests, not to mention the costs.”

It was a quarter after eight and Sarah was now firmly ensconced in Doctor Dudley’s chilled examining room. The vet went on, warming to his subject, his bald head gleaming under the fluorescent lights, his thick lips curling up like some quiz kid who finally got a question on his favorite obscure topic.

“There’s the panel of chemical toxicology if one wanted to go that far. I also told her we could examine the stomach contents, the liver, kidney, heart and brain. Plus the blood from the carcass and the urine.”

"That's what you told Katie? That's the way you talked to her?"

Breaking into an even broader smile, the vet said, "Absolutely. I was perfectly candid, gave her the whole spectrum. But she would have none of it. She just burst into tears."

The bear-like golden retriever looked up from the low-hanging scale and seemed to smile as broadly as the vet. The acrid smells coming from the open vats of formaldehyde were beginning to curdle Sarah's stomach – that, and the gleeful descriptions of canine death.

"Okay, okay," said Sarah. "Let's just cut to possible ways and means."

"Without conclusive proof?"

"Skip the proof for now. Just give me some possibilities. If it were poisoning, I mean."

"Ways and means, eh?"

"Yes."

"Well, that's endless. Decaying vegetation, black leaves, toadstools, molds--now we're talking about fungal and bacterial toxins resulting in liver failure and kidney failure. Wait, wait … oh, I know a good one: antifreeze. Dogs love it, tastes sweet.

Had a case just a few weeks ago. The poison got into the blood stream and before you knew it--"

"Does any of that fit the circumstances?"

"Possibly. The dog was almost four months old. No telling what it could have gotten into, especially if it was neglected."

"It was not neglected. It was probably mothered and cuddled to pieces."

Dudley went cold for a moment, obviously having no patience for open displays of feeling. Then, as if erasing Sarah's last comment, he was off and running again. "There were no symptoms, no warnings, no previous signs. For a St. Bernard of that age and condition to expire that quickly, it would take something like digitalis."

"The heart medicine?"

"Precisely. An overdose would make the heart give out."

"Pills?"

Dragging the overweight golden retriever off the stainless steel scale, the vet softened his tone, his voice fading as though recalling something that had actually touched him personally. "There are also natural toxins . . . like common foxglove leaves. If they're dry, chopped up, mixed in with meat, in no time flat, his heart races like crazy and he's gone."

Eyeing Sarah and then checking back at the beaming golden face, the vet added, "Being overweight does it too. Slower, but sooner or later it does the trick."

"Thanks," said Sarah, grabbing her leather bag, easing her way through the grayish green waiting room. She glanced back at the retriever. She knew next to nothing about the world of veterinarians and pets. She began to wonder about the fragility of all creatures great and small, glanced back one last time, pivoted and smacked into a tiny bespectacled woman cradling an orange kitten. After a round of mutual apologies, she hopped into her car and headed toward Waybury, and the town hall.

Out of habit, she reached under the dashboard for her handset, pressed the power button and checked the display. The signal held at three bars, blinked and faded to two. Reaching inside her leather tote bag produced the same result. The indicator confirmed the fact that when wending one's way down and around the hills between Sharon and Canaan or traipsing around by foot, a cell phone or car phone would do you no good.

"Now let me get this straight," said Sarah. "There was a trooper on the scene who filed this cursory report."

Selectman and former trooper Will Gibble shook his square face once again. "No, Miss Bucklin, it wasn't cursory." For the about the twentieth time, he glanced at his rectangular watch with the bright steel case and shuffled the papers inside a file folder.

It was now almost ten a.m. Sarah had been sitting in Gibble's oak- paneled office for twenty minutes batting zero. The upshot was that there was no law officer on the case because there was no certifiable crime.

"Will that be all, Miss Bucklin?" said Gibble, leaning back on his matching oak captain's chair.

At this point, Sarah felt she was dealing with a cartoonist's sketch of a public official--a dash for a mouth, two slits for the eyes, salt-and-pepper closely cropped hair with matching sideburns drawn neatly on both sides, a lantern jaw and complementary straight lines etching in the torso. If they ever issued a missing person's report on Gibble, it would read: early forties, gray suit, nondescript features, tall and lean with no discernable marks or characteristics.

Here Sarah stopped herself, as she often did, to tell herself to stop making snap judgments. It was a bad habit, a quick mental filing system when under pressure. Reminding herself to knock it off made little difference, but she did it anyway.

"Come on," Sarah said as Gibble adjusted his watchstrap, "it's not open and shut and you know it."

Once more Gibble slid the "Police Blotter" clipping from the *Lakeville Register* across the polished wooden desk.

Sarah slid the item about Katie's "accident" back onto Gibble's blotter, reached into her floppy leather bag and dealt Katie's letters like playing cards atop the clipping. "Let's add up some of the details again," said Sarah. "Possible poisoning of her puppy plus swiping her car keys and checkbook. Then put totally out of the way so she can't run her summer theater. Let's run it by that way and see what we get."

In reply, Gibble replaced the newspaper clipping and fixed his bright eyes directly onto Sarah's face. "Tell me, Miss Bucklin, are you a reporter or a story teller?"

Sarah took in the remark, let it hang there for a second and went on. "Okay, let's put it another way. Katie's lying there, at this moment, hanging by a thread waiting for a little reassurance. I'll back off and bow to your expertise. I'll even settle for telling her you're on the case and things are about to move."

The bright eyes didn't budge. They kept boring a hole through Sarah's forehead.

"You see," Sarah continued, "she's gullible. Read the letters. Inside that little pixie brain she probably believes it's some kind of punishment. For being in a play about witches a long time ago while her parents drowned. I mean, she talks a good game about being a free spirit and all, but by coming back here and doing the same play again . . . What I'm saying is, on the surface she thought she was breaking the spell but underneath she feared she might've been defying God or something. So right now she's suffering in many ways. Can you see that? And even if you can't, it's a fact that Katie, as nimble as they come, could never fall into a cistern. It doesn't add up."

After an interminable pause, Sarah snatched up the letters, stuffed them back in her bag and blurted out, "Okay, what would it take?"

"For what?"

"Look, if I go to Canaan and confront that trooper or anybody else at the barracks, they'll put me off and call you. Unless you've been jerking me around, that's the deal."

"Yup, that's why they elected me: two for one. I do the selectman's work and field the complaints."

“We know, we know. So how do I get you to get someone on the stick?”

Sitting up ramrod straight, Gibble sent his clear gaze just past Sarah’s left ear, presumably onto some imaginary chart. He then began to recite by rote. “Procedures would be initiated if a veritable shadow were cast on preliminary findings. If hard facts, so to speak, turned up to the contrary… As it stands, the paramedics have corroborated the trooper’s statement. The injuries were totally commensurate with the incident. As for the previous allegations—Mrs. Haddam called me about the missing keys and checkbook--there too we have nothing to go on. No witnesses, no primary source, no evidence.”

“And the dog. Dr. Dudley said that--”

“Do we have the cache of digitalis you mentioned? No. Do we have anything to support any of these speculations? Do we even have a hint of any misgivings on the part of that scene painter or whatever he is?”

“Kevin.”

“Exactly.” Gibble rose abruptly, slid open the top drawer of a file cabinet, shuffled a few folders and then, raising the pitch of his voice a notch, said, “Is he keeping something from us? Did he come across anything before or after he pulled Mrs.

Haddam out? That conceivably would be the kind of shadow we're talking about."

"In other words, somebody is going to have to dig and do your prep work for you."

Gibble stared deeply into the metal drawer. "Tell me again what kind of reporting you do."

Sarah saw it coming but answered anyway. "Features."

"Ah."

"That's right, no police beat, no fast-breaking fire-bombings, shootouts or murders. That's why I keep bringing up this sappy stuff like Katie's pain and righting a wrong."

"Uh-huh," said Gibble, his voice regaining its resonant timbre.

"What if she dies, Mr. Gibble?"

"Let's keep this on a procedural level, shall we?"

"Right. Sorry I asked."

"Now if you'll excuse me, I'm only contracted till noon." Handing her her shoulder bag, Gibble steered Sarah out of his oak-paneled world, past the elderly lady typist pecking away.

In the cramped foyer, just inside the front door, Sarah tugged at the sleeve of his impeccably neat charcoal jacket, restraining him from bolting back to his files. "Give me something," Sarah said. "What pictures can I take? What can I pry open just a smidge that would do the trick?"

Brushing himself free, Gibble lingered for a moment. "If she had defense wounds: broken fingernails, signs of abuse other than those resulting from the fall. If, let's say, a retaining rod was found--something that should've prevented her from dropping through, things like that…"

"What about Kevin?"

"If he came into the barracks and made a statement pointing to or suggesting an assault. But even then we're talking probable cause that could hold up while the accused has his or her lawyer sue for slander. Then again, this is all conjecture."

As he strode back past the elderly typist, Sarah called after him. "Suppose I can't get any of that? Suppose I actually do confront the trooper who filed the report?"

"Won't be back on shift till Monday night." Gibble had one foot inside his office when he turned back one last time. "I can understand your frustration, believe me. Happens all the time."

"Tell me something," said Sarah, taking a few steps toward him. "Has anything set you in motion? I mean in recent history?"

No answer until, finally, Gibble said, "Willy."

"Willy?"

"Our one clear-cut felony. Textbook, you might say. As a guideline for productive use of police time, Willy often comes to mind."

Not knowing what to make of this last remark, Sarah felt it was time to cut her losses and back off. She countered Gibble's cool gaze with a hard glare of her own.

"Sorry about your friend," Gibble added. "But in cases where there is no case, there's not much you can do."

Gibble turned on his heels, sauntered into his office and squeezed the door shut. The spinster froze at her typewriter, forced a brittle smile and waved goodbye. Sarah didn't reply. She traversed the short flight of steps, crossed the street and leaned against the hood of her car. A heady scent of lilac filled the air. A dozen or so speckled birds fluttered across the clean sheet of blue sky, twittering away, and then tested the reaches of a nearby maple; as if there were possibilities elsewhere.

But where? A major felony by some character named Willy led Sarah's mind back to Gibble's notion of defense wounds. Defense wounds led to thoughts of further harm.

Turning the corner, Sarah hurried up the rickety flight of stairs into the lobby of the inn. Spotting a pay phone over to her right, she dialed the hospital. After being put on hold, she eventually learned that Katie's condition hadn't changed; it was still touch and go. No unusual incident had occurred since the little run-in with Kevin. Nothing had happened at all.

What now? Before she had a chance to answer her own question, she felt a light tap on her shoulder. A half turn and she was confronted with Doreen's wrinkled face, lavender eye shadow over the one good eye, chopped bangs and triangular sideburns. No earrings this time and her sack dress was a muted green.

"Just read about your friend in the weekly. First time, in I don't know when, there was actual news in that paper. Must be at least seven years."

"Since Willy?"

Doreen's good eye seemed to widen and flare. Quickly recovering, Doreen said, "Yes sir, it's been quite a while."

Sarah adjusted her shoulder bag, waiting for the rest of it.

"Look, hon," Doreen went on, the lavender stain over her good eye flickering, "no use duckin' it. From the girl in the dinette I learn you're a reporter."

"Not really."

"Hey, why you makin' this so hard? You're gonna need help if there's somethin' cookin'. And you're gonna need help if there ain't so's you can get back to New Haven."

"No thanks. Thanks all the same."

Doreen's overworked good eye began to droop. "Hold the phone, hon." She sidled behind the mahogany counter. Four deep swigs and she was back, her good eye a tad steadier.

"Now then, let's look at it this way," Doreen said, picking up the pace. "This is the absolute smallest spot in Connecticut, did you know that?"

"Nope." Looking for a quick way out, Sarah's glances settled on the front screen door.

"Well, if you think about it, the smallness gets to certain people. They're just itchin' to do somethin' big. You get my meaning?"

"Not yet."

"Then try this. You got a playhouse and winery that never can be. And you got this Russell, this Katie's older stepbrother and his lame revival."

"Revival?"

"Ah, got your attention, huh?"

At this point, Sarah gave Doreen no more slack, assuming she would either catch on or run out of steam.

"Well," Doreen went on, "you can go around half-cocked lookin' here, lookin' there, wastin' time. Or you can shoot for the real story." Doreen continued in this vein until Sarah could wait it out no longer and asked what she was after.

"Things to come to somethin'. Or left alone. 'Cause if it don't come to somethin', what's the point, right? I might as well go back to my soap operas and what's on the stupid cable TV and you might as well go on home."

"And why do you want that so much?"

"Want what?"

"For me to come up empty and clear out."

"I never."

Doreen shuffled back over to the front desk, sipped her elixir and winked. "I shouldn't take you for granted, huh? You got things clickin' up there. Makes us two of a kind, now don't it?"

"You bet. Are we finished?"

"I mean, I don't figure you for stupid. That's all I meant to say."

"Thanks."

Doreen tried her best not to speak, not to carry on any further, but it was too much for her. "Ain't you even gonna ask me about the map? Ain't you gonna ask how I know every detail of the place?"

"No."

Sarah padded over to the screen door but something about Doreen's grinning stopped her. "All right, what now?"

Doreen pointed a lavender fingernail at the notepad sticking up from Sarah's open bag. "There is no way you can disregard me and you know it."

Sarah shrugged and, for no reason, plucked out the pad and a pen. "Shoot."

"Hit me with a topic."

Half-seriously Sarah said, "Nasty pranks."

Doreen skirted back to the front desk, leaned back on her flint elbows and chuckled. "That's good -- that's rich."

"Well?"

Doreen licked her chapped lips and adjusted her eye patch. "Well, first they were in my mailbox 'cause I told on her once. Then they showed up on some neighbor's back swing after the neighbor shooed her away from her sixteen-year-old son."

"What showed up?"

"Little dead critters. I guess you can figure who the culprit is."

"Hyper twelve-year-old Alice."

"You got it. And now I got it."

"What's that, Doreen?"

"Uh-uh-uh-uh. That's not how we play the game." Chuckling, she scuffed away, fighting her clinging sack dress as she moved off into the mahogany shadows.

Still lingering by the front door, Sarah felt a keen awareness of time passing. The way things stood, it could have all started with Alice. It could have started with any one of a handful of people. Or, as Gibble was strongly suggesting, all of Katie's problems were fueled solely by her own overworked imagination. And there was nothing more to this case than meets the eye.

Sarah went back to her car, shifted into gear and headed out for the estate. She wanted some help, she didn't know whom to trust; she wanted to get something done. "Enough of this. See for yourself," she muttered under her breath. Deciding to give Katie at least the benefit of the doubt.

Ignoring the flutter of the worn lifters, she took the first steep grade in second gear and kept a steady pressure on the pedal. She also ignored the flutters in her stomach. The kind she got lately when forced to walk down the side streets off Chapel and Crown. When anything could be coming around the corner.

Six

een from the dirt driveway, Katie's estate consisted mainly of a jungle of wild honeysuckle masking a two-story sprawl of white clapboard, flaked blue-green shutters and a file of brick chimneys. One yellow bulldozer blocked off a pitted road about thirty yards to the right. Thick oak trees joined the free-spirited honeysuckle far to the left. No other houses were in sight. Only the bridal veil bush directly in front of Sarah's parked car gave any hint of habitation. Its even sprays of delicate white flowers seemed cultivated, a remnant perhaps of some earlier time when plantings had been selected and nurtured with great care.

The sky turned hazy as Sarah stepped out of her beige Accord, as if someone had drawn a milky shade, turning the air muggy and warm. Letting her eyes stray across the scene, Sarah decided to change her shoes. If the front of the compound was any indication, it was going to take a bit of tramping to get to the scene of the incident, from which point she could work forward or back and mosey around.

It was just about noon. It was still Saturday. She had been engaged in her first ever attempt at detection for one full morning. Pulling on her beat-up hiking shoes from out of the trunk only made her feel even more self-conscious. Cinderella and all true princesses wore a dainty size five. They didn't sport a size nine-wide set of clodhoppers.

Tying her laces, she debated about the camera. She scrapped the idea in favor of the can of mace nestled in the corner of her glove compartment. Given the encounters she'd had with assorted street characters, any trek alone in foreign territory called for some kind of edge. Slipping the mace inside her blazer pocket, it dawned on her that she had to gain lawful entry. The obvious means was to latch on to Russell and establish her position acting on Katie's behalf. And then poke around.

But did she really need the mace? Was there really any danger, any threat of anything? Probably not. Humoring the irrational edgy feeling, she patted her blazer pocket as if the mace were a good luck charm, chuckled to herself and moved on.

Scuffing up the asphalt drive, she paused for a second and glanced at Doreen's makeshift map. The location of Russell's cottage was underlined and given an asterisk, like the first spot on a guided tour. She noted a fork veering off to the right in the distance, ostensibly leading to the playhouse, and made out what appeared to be some rubble or debris. She shrugged it off for now. Neither the playhouse nor the fork had been marked very clearly. Just indicated by a few dotted lines and a cursory box.

Continuing on, she noticed the lean, muscular form on the roof above her on her left. He was shirtless, tan, wearing white jeans--like a surfer, riding a low, buckling black wave. She moved past another bridal veil, its plump blooms giving off a pungent, almost sickening smell.

Lengthening her stride, letting her eyes wander, she scanned Katie's entire domain. Directly ahead was the scraggly roll of the back lawn. Like the condition of the main house, the grounds were weather-beaten and ragged. So, Sarah guessed, was Katie's nearby playhouse. So was it all. Squinting into the flickering tracery of shapes, she noted what Doreen indicated were the locations of the barn apartments, a rose garden, vineyard and pond.

From somewhere a deep "Aah" filtered through the haze and broke the silence. It came from the guest cottage about fifty yards in front of her, just beyond the sloping lawn. The singing sigh had an old familiar ring to it, mellifluous and mellow. Katie's older stepbrother Russell was definitely at home.

Traipsing across the spongy grass, which must have been sprouting out of habit, totally unaware that April had been much too dry, Sarah approached the flagstone terrace that rimmed the miniature one-story Cape, its gable roof as high as its span. She scraped the bits of black dirt from the soles of her hiking boots on the brick stoop and added to her wish list. Hoping, perhaps, she could catch Russell off guard, eke out some information, some sign in Katie's favor. Or at least find some point of dead reckoning. From there the pieces would fall into place like they always did. Like it or not, for better or worse, there would be a story to tell. And, like it or not, for better or worse, once she got into gear Sarah had to find a beginning, middle and end and get it right.

The front door was slightly ajar. The deep sighs became a drone and then a low rumbling incantation.

"Russell?" She knocked a few times on the jamb, slipped inside, past the brick fireplace, to the right, down the brief hallway and stopped short. There, on the cot in the single bedroom, Russell was propped up against the wall, his bulky form rigid, his heavy legs crossed, like some blown-up Hindu fakir. Only his quiet gaze at the beams that ran across the ceiling overhead indicated he was both alive and awake.

Sarah said,"Russell?" again but received no reply. Only when she rapped her knuckles on the chipped green nightstand did Russell deign to speak.

"Ah, Sarah. I thought . . . perhaps. And lo and behold, here you are." As ever, his tone was long-suffering and paternal, like a biblical shepherd who waited patiently for his flock to come home. That is, as long as he could keep prodding them to get with it and finally tow the line.

"Can we skip the ministerial tone, Russell? Would you mind?"

"Relinquish my hopes, you mean? Toss aside my vision? As you may or may not be aware, I've been meditating."

"Uh-huh, right," said Sarah, wanting to dispense with the preliminaries but knowing full well she couldn't.

Russell turned his blotched ruddy face toward her and displayed that benign secret smile of his. Then he uncrossed his legs, stretched and yawned and widened the smile just a tad.

Sarah tried again, peppering him with small talk, catching up on the news--the usual. If she confronted him again directly, he would flake out on her, spout scripture and homilies and she would be back to square one.

"So?" Sarah went on. "What's the story? I thought you were looking into some Assembly of God opening down in Waterbury?"

Russell arched one of his steel wool eyebrows, stroked his curly gray beard and said, "Still up in the air."

"I hear in the meantime you're going to toss in a revival."

Arching both steel wool eyebrows, Russell said, "And where did you get that notion?"

"Oh, somebody's who's got one good eye and tends bar."

"Doreen."

"Yep. That's the one."

"Ah." Another stroke of the beard and Russell said, "It's true that I've been chatting with some people on Channel Twelve. You know, the one in Hartford. Nothing firm as yet but it looks promising."

Sarah shook her head, tried to stifle the thought but blurted it out anyway. "Even though you know that TV evangelism went out with *The Moral Majority*. Give me a break."

Russell fell silent as if someone had uttered some unspeakable blasphemy. Just as suddenly, he rose to his full six-foot-four, towering over the bed furniture like something out of a fairy tale. Another of his deep resonant sighs and he snapped out of his torpor and shifted into his purposeful saving-the-misguided-multitudes mode.

"Look behind you, Sarah. Look around. It doesn't take much to see that this property is a Sleepy Hollow, a microcosm of a Tarrytown where the devil tarries. A perfect metaphor of how easy it is to be lulled into sloth. To shrug things off as if everything in this world just happens. Heisenberg's uncertainty principle: everything is chance. Terrorism and all the rampant evil in the world is just an accident."

Taking this last comment as an opening, Sarah related how she and Katie had discussed this very topic within the past six weeks over some strong Kenya AA at the Starbucks coffee pavilion inside the co-op at Yale. And Sarah had convinced Katie that there was no logical link between a juicy part in a dark play and the bad things that happen to good people. If she wanted to take another stab at playing Barbara Allen, if she wanted to open a playhouse—if she wanted to do anything, she should do it and rid herself of the silly notion there was a cloud hanging over her.

Russell then countered with a series of quasi facts about all the misfortunes that befell actors who played in productions of *Macbeth*, underscoring some other quasi fact that many of them had played one of the witches.

"Right," said Sarah. "Now we're into it. Katie wrote me that you were working on her again. Using anything and everything to bring it up, to continue to cause her grief."

"How so?"

"Come on. As if that old thing *wasn't* an accident. As if your parents didn't just drown, as if it were some kind of unfinished business. It was seventeen years ago, Russell. I mean, get a grip."

"Of course. And it would have made no difference if Katie had manned the tiller? Knowing full well that Mother was hopeless on a boat and Dad wasn't much better. When the winds suddenly shifted and the gale came on. Tell me it wouldn't have helped if Katie had abandoned that godless play and been at her place. Tell me I should just let it go. Let everything go."

"Oh sure, absolutely. It's all part of a continuous satanic plot."

"She forgets. Everybody forgets. Or even worse, you do something and you take it all back. And to prove she's absolved, she goes and takes your advice. She comes up here and starts her season with the same demonic role. Why not? La-di-da."

Russell caught himself waving his arms around as if swatting away bees. Clasping his hands, he sucked in his breath, held it in for a second and let out one of his patented long-suffering sighs. Then they both held still for a while, realizing it was one more variation on the same theme and, as always, they'd gotten absolutely nowhere.

"Just wish people would weigh the consequences of their actions," said Russell, regaining his composure, trying to get in the last word. "Call a spade a spade." Shambling out of the tiny bedroom, he threaded his way down the cramped hallway and popped into the equally cramped kitchen. "Care for some herbal tea? Iced? Red Zinger? Any kind you like."

"What actions, exactly?" said Sarah, following after him. Reminded how he had yanked Katie out of the "Moon" production immediately after his mother and father drowned in nearby Twin Lakes. Then yet again in high school on the shore, claiming that she was duped by demon spirits and, in the words of the play script, ". . . never could be pure, never could be true."

"What actions?" Sarah repeated, leaning up against the old porcelain sink, trying to sound casual. "What happened this time?"

"Oh . . . nothing."

"Come on, I want to hear. Honest."

Sarah kept coaxing him, teasing, making him shrug.

"Well," said Russell finally, "if it helps open your eyes . . ."

"Try me."

Russell's ruddy face pivoted, like some kind of radar device homing in on an object within close proximity. "I was just standing by, mind you. Not particularly looking for anything."

A little more nudging as Russell prepared the iced tea and, slowly but surely, his little tale seeped out. It centered on the "surfer" on the roof whose name it seems was Mark.

As Russell went on, Sarah, ever the consummate story editor, erased Russell's biased asides and circumlocutions, took notes and reconstructed the incident in her mind's eye as one continuous scene:

Flustered over her missing car keys and checkbook, Katie was already fuming when she heard a grinding echo. The sound came from beyond the tree-line and the guest cottage, well past the point where the drive at the side of the estate turned into a Y-fork.

Hurrying outside, she worked her way through the blockade of prickly yellow forsythia, and came upon Mark astride the yellow bulldozer, plowing heaps of asphalt and gravel right and left. By the time she got his attention and made him shut off the howling engine, the playhouse road was impassable. Katie reminded Mark that they were going to talk about it first, plus figure some way they could put in a concession stand and extra parking. Mark claimed that with all the potholes, there was no way anyone could get to the theater anyway without breaking an axle. All the while, he had stared at Katie's hips and breasts, grinning, recalling that the former owner from Long Island had a cute little bod and also had no clue.

By this time, Mark had pushed up the sleeves of his yellow sweatshirt and flexed the long muscles of his arms, swiveled around, looked Katie in the eye and winked. Katie responded by telling him to patch up the access road or get fired and underscored the fact that she never hired him in the first place. Somehow there was some mix-up or assumption that he just came with the place.

Loosing his cool, Mark insulted both Katie and her husband, calling Tommy a wimp and yelling, "You're hopeless. You're stupid. Neither one of you knows which end is up."

He then hopped off the dozer, threw up his arms as if begging for forgiveness, hovered directly over her and kept looking her up and down. She backed away into the prickly forsythia as he shuffled after her, shaking his head, grinning away. Pinned against the bushes, she tried to twist away as Mark hovered over her once again. In that same moment, she caught a glimpse of Tommy's slight form. He was standing just beyond the bulldozer about fifteen yards away, glancing at her sideways, his sandy hair and soft features held in profile. In that same instant, he possibly no longer looked like the calm, privileged, proverbial rich-boy-next-door.

In Sarah's mind the sequence probably ended with Mark back on the dozer and Katie and Tommy silently wending their way back to the main house. Then again, it could have ended differently. The jangle of ice cubes in Russell's glass of tea broke Sarah's train of thought.

"Well?" said Russell. "Now what do you have to say?"

Sarah ambled into the doll-sized living room, Russell padding directly behind her. Positioning herself by the mantle above the charred fireplace, Sarah said, "Nothing, Russell. I'm just listening, taking it all in."

"Come now. You have to admit there is a pattern. Those who bring things upon themselves."

"Guess what? You're doing it again."

"But it's so obvious. Take Kevin for a perfect example. A failed actor, painter and handyman who has been smitten. Probably up at the playhouse mooning over Katie as we speak. Part and parcel of the aftermath of her actions."

"Now you're pushing it."

"I am indeed."

In the next pregnant pause, Sarah looked down at the fireplace, toyed with a cast iron poker, spotted a split hickory branch with a forked end and snatched it up.

"Divining rod," said Russell. "Broken, useless. Yet another case in point."

"Give it a rest, will you? Not everything in this life is grist for your mill."

Russell smiled his long-suffering smile. Sarah absentmindedly rubbed the soot off the smooth forked length of wood. Then she worked her way up the entire length, pausing at the rounded grip, trying to make out the carved letters.

"Of course," Russell went on, unable to contain himself, "Katie never told Tommy that the vineyard was a sham. No divining rod could help bring it back to life. No source of water, and the location of the old cistern was a total mystery. But did that dawn on her? Or the fact that there was a drought going on? Or that the vines had to be pruned back in winter and the fruit buds had been knocked off? Did Katie ever stop to think about anything?"

"You know what a hammer mill is, Russell? You hand-feed it a bit at a time. No more."

"Come again?"

"Otherwise everything gets all clogged up and turns to mush. Word to the wise from my first Journalism prof."

"Interesting. I'll have to remember that." Deflecting, Russell shambled back into the little kitchen and replenished his glass of iced tea. In the interim, Sarah rubbed a little harder until she could make out the letters on the hardwood handle. They spelled "Willy." The same name Gibble had mentioned back at the town hall.

"Truce," said Russell, returning, glass in hand, holding up one oversized palm in some gesture of peace and forgiveness.

Draining her glass of iced Red Zinger, replacing the diving rod in the fireplace, Sarah said, "Good. Now, quietly, ever so gently reassure me. Tell me how you've been visiting Katie and given her comfort."

"I've prayed."

"No, no, Russell. You know that way way down deep in her kiddie brain she believes in your wondrous sins of omission and commission."

"Hopefully."

"And so, being the good Christian that you are . . ."

"But it's not up to me to sweep everything away."

"Terrific, Russell. Just great."

Using his most mellifluous tones, Russell said, "Did you know, Sarah, that 'New Englanders are a people of God moving into the devil's territory.' Cotton Mather, 1692. We have a covenant. We have broken it. Waybury is a parable, if you will. That's why I consented to relate that story. So that you might begin to finally understand and perhaps offer a little aid."

Russell began to fade back into his pastor-leading-the-poor-blighted-flock routine. Giving up, Sarah finally said, "Okay okay, never mind. Just show me where Katie fell. The exact spot, I mean."

Russell shook his big bear of a head. "Why?"

"Why not?"

The steel wool eyebrows raised up. Sarah added, "Why do you think I'm here?"

Russell swirled the ice cubes with his finger and rubbed the glass against one of his blotchy cheeks. "Those misguided messages from Katie, I suppose."

"Look, somebody has to look out for her. Luckily I wasn't counting too much on you."

"Oh dear," said Russell, emitting another sigh. "Just when I thought you might be starting to comprehend."

"I get it. As always, you have to make it so damn hard."

They sparred a bit longer until Russell shook his head, clunked his glass on the mantel and said, "Just remember, Sarah, this isn't the movies." The remark meant what it had always meant. Nearly once a week Sarah could be found in the back row of some multiplex or art cinema, taking in a variety of conflicts and situations. But in no danger of smacking up against any of them and coming undone.

As a retort, Sarah fired back with the same old response. "At the movies you get to appreciate multiple shots, multiple plot lines and multiple views. You ought to try it sometime." At the same time she began to worry about all the possible shots and plot lines surrounding this case—if that's what it actually was.

After a second truce, she prodded a bit more about the location of the scene of the accident until he gave in and pointed her in the right direction. He also agreed to let Tommy know she was on the grounds. Offhandedly, he slipped in a query about her plans, wanted to know when she'd be back at work in New Haven. In reply, Sarah asked about his plans for forgiving Katie and suggested they both go to the hospital first chance. As expected, neither gave an inch.

A moment later, standing outside the cottage, Sarah plucked out her notepad and scribbled an afterthought about Mark and the access road to the playhouse. Then she padded off, shielding her eyes from the hazy sunlight, stopped again and jotted down the name "Willy."

Hold it, she thought. This non-assignment assignment deals with tangibles, remember? Use your eyes; see for yourself. Start with Katie's fall.

Seven

eading along what must have been the course of Katie's near-fatal jog, Sarah left the cottage, heading west, passing the red barn with apartments above to her left and made a beeline: through the center of an overgrown flower garden gone to seed, reeking with the scent of lilacs, the lavender spikes bursting above yellowish shoots and briars; proceeding into the milky haze, down a beaten path to a file of stakes and trellises, the thick gnarled vines twisting around the posts and latticework like garlands of snakes, seemingly attempting to splinter and drag the pieces of wood down into the rich black dirt.

Halting at the battered vineyard, she came upon mounds of earth and deep ditches, as if someone had been frantically digging for something they'd lost.

Tommy? It was his project. But it was hard to connect him with this coarse, scraggy jungle. Sarah's thoughts began to return to the wedding reception a few weeks back on the manicured lawn of his parents' home in Westport.

Tommy had sat out most of the dances, safely ensconced under the striped yellow and green tent. In the meantime, Katie had continued to jounce and twirl nearby to the strains of the six-piece band cranking out her favorite oldies but goodies. Through it all, Tommy's fine sandy hair stayed perfectly in place, his blue eyes soft and gentle, his powder-blue suit and matching tie unruffled. Even when Sarah had plopped down opposite him in a white wicker chair and asked all sorts of leading questions, his responses were laconic and uncommitted, his tone pleasant, a bit shy and unwavering. As if he were Katie's secret fantasy and hers alone.

From time to time, Katie embraced him from behind, her eyes closed, her slender arms encircling his neck. And when they stood together--both under five-foot-six, appearing like fairy tale ornaments on a cake--it all seemed totally unreal.

And nothing altered Sarah's general impressions, not a jot. Even when Sarah presented Tommy with the big cuddly puppy, Katie squealed and Tommy retained the same fixed smile. Moments later he was back at his perch while Katie resumed her frolic, the puppy in her arms, doing a little time step to a thumping version of *Dancin' in the Street*. As Katie dissolved into a blur of flailing arms and stomping feet, Tommy's demeanor held steady, as it did when Katie returned, whirling past him, lip-syncing, "I've got sunshine on a cloudy day." That particular song was still playing when Katie announced to all within earshot that some old childhood spell had been broken, the clouds had lifted, the "dark of the moon" had no choice but to brighten and twinkle. Tommy added a nod to his benign smile and applauded unobtrusively.

Afterwards, when Tommy had let it slip that he would be engaging in a little cloud-lifting and resurrection of his own, his noncommittal expression remained that of a young squire posing for a portrait, on his best behavior all the while.

The wedding day was the first and last time Sarah had ever laid eyes on Tommy. Even now it was all she could do to conjure up a vague image. There was no way to look for signs of his handiwork in the nearby mounds and ditches. In point of fact, it was hard to imagine his doing any work at all.

Scouring her bag for a sugarless Kiwi candy drop, Sarah proceeded on the beaten path, making a mental note that all that could be said was that Tommy had doubtless asked someone to hunt for a lost well within the past few weeks.

Just ahead, Sarah noticed a divining rod attached to a tall trellis. A good one, not split and charred like the one with Willy's inscription. Perfectly straight, set at a right angle, flecked at the forked tip with drops of Day-Glo yellow. It appeared to be pointed at sawhorses draped with red flags. The sawhorses barricaded a sheet of plywood just large enough to cover the top of a large cistern, ostensibly signaling the end of Tommy's search.

If Sarah had brought a crowbar, she could have investigated further. For now all she could do was stand there and imagine the scene in the dark with the cistern uncovered, Katie swerving while running at full tilt and suddenly dropping through.

Sarah went back to the divining rod and examined it more closely. Sure enough, the grip and signature were identical to the one resting in the cottage fireplace.

The haze grew brighter, weighing down on her, smudging her view. It gradually occurred to her that the only way to take this case-which-wasn't-a-case off hold, was to discredit the trooper's report. Said report stated--to wit, for the umpteenth time--that Katie's fall was commensurate with her psychological state and the negligent act of jogging at full tilt (which was her custom for the past couple of years), while disregarding sawhorses and red warning flags; in the rain, under darkening nightfall. Therefore, unless a piece of provocative evidence or testimony was produced forthwith to the contrary, the report would stand as written. Or, continuing in Gibble's lexicon and underscoring his directive, the only thing that would make a difference was something tangible that would cast a shadow. Anything else was just so much drivel and hot air.

Tramping around in a wide arc, feeling her mascara run into her eyes from the shimmering heat waves, she worked her way down to the pond. What better place to toss away some telltale object? If there was such a thing… Wiping her brow again, she stared into the glut of lily pods and brackish water. She prodded around with a broken branch, muddying the area even more. The dankness brought to mind Katie's probable fate. It also brought to mind something Jan, Sarah's buddy on the crime beat, once said. Crime stories were totally different than features. Something was always wrong: looked wrong, felt wrong, smelled wrong and even tasted wrong.

Okay, Sarah thought, something definitely seems off. So, what do we need? Answer: evidence or testimony. And what do we have? Nothing. And nothing can be gained from aimlessly poking around.

The notion of Kevin--the moonstruck actor/set painter and only witness --seemed to be an obvious next step. He was supposedly dabbling just across the way. If Kevin could continue to moon over Katie in the hospital, he could certainly come forth, do some corroborating and help her rise out of her pitch black hole. Besides, at the moment, besides jotting down notes about the sawhorses, Willy's divining rod, etc. Sarah couldn't think of anything better to do.

Hurrying on, Sarah tried to be positive, as if she knew what she was doing. Talking to Kevin was Gibble's idea. If in some way it proved to be constructive, she could get some much deserved lunch while the police began to do what they should have been doing this whole time. And she could stay on the sidelines where she belonged.

She crossed the open field beyond the trellises and pond, wading through the knee-high thickets of saw grass as the white converted barn of a playhouse loomed up ahead. Pausing frequently in the milky heat to mop her brow, she finally reached the fringes of the theater area, filed past the hut-like costume shop and mounted the plank steps into the hollow recesses backstage. Immediately she spied the spindly shadow accosting a huge stretch of hanging muslin. She paused to catch her breath, letting it rise and fall, wiping the damp perspiration from her neck with her loose cotton sleeve. She then brushed by the black velour wings and took in the scene.

The work lights overhead glinted on the backdrop onstage, wet with a pale milky wash, the galvanized buckets and Kevin's gyrating frame. On the palette table to his right lay bowls of whiting, dry yellows, reds, blues, greens, browns and blacks.

Strewn about the spattered stand, long-handled and short-handled brushes lay in wait.

As always, Sarah was uncertain about approaching strangers, especially those like Kevin who were unsocial and wary. Should she gloss over their little run-in at the hospital and apologize for spooking him? Or should she ease into it by kidding him about the roles she'd seem him play on the Connecticut shore: the gangling slow-witted kid in *The Rainmaker*; the crazed boy who put out horses' eyes in *Equus*; the deadbeat who wanted to end it all in *The Zoo Story*; and the wild young priest who tried to shake up the Catholic church in *Mass Appeal*. And then, when she spotted an opening--like she had just experienced with Russell--should she ask about his recent rehearsals as the witch boy who dug up graves and longed to caress a human girl? Should she use the *Dark of the Moon* ploy and move in from there?

"Okay, okay, let's try another tack," said Sarah. All of her lame ploys had failed. She'd been trying to get some kind of give-and-take going for the past fifteen minutes. Glaring at Kevin's beanpole form as it flitted around her, Sarah was starting to believe he was unable to talk at all unless given lines to speak. And since all of his roles were nut cases or close to it, the whole exercise was starting to appear hopeless.

"Like I said," Sarah went on, "it's not like you're a suspect or anything. You don't even have to talk to me, just ex duty officer Will Gibble. Throw a little mud on the trooper's report. Help Katie out. What do you say?"

"Mmmm," Kevin said, brush in hand, turning his narrow face toward her.

"What is that supposed to be? A reply?"

Kevin rolled his furtive eyes, ran his fingers through his long, scraggly chestnut hair and cocked his head like a wary wolf at the edge of a poultry farm.

Sarah edged closer to Kevin's side, still trying to make some eye contact. Countering, Kevin dragged over a tall wooden stepladder and continued warding Sarah off.

"Talk to me, Kevin. I mean, what have you got to lose?"

"Well," Kevin said, dipping a longhaired priming brush into a milky-gray pail tinged with yellow ochre, "that depends."

"On what, pray tell?"

"Tommy."

"Meaning?"

"And how Katie does."

"Go on."

"That kind of stuff."

"What kind of stuff? Why can't you just say, 'There's nothing more than what I told the trooper?' Or 'there is more but I'm holding back.'? Why is that so hard?"

Ignoring her, switching the priming brush to his left hand, Kevin climbed to the top of the drop and laid in streaks of ochre tint.

"How about this, Kevin? I talk; you listen. If I'm on the right track, you nod. If not, you shake your head."

Shrugging, Kevin hopped down the ladder, dropped the brush in a bucket of water, went over to the palette table and began mixing raw sienna with cobalt.

"Terrific," said Sarah. "Ready? Listening? Let's say Katie was distraught. Her usual run to clear the cobwebs out of her head was worsened by the fact that Mark had just torn up the road to this playhouse. And, probably, she was headed up here. Make sense?"

Back on the ladder, streaking in a vibrant gray in the center of the sky-drop, Kevin said, "Later, huh? Okay?"

"Oh, that's cute. That's real cute. What should I do, get Tommy to ask you? Pressure you? Is that the ticket?"

Grinning, Kevin feathered the edges of the graying sky and began muttering to himself. "Right. You want action, Tommy's your man."

"I'm serious." Straining for something, anything, Sarah said, "This Mark character then. He's the caretaker. Suppose I go to him?"

From her vantage point looking up, Sarah noted a definite twitch in Kevin's left cheek. Checking his digital plastic watch, he muttered again, this time something totally incoherent and plied the paint in sweeping arcs, working much faster. He then hurried down the ladder and plucked out some special-lavender and no-color pink lighting gels from a nearby metal box. Peeking through them, he tested the probable effect of stage lighting on his work. Obviously frustrated now, Sarah repeated her threats to go to Mark or Tommy but to no avail.

Going back to his palette table, mixing in some burnt umber and ultramarine blue, Kevin turned his angular face toward Sarah and hunched his narrow shoulders as if asking, Well? what are you still hanging around for?

Sarah said, "Humor me, will you? You said it depends on Tommy and then you laugh at him. But when I mentioned Mark--"

"Just give it a rest." His mane of straggly hair flipped around as he shook his head. He climbed back up the ladder and stroked another wet swath of vibrant gray across the stretch of cloth.

"Thanks, Kevin. For all your help and concern."

As Kevin continued to shrug her off, Sarah began babbling about the backdrop, suggesting that Katie would have insisted on light clouds, patches of blue and dabs of bright silver on the moon. Flustered even more, still hopelessly trying to disarm him, she rambled on about what she vaguely remembered about the rest of the set from the Shoreline High School production: a peak of a ridge in the Smoky Mountains, a clearing in the woods, the interior of the church in Buck Creek--all the while reminded of Russell and sin. Plus certain lyrics in the theme song like ". . . and many men did Barbara love, but never was she true."

At a loss, Sarah flipped through her notes. She had begun the day with two factors in mind: a poisoned puppy and a near fatal fall. Doggedly, she went back to number one.

"Hey, Kevin, about the puppy . . . I have a vested interest, bought him as a wedding present. What happened to him?" Reaching even farther, she added, "I know you know."

Yet another shrug, more hurried brush strokes, more prodding from Sarah and Kevin finally said, "Nothing to do with me. Found him under the overhang, that's all."

"You found him?"

"She called, I came down."

"From where?"

"My room."

"You mean the barn? Is that what you're talking about?"

"Uh-huh."

"When did this happen?"

"After we talked about this drop, after I walked her back ..."

Sarah held still and turned away from him. Somehow, at long last, he was talking to her and she didn't want to do anything to spook him. Little by little he let more and more eke out as Sarah kept her focus solely on the movements of his brush. Ever the consummate moviegoer, she mulled over the bits and pieces and began to fashion another flashback starting with an opening shot:

Under a moonless sky, Kevin was traipsing along beside Katie, often breaking into a wolf-lope ahead of her, scouting around protectively, self-conscious without something to do. Every now and then, flicking his shaggy mane, he glanced back, finding his hands to be a problem, sometimes rubbing them, sometimes hooking them into the front pockets of his jeans. At first glance it appeared to be a repetition of a casual ritual, the same ol' trek back for Katie: heading east up through the scraggly field, past the trampled vineyard and the jutting stakes, then through the overgrown garden to the overhang and the barn apartments. Then a friendly goodbye to Kevin, a lively barking greeting just ahead, another hundred yards past the guest cottage, a loving goodnight to Arthur, up the slope of the back lawn, into the main house, up the stairs to Tommy and bed.

But there was no sound from Arthur, no hoarse bark, no nothing. Katie passed the pitch and square cut of the little Cape Cod with stepbrother Russell contained, approached the lawn and the looming old colonial and listened closely, almost straining for the clink of Arthur's tether. But there was still nothing. Not a yelp, not a scratch.

Reaching the back yard, Katie must have paused a few hundred feet from the oversized doghouse, called, whistled and clapped. Then looked inside. She probably circled the rambling main house, still calling, whistling and clapping, her search growing wilder as she backtracked to the cottage and then the barn, sensing something under the hayloft, turning her eyes away but then snapping them back, thinking that big puppy Arthur probably had gotten loose, run around like crazy, worn himself out, eaten some spring grass, spit up and was sick. Her eyes then taking over, drawing her closer to the plump tan and white form slumped in the deep shadows, jostling Arthur's rigid shoulders, rocking him back and forth, hugging his thick neck, begging him to move. Then holding his blocky head in her lap, waiting for some sign of life, or for Kevin to come out and fix it, or for hubby Tommy to intercede and show her what to do.

But Katie knew very well what the story was, knew all along. Sweet puppy Arthur was dead.

Sarah was so caught up in the movie in her mind, coloring it shamelessly, she barely noticed Kevin slipping away. She stayed with the incident and the question of the puppy's poisoning until the voice coming from behind, outside the front of the theater somewhere, became more insistent and annoying as well. Forgoing Gibble's directives about hard evidence and telling testimony, giving in to her curiosity, she turned around and walked past the wooden seats as the rafters overhead began to echo the wacky monologue.

Slipping into the theatre lobby, Sarah wondered what in God's name pubescent Alice was up to. And whether she might, by some fluke, be an integral part of it all. It was as if Sarah had stepped further back from the scenarios in her mind and caught a glimpse of the coming attractions--as if the clutter of shots and sequences fit together somehow, as if there really was a criminal case. At any rate, Sarah found herself wanting to know more: a lot more.

Eight

In front of the white barn theater, about twenty feet away from the jutting marquee, Alice held an imaginary microphone and continued to prance around.

"Yeah, well what can I say? I mean, you caught me readin' the Witch Girl part with Kevin--yeah, that's right, *me* totally twelve, just about thirteen, goin' on womanhood. No wonder you chose me to represent my peers."

Strutting around beneath the milky haze like some bony hooker, Alice paused and looked about, obviously expecting someone.

It was now ten after one. Despite her gnawing hunger, Sarah held perfectly still, peering through a raised window inside the lobby by the ticket booth, not knowing what to make of Alice's act.

"Of course none of this bothers me," Alice went on, turning sideways in Sarah's direction, answering the query of some invisible TV host. "What's your problem? Chasing after a dude twice my age--that's nothin', man. That's like, So what else is new?"

Soon, Alice's non-stop patter shifted to an apparent Q&A session with Russell. Then she paused in mid sentence, holding a spidery finger to her lips. "Hey, wait a minute," she muttered. "This could be used as blackmail. Get me in trouble with grease-monkey-dad Benjamin. I mean, how do I know once it gets on the tube?"

"Right," Alice answered herself. "It's a crusade. I am a whatchamacallit, a symptom of a great illness. Like you are a doctor. Right, whatever."

After another exchange with imaginary Russell, Alice yelled, "So hey, I got it. I'll tell you about the other guys, not me."

Alice twisted all the way around, threw out a scrawny hip and positioned herself for fantasy arc lamps highlighting her scraggy features and mousy hair. In relief against the pale sky, the red of Alice's T-shirt seemed to leap out, underscoring her scrawny frame. In that same moment, to Sarah's mind, she went from hooker to starving waif.

"I'll tell about the girls I hate," said Alice, holding her pose. "The ones who talk about it night and day and want it but won't do nothin', don't have the guts."

Alice carried on about a girl named Marie who was always sneaking a peak at her parents' X-rated videos. The moment Alice's bony knees began to twitch and a look of mischief flashed across her face, Sarah could take no more. If there was any point to this charade, now was the time to find out.

The second Sarah strode through the open entranceway, Alice froze and her body went limp like some discarded rag doll.

"Auditioning?" said Sarah for want of any better opening line.

"What's it to you?"

"For Russell? I don't believe it," said Sarah by Alice's side.

"And I don't believe you've got the nerve to bust in and give me some grief. What is this? I got business here, do you mind? If you want to talk woman talk, swell. But not now. And without the attitude."

Sarah chuckled despite herself. She couldn't believe that even with this hyper kid who wanted desperately to make friends, she was off to a bad start.

Alice checked her watch. Sarah checked hers. Ten more minutes had gone down the drain. Sarah unbuttoned her blazer and mopped her brow. Alice tugged on the neck of her oversized T-shirt. Sarah popped a sugarless candy drop in her mouth. Alice sidled over to a grassy verge, plucked up a dandelion shoot, returned to her original position and sucked on it. They were both standing in profile now about fifteen yards in front of the open entrance doors and about six yards apart.

Glancing up over her left shoulder, Sarah noted an unlit sign up on the marquee, the neon tubing forming the words "Revival." Alice followed suit and rolled her eyes.

Mopping her brow again, Sarah eased under the shade of the overhanging marquee. Alice scuffed back to the verge and plopped down under the branches of a nearby shrub: Mexican standoff, number four.

Sarah chuckled again and tossed Alice a candy drop. Alice got up, retrieved it, plopped it in her mouth and smirked back.

"You and Kevin, eh?" said Sarah.

"How did you guess?"

"You told me."

"Oh yeah."

"And you just blurted out he's twice your age."

"Uh-huh."

"And that's okay?"

Too restless to stay hunkered down under the shrub any longer, Alice jerked herself up and started to pace back and forth. Looking off into the scraggly field beyond, Alice said, "He needs me. He's got problems as any dork can see. And we get along so-o-o great." Walking toward Sarah, she hit the word "so-o-o" loudly enough for the whole world to hear.

"Problems, huh?" said Sarah, trying to sound offhand.

"Yeah. If you open your eyes, if you're not some alien poking around just arrived yesterday, you'd see that. If you knew him real good, you'd know."

"I see."

"Very funny. You don't see, man. That's the whole point." Alice went back to her cool-beyond-my-years mode, this time strutting around on a worn patch of grass. "You seen his motorcycle? I'll bet not. You seen him tryin' to rev up the steep grades, his worn tires hitting the potholes, the carburetor fighting him all the way? You seen him twistin' the throttle harder, flicking his wrist back and forth? The pull-plunger at the least has got to be fixed on that piece of crap my ol' man conned him into. Kevin owes his shirt on it, poor guy. But I'll think of something. I mean hey, all the things I know."

"Your ol' man conned him? You mean Benjamin, right?"

"Yeah, beer-belly Benjamin. The same dude who busts into the inn last night and cranks my arm just 'cause I wanna know what you are up to which may have something to do with me and Kevin maybe."

Sarah whipped out her note pad, beginning to see another angle. Up to this point, she had noted incidents and questionable signs, including the divining rod pointing to the swath between the red-flagged sawhorses. If she could add to the list, pile up some more pointers, motives and circumstances, she might get a rise out of Gibble. Get the ball rolling. "So Kevin's got money problems," said Sarah. "How's your father handling it?"

"How do you think? Kevin squeals into the garage, whizzin' by the ol' Dodge, the rusted ram whatsis on top of the hood missin' his ribs by inches. Which means it's even worse--the brakes are shot. Which means the repair bill's even more than what he owed on the cheesy bike in the first place. Which means ol' daddy Benjamin is antsy as hell."

Letting Alice jabber on, asking her one or two little questions, Sarah speculated that this little scene took place the morning after the poisoning of the puppy, perhaps some six hours before Katie's last run.

"So," Alice continued, warming to the subject, "I says 'Hi', wigglin' my hips a little, fannin' my hair back, clippin' it into a ponytail. You know what I mean. Had this big floppy white T-shirt way down my jeans, red letters that say 'Take Me' plastered over my breasts. Just to make Kevin feel better, you know? Get his mind off things. When I say, 'Wanna hear a dirty joke?' ol' Benjamin comes out screamin' 'Shut your face, Alice' and lays into Kevin about his tab."

Sarah continued to hang back, hoping to get some inkling of Kevin's state of mind that day and, if she could sift through Alice's loopy flights of fancy, get a bead on why he was so reluctant to talk about Katie's fall or its aftermath.

"So," Alice said, jabbering faster and faster, pulling the banana clip out of her hair and slapping it against her palm. "I tell the joke anyways. You see, this rough guy grabs this tender babe like me. And he says real gruff, 'I want what I want when I want it.' And she says back--are you ready for this? She says, 'I'll give you what I got when I get it.' . . . Get it, get it?"

Leaning back against the theater-entrance doorjamb, Sarah faked a smile. She checked her watch again and tried to disregard the insistent hunger pangs.

"Then ol' Benjamin tosses his rusty rag and shakes me. Says I got a foul mouth, says Kevin ain't interested, and then lays into Kevin about payin' up or else: eight-fifty for the bike and two-fifty for the repairs. Then adds droppin' the bowl, taking off the lid, slingin' in a gasket or takin' the whole choke part for one-fifty more. Plus, if Kevin don't deal with the brakes, he's goin' nowhere. Money-wise and bike-wise he is totally up the kazoo."

"Hold it," Sarah cut in. "What about working on the estate and painting the drop and acting and--?"

"Yeah, right, sure." Alice's entire frame was gyrating now as she slapped the banana clip harder against her palm. "Mark says he's gonna beat his butt 'cause he didn't do a lick of work, didn't finish any of his chores and all. Ol' Katie pooh says he'll get paid as soon as she pays off her expenses from the proceeds of the shows and look where she is. And Tommy -- what a waste, man. He goes around in a fog--so nice, so neat, so spaced-out. Worryin' about his nowhere grape patch and doesn't want to know about nothin'. So what does that leave? I mean, who does he turn to for some much needed coin. I mean, what do we do?"

Checking her watch frantically, gazing back at the field every few seconds, Alice continued to run off at the mouth, as if trying to catch up with something that was speeding away. "So I says to Kevin, right in front of ol' Benjamin--I mean, I was tryin' to get some kind of line on where we stand, you know? I says, 'Look, we can talk about your problems or I can help you with your lines. Whatever you need.' And he says, 'No point.' Like he was thinkin' of splittin' or somethin'."

Jabbering out of control now, Alice told how they first got together: her offering to read the other parts, especially in one particular scene in which the Conjur Woman proclaims, "All you got to do is promise and you git the thing you wants, the blue-eyed gal'." Then Kevin as the Witch Boy answers, "No more ridin' with my eagle, black against the moonlight . . ." But, for some reason, it appears that lately Kevin had been drawing a blank: unable to repeat the digging in the graveyard speech. Or the "I'll miss the moonlight" lines and "What if there's no way the blue-eyed gal can be true?"

Off on a sudden tangent, Alice asked Sarah if Russell could be right. And plays like *Macbeth* and *Dark of the Moon* are some kind of warning. Even though, to Alice's mind, the moon play was just a takeoff on *Romeo and Juliet*. The only difference being that it took place in the Deep South and this time Romeo was a witch boy. Still and all, there was a bad prophesy in it, like the cauldron thing in *Macbeth*.

"So," Alice blurted out, not waiting for an answer, marching over and staring right in Sarah's face, "what I'm sayin' is, he's been clamming up on me, lookin' weird. And I got so pissed I yelled out, 'Say it. Say you'd rather hang with me, Kevin. Especially after all I done and all.' And he takes off. Guns the bike, leavin' me in the watchamacallit."

"Lurch," Sarah said, looking into Alice's sliver of a face. "Acting strange right before digging Katie out."

"Who said? who said?" Alice spun away and loped back over to the verge, scuffing the dandelions with her floppy sneakers. "What are you doin', man? What we're talkin' is woman's stuff not detective crap. Why are you here anyways? What are you drivin' at?"

"I'm just listening," said Sarah, moving out into the haze, feeling a bit lightheaded, trying to close in on something. "Listening to you tell me about Kevin."

"Hey look," Alice said, digging the toe of her sneaker into the dandelion roots, sending up a spray of sandy dirt, "I took a chance on you, man. I mean, who else is there to find out about this stuff 'cept dopey one-eye boozer Doreen? I figure you for somebody who's been around the block and . . . I mean, this is my first time for rice cakes."

"And I've got somebody waiting for me in a hospital who doesn't have all day. And if you'll level with me, maybe you can do some good."

"Right. What do I matter? Forget it. Just furr-get it. I got business."

"What's going on, Alice?"

"Yeah. Wouldn't you like to know."

Alice bolted away and headed back toward the open field. Sarah hurried after her. A swarm of needle-like insects whirred out of a clump of lavender wildflowers. Whipping her blazer over her head, Sarah batted them away, losing her balance and then regaining it, trudging on after Alice who was now scampering dead ahead through the high saw grass.

Sarah rushed forward, losing ground, following in Alice's wake where the waist-high weeds and grasses were tamped down. Still way ahead, getting a little too cute, Alice zigzagged off the beaten path and twisted something. Wincing and yelling, she hopped around, kneading her thigh with both hands.

"Terrific," Sarah said, finally cornering her against a thicket of brambles. "Nothing like a good heart to heart."

"In your ear."

"Now now. As we were saying--"

Gingerly putting her weight on one leg then another, Alice said, "I was saying about <u>me</u>, get it? Me!"

"Absolutely. What you've done for Kevin. And perhaps the ways you've tried to get rid of your chief rival."

"I don't know what you're talkin' about," said Alice, screwing up her beady eyes. Turning back toward the playhouse, checking her watch yet again and peering hard, Alice said, "What is this? Where are they? Later,man."

Alice straightened up and began to bob and weave, looking for an opening. Sarah shifted directly in front of her and said, "Why not now? Maybe I'll cross you off my list."

"Oh whoop-ti-doo."

Alice tried to sidestep but Sarah pressed her back. Still flicking her beady eyes left and right, Alice undid her banana clip and held it like a dagger. Sarah snatched it away.

"What was that?" said Sarah. "Some kind of threat?"

"You got it."

"In line with swiping keys and checkbooks? And leaving dead squirrels?"

"Like hell. Show me some facts, man."

"You show me," Sarah said.

"Take a hike. And give me back my clip."

"Just between the two of us."

"Stuff it. If Benjamin hears you been hasslin' me, you better watch your back. 'Cause he's got more than garage stuff, believe me. He's got guns and you name it."

Letting that one pass, Sarah said, "Okay. Tell me how you feel about Katie and we'll call it quits."

"Right, sure." Alice shoved Sarah aside. Sprinting past her before Sarah could regain her balance, Alice raced back through the swath of tamped-down grass to the playhouse. Sarah lingered in the glare of the shimmering haze as the hunger pangs took over. She tried to slough them off one more time but it was no use. Reaching into her shoulder bag, she rummaged around until she came up with a packet of dried fruit. As she ate, she wondered what had gotten into her. She hadn't run after anybody like that since she was a kid. It was simply not her style.

Plopping down onto a bed of clover, munching some dried apricots, she pulled back and made some more notes: drawing arrows between teen-like crush, his Witch Boy role, money needs and Katie. She also included his possible use of desperate, gullible Alice. As she jotted down her findings, she noticed that the neat columns had given way to scribbles, scrawls and splotches. She obviously needed a break.

Putting away her pad and pen, she closed her eyes and rested her brain, allowing her thoughts to meander and drift. Her mind returned to those bygone moments of symmetry when everything seemed to be in its right place. She thought of her boyfriend, the English instructor at New Haven Community Technical College, who would be coming home in a few days. Which meant more polishing of his Civil War Poetry manuscript, writings that reflected a much simpler time. She vaguely remembered one of the poems . . . someone named Timrod was orating like Marlon Brando in the movie version of *Julius Ceasar*:

> ". . . Call thy children of the hill,
> Wake swamp and river, coast and rill,
> Rouse all thy strength and all thy skill,
> Carolina!"

Timrod led her to Whitman's ode to the fallen:

> "The moon gives you light,
> And the bugles and the drums give you music,
> And my heart, O my soldiers, my veterans,
> My heart gives you love."

Sarah felt calmer. The little muscles around her mouth were relaxed, her eye lids were definitely softer. Flicking her eyes open, Sarah said aloud, "'Carolina? . . . The moon gives you light'? Back to the play again?" Sighing, she added, "Right. Okay, that's it, everybody up."

Surveying the area, at a loss as to what to do next, she caught sight of a few flashes and glints coming from the direction of the backstage area. Moving closer, the glints began to take on a definite shape. Soon she could make out what appeared to be a rather large movie camera. She recalled

Alice's talk show act and realized she had never found out exactly what Russell was up to. More forays into the world of sin? Or something else like capitalizing on Katie's plight?

Swallowing the last handful of raisins, she wondered if Russell was right. Perhaps she had seen far too many films. However, at the same time, the movies she appreciated were not a waste. They had a logic to them, a pattern, a form. You could always ask yourself, Where is this going? And rest assured there was a destination. The screenwriter had a payoff in mind. The director had a sense of integrity. It was all worth the effort.

Okay, Sarah thought, walking through the swath of weeds. Check it out. Include it as a possibility or chuck it. Get past the shopping list of inklings.

Nine

esting backstage by one of the velvet-black wings, Sarah waited for the kicker. By this time, Alice had split. Walked out over the issue of payment. She had settled for compensation for time spent and stalked off the shoot, insinuating that Russell had been leading her on. Her exit had not only unnerved Russell, it had also dismayed the balding and squat cameraman: a boy-man sporting rimless glasses, a baby blue polo shirt with a monogrammed orange pocket and yellow baggy pants. It had taken said cinematographer, foley artist, best boy, gaffer and grip all rolled into one, a good fifteen minutes to pack up, his outfit replete with enough lenses and sound attachments to film an epic. In a huff, he too had accused Russell of misrepresentation and scurried off. Whatever Russell was up to was part sham and, evidently, part red herring as well.

Still sitting, tapping her fingers on the clear-lacquered wooden arm of a director's chair, Sarah could no longer put up with Russell's evasions, quips and homilies. In the interim since their last meeting they had lost ground and he was treating her like Katie's little playmate of old, someone who had no idea what grownups have to go through. By this point, Sarah had whiled away a good thirty minutes. It was now a few minutes after two.

"Quit it," Sarah finally said, springing to her feet. "Quit jerking me around. There is no link to *Macbeth*. No connection to a southern play written during World War II which is just an umpteenth version of an old ballad. Which, taken together, has nothing to do with anything except as another way to keep me in the dark."

In response, Russell asked her opinion about morality and restraint in the face of darker urges. Could she at least admit that she'd experienced the magic hour between waking and dreaming? Could she at least admit that she'd been led into temptation and often witnessed storm clouds gathering?

Sarah rolled her eyes. At the same time, for one second, some part of her felt a twinge of recognition.

"So," said Sarah, instantly coming to her senses, "the only thing we've got so far is a fondness for antiques."

"Oh?" said Russell, now giving her his full attention.

"Old ballads and plays, an old vineyard gone to seed and, in your case, the same tired fixation for that ol' time religion. Only difference is, this time you'd like to get it on film."

Russell ambled around, buttoning and unbuttoning his oversized white cotton jacket, running his massive hands through his gray crinkly hair.

Following right behind him, Sarah added, "But—and this is key--where oh where is the brother whose stepsister may not make it through the night?"

"Casual sex, Sarah," said Russell, pivoting, holding his ground, eyeing her face to face. "Where oh where is the concern for that? And rampant infidelity--here, there, everywhere. Then we've got --"

"That's it, Russell. Keep deflecting. That's what you're good at."

Thrown for a second, Russell began to paw the air. Then he got back on track. "I am not deflecting. I am directly on target. Intervention, that's what this is all about. Alice, the same age Katie was, afflicted with misguided notions. Believing the pittance I was hoping to pay her for her video testimony would detain her lust object: as if Benjamin would accept the one hundred dollars and wait for the rest. As if Kevin would take the money from her. Yes, the same age as Katie when you-know-what."

"Drop it," Sarah said, folding up the chair, all but giving up. "Can the time warp, drop the games and give me a break."

Russell tried to smile but his ruddy complexion grew redder and his full lips tightened. “Games?” Russell said. “You think this is all a game?”

“Obviously. Right off the bat you toss me a curve with some fabricated triangle between Katie, this Mark character and Tommy. And throw Kevin in to boot.”

“Yes . . . Kevin . . . very good, very good.”

“Anything to slough me off, even refuse to consider Katie’s condition so you can do your whacko thing with Alice and take over her playhouse.”

“Excuse me?”

“Oh please. We’ve got part of a neon sign sticking out on the marquee. We’ve got live footage for your snake oil and revival show. The least you can do is admit it.”

Russell clenched a fist and then quickly walked offstage, returned with a Thermos, emitted one of his deep, patented sighs, straightened up the director’s chair, took three interminably long sips of iced tea and sank deep into the canvas seat. It was ploy number three. During an impasse, he customarily would ease off and busy himself. When he was unsure of his next move, he would babble. When he felt confronted and had difficulty containing his anger, as he did now, the response pattern switched. Sure enough, he set the Thermos on the stage floor, reached into his pocket and drew out his white clay pipe, the one with the tiny bowl and long slender stem. Russell didn't smoke. With this prop, his hammy fist was forced to relax to keep from crushing the fragile bowl. Continuing to employ this device, his limpid eyes floating up and scanning Kevin's murky drop, he managed to cross one ankle over the other, doing his damnedest to appear casual and totally in control of his flexing fingers as they caressed the pipe bowl.

One more sigh as Russell segued into his chiding mode, eyes still on the backdrop, his voice weary, the impatience and anger not quite contained. "Sarah, what if I told you we are basically on the same page?"

Russell placed the stem in his mouth and sucked on it. This part of the ploy was patently learned from other pipe smokers and designed to keep listeners hanging and at bay. Other variations included tamping down the tobacco, fiddling with matches and cleaning the bowl. Anything short of actually smoking would do as he calculated his next tactic.

"If only you weren't so matter-of-fact," Russell continued, his tired eyes still gazing up, still buying time before he could once again go on the offensive. "So flippant, so offhand. Like the time you toyed with that do-it-yourself religion. You know, at the Shoreline Unitarian Church where, in some casual way, one comes up with ones own theology."

Sarah countered, unable to wait it out a second longer. "That's it, keep it up. Look down; look away. Forget all the Assembly of God churches that either gave you the sack or shunted you from pillar to post. Block out the fact that, as of six weeks ago, right before Katie's wedding, you had no prospects. Zero. Keep deflecting and keep trying to bill yourself as a missionary for God."

As if she had finally prodded something loose, the routine snapped. It was imperceptible at first, but Sarah soon noticed that Russell was no longer looking heavenward; his round eyes were gazing directly at her. And his tone was flat.

"Call it what you will. Then accept the pattern, accept current events; accept the facts."

"Great. Terrific. Tell me the truth and I'll let her know she's blameless."

Springing to his full giant size, turning his back on her, Russell said, "When you're ready to listen, maybe we'll continue." Tapping the long tapering pipe stem on his lips, he added, "I really don't have the time."

"Right," said Sarah. "But plenty of time for this phony documentary. And bulldozing the lot for that church auditorium that never got built while Katie was getting married."

"What does that have to do with anything?"

"Nothing. Everything." said Sarah, putting away her notes. "You and this guy Mark. Two of a kind; both hell bent on plowing things under."

The snap of the clay pipe startled them both. The ensuing silence was palpable. They both gazed at the bowl in the palm of Russell's right hand and the jagged reed-like stem in his left.

Pocketing the pieces inside his billowing jacket, Russell sauntered out of the backstage entrance into the muggy heat. Keeping pace, just as silent, Sarah followed behind. As he threaded his way through the beaten path, Russell kept stretching and flexing his fingers as if yearning to throttle some offensive substance.

Passing by the dingy ripples of the pond, little by little, Russell resumed his mellow sermonizing, covering his tracks as it were, dismissing anything that might be misconstrued. Pointing to the stagnant water, he said, "You see? The well has been poisoned. Once you pull God out, it all seeps in."

"Absolutely," Sarah said, shrugging him off. "Whatever you say."

A moment later, out of breath trying to keep up with him, Sarah began to hang back, her legs aching from all the tramping back and forth in her hiking boots. The heady smell of lilac filled the air as they filed by the site of the incident. Heat lightning flashed across the clotted sky, the dim sunlight pulsing like a fading signal.

"So what will it take?" said Russell, over his shoulder, intoning, working on his resonance. Stroking his beard, weaving through the vineyard stakes, he asked again. "What will it take to cure this sleeping sickness? This fatal virus?"

"Russell," said Sarah, as they reached the full sweetness of the lilac spikes. "The only thing close to death is Katie. Got it?"

Russell stopped beside the tangle of shoots and spikes. Sarah bent down to tie the laces of her boots, warding off the cloying scent, hazy heat and abiding hunger.

"So," said Russell, abruptly changing the subject. "When did you say you'd be heading back? To New Haven, I mean?"

"I didn't."

"But your job?"

"Don't worry about it." Sarah reminded herself that she had till noon tomorrow to make up her mind about the editing position but she certainly wasn't going to tell Russell. Not after his shuffle, tap dance and smokescreen act.

"Still and all," Russell said, switching gears again, "it's a pity you can't help. Turn your focus on Mark, Tommy and Kevin. Put their antics up on a screen."

"Good ploy. Loan me your cameraman, the aging cherub with the huge lenses. Let's get it all on film including you."

Without warning, Russell was off again, breaking into a diatribe about the countless pornographic web sites available to any youngster with the click of a mouse. He mentioned the shock value of rock music, the in-your-face lyrics, the cynicism of what passes for humor in all phases of the entertainment industry. He added the dog-eat-dog materialism to his list and labeled it Darwinism, claiming that people nowadays—even though they gave lip service to the idea—really had no handle on the relative importance of things. He went back to cynicism; a topic that seemed to unsettle him the most.

Then he stopped rambling. For a fleeting instant, there was another possibility of an actual exchange. But the moment passed and the chance was gone.

Without warning, Russell turned sharply on his heels and headed past the barn apartments toward the sprawling main house. As he quickened his pace, he threw up his hands and called out, "What is the use?"

Calling back, Sarah said, "Did you tell Tommy I'm around? Did you at least do that?"

Russell seemed to nod, pausing for a moment, cocking his shaggy head to the right and then the left as if scanning the terrain, and then hurried off.

By the time Sarah reached the shade of the barn's narrow overhang, she was ready to reconsider her options. She could stop sputtering and spinning her wheels and turn in what little she had. See what Gibble had to say and take it from there.

Looking over her notes, the only thing she could check off as a tangible were the flecks of Day-Glo at the forked tip of the diving rod. Perhaps they represented some kind of traffic signal of misdirection. Prompted Katie to make a nightly mad dash down her customary path, in the dark and pouring rain, suddenly veer to the left, stumble and plunge. In combination with the even marks left by the dragged sawhorses, coupled with the red flags, it was conceivable that someone had set up a detour. And it was also possible that these telltale signs weren't left there because of an oversight but, since the incident was dismissed as an accident, there was no need to cover up anything more than the cistern.

She thought of getting her camera to record her findings. But for some reason she sensed there was no time. She worked her way back through the tangle of vines, stakes and trellises to the spot. She scoured the area looking high and low, retracing her steps. The results were the same. The mounted divining rod was gone. So were the deep and even sawhorse tracks and the mounds of dirt and deep pits as well. All that remained were a dozen or so patches of freshly tamped-down earth.

She plopped down, nestling herself in a thicket of grape leaves. She made no more notes, not about what had just happened, not about Russell, his cameraman and Alice, nor about the way Russell had snapped his pipe. She put aside the fact that she hadn't touched base with Tommy, let alone exchanged one word with Mark or seen him up close. She scuttled the rest of her rounds, feeling that it was all moving beyond her in ways that not even she, the consummate moviegoer, could imagine.

Ten

All morning Tommy had traipsed around the main house, weary of the ramshackle colonial; weary of the mildew odor that followed him through each paisley-wallpapered room; weary of spotting his bland reflection in every cross-hatched window: two pleasant eyes, pleasant nose, pleasant mouth. Tired of his customary way of letting everything slide, letting everything go by, just going along. There had to be more colors in life than pale blue, more interesting states of being than an even keel.

Even Katie's condition--the critical shape she was in, the doubtful prognosis--had been placed at arms length: like unfortunate information on the six o'clock news.

By noon, he had finally found a way to stir himself. It involved actually raising the vineyard from decay, accomplishing something and perhaps, at last, making his mark. To cease being so nice, so "that's-too-bad-but-let's not-make-a-fuss" about everything.

Now, sitting in the study, he went over his argument, the exact words and phrases he would use in accomplishing the first order of business--firing Mark. He leafed once more through the dog-eared journal, the one he had searched for and finally located amid the cellar debris. According to these jottings and inscriptions, the vintner who had originated this particular strain of grapes was named Willy. The self-same person the realty agent had lauded for his expertise and renown in the not so distant past. If he, Tommy, could become pro-active as they say, it would have been worth every penny he had sunk into this place, worth the last vestiges of his inheritance.

But was it worth everything that had happened? Thoughts of Katie rotting away in that hospital, thoughts he had tried to put aside, filtered into his consciousness. So did thoughts of Mark and Katie and the scratches on Mark's face. If he could pull off the firing venture, he could start to gain a little self-respect. Feel vital and alive. Perhaps come to terms with everything.

He riffled again through the notations. It was past two-thirty and the stifling heat seemed to be closing in again, like another obstacle he would have to overcome. He rolled up the sleeves of his white oxford buttoned-down shirt and undid the second button. Presently, voices drifted in from the kitchen. Shutting the door would only make the mugginess worse. The single crosshatched window was open as wide as it would go. It was no use. The voices rose annoyingly, marring any chance to polish the arguments he would use with Mark.

"Keep away from the dang dozer, Russell," said Mark, yelling out in that fake country-western drawl of his.

"You don't understand," Russell intoned. "I've had experience. I've cleared out land, I assure you. For a church auditorium on the Shore, in point of fact."

"I don't care what you did. Just keep your paws off."

"Look, Mark, the road has to be cleared anyway to utilize the playhouse."

"Look, if you don't kiss off, so help me . . ."

The voices trailed off for a few moments and then trickled back, more insistent than ever. Tommy decided then and there that he had to get Russell off the property as well. And Kevin. He had to totally clean house and control things. Unencumbered. Otherwise the whole enterprise, like everything else he had ventured these past years, would come to naught.

A whirring noise drifted into the study, mixing in with the heated tones. Doubtless the sound came from the food processor Katie had insisted on buying to go with their "country look."

Tommy rose from the Ottoman clutching the journal. He smoothed his wispy hair and hitched up his chinos just above his waist to gird himself for a firm exchange. Ready as could be, he strode past the dining room, paused by the kitchen and peered in.

Grinding up strips of carrots, beets and celery stalks, Mark cocked his sunburned face and poked a finger at Russell, the scar from the scratches by his left temple more prominent than ever. Framed in the doorway, Tommy lowered his eyes, not knowing quite what to do.

"Ah," said Russell stepping forward, his bulk looming over Tommy's shortish form. "Just in time. Certainly it makes no difference to you if I use the bulldozer. Tell Mark it's your prerogative."

"If you don't goddamn get off it, Russell . . . I mean, don't mess with me. You got it?"

Continuing to hover over Tommy, Russell said, "Well? Will you kindly intercede and end this silliness?"

Letting the food processor grind away, Mark turned Russell completely around. "Listen, pal, I got news. You got no call, no rights, no nothin'. You are a deadbeat squatter, that is all."

Still at a loss, Tommy watched Russell and Mark square off, standing toe to toe in profile, both almost the same height, bulk against muscle. Breaking the silence, Russell rubbed his hands together, making a kind of popping noise. He emitted a rumbling groan, spun back around and padded out, almost knocking Tommy over.

Chuckling, calling after Russell, Mark said, "Tommy here's silence is your answer, fan-tan. Like I told you, you ain't usin' the dozer, ain't touchin' nothin'. So you might as well split."

Mark ambled back to the processor, which was still whirring away atop the long butcher-block counter. In turn, Tommy eased in, braced himself and finally spoke, the words practically stuck in his throat. "As it happens . . . as Russell just pointed out this is still my house, Mark . . . still my property."

Mark said nothing; his lips reverting back to his usual cocky leer as he wiped the vegetable drool into the sink.

Holding up the battered old journal, Tommy went on. "What I mean to say is . . . obviously nothing is going right with you here, the arrangement doesn't work. And besides, I have the original vintner's notes to um . . . back me up."

"What are you sayin'? Who you talkin' about?"

"His name was Willy. Surely, given your history with the place, you must have known him."

Mark ignored him, inserting more assorted vegetable slices into the slot.

"Willy. I said his name was Willy."

The leer dissolved. "I don't wanna hear it, okay? Got no time."

"Then you have to make time. As I suspected, the pruning has to be finished before bud-break. The middle of May in point of fact."

"I said I don't wanna hear it."

"I'm sorry, Mark. But it looks like . . ." Tommy took a breath and forced himself to spell it out. He couldn't just keep hanging back. Not after all this, and not when he now knew what had to be done. "You see, I'm going to have to bring someone in with a viticulture background. Someone who can tell the strength and size of the wood, determine its health. And determine exactly how many buds to leave on each vine."

Mark glared at him.

Pointing at the underlined passages in the journal, Tommy added, "It has to be done now: while they're in the dormant stage: while they still haven't used up their stored energy. Look here! That's what this Willy fellow notes. And he surely knows, judging from all these entries. He was the creator of the vineyard and the strain of vine, as you must know."

Mark's T-shirt was now stained with the rusty-colored mixture, his pectoral muscles flexing as if ready to take out his frustrations on the food processor. Instead, he grabbed the journal out of Tommy's hand and pitched it through the open kitchen window. "Are you threatenin' me, is that it?"

"No," said Tommy, his eyes darting in all directions. "You mustn't take this personally."

"Really?"

"Yes. It's not just you. There's no need for Kevin either, now that the play's been canceled."

"Brilliant. There was no need for him ever."

"Although he did locate the cistern."

"I goddamn located the cistern. And I'll be glad to boot Kevin the hell out."

"Yes, well . . ." The familiar mechanism was seeping in: backing off, stepping aside, letting others take charge and deal with messy things.

Pulling himself up so that he didn't feel so much shorter than Mark, so much slighter, Tommy kept his eyes trained on the open window so as to avoid Mark's sunburned face, and tried to press on. "As I was explaining, I have to get an expert in. And as this Willy points out, pumps must be installed plus pipes and hoses. A full water distribution system, gravity fed, controlling the exact seepage if the vineyard is to succeed."

"What is that supposed to mean?"

Straining to stay on track, Tommy said, "For one, it means I have to put in a tank high above the vineyard. And since I couldn't bear using the cistern, I'll have to hire people."

"Hire? Hire? What are you talkin'--the goddamn army corps of engineers?" The processor seemed to vibrate and shake more insistently, jiggling close to the edge of the counter.

"The bottom line is . . . I don't need a caretaker. What I need is, what I've decided to do is . . ."

"Just like Russell, you are doin' nothin', man. 'Cause you don't know crap, what you read is crap and, except for getting' rid of the rest of the dead wood around here, you only wastin' time."

"I'm sorry."

"You got that right. Sorry as they come." Mark switched off the processor, poured the juice concoction in a tumbler and moved straight to Tommy's side. "Why don't you put the house on the market like you said and be done?"

"I never."

"I suggested it, you nodded."

"But that was before I . . . I . . ."

"Before you what?" said Mark, holding up a glass of goopy liquid as he inched even closer. "Look, it's over, dum-dum. Might as well clear out. Cut your losses."

Tommy tried to slip out of it. Find some means of accommodation. But the scratches on Mark's temple, the marks Katie must have made, were staring him right in his face. Reflexively, he slapped the glass with the back of his hand. Juice splattered in Mark's eyes, all over his neck and T-shirt. His thick forearm caught Tommy in the throat, driving him back, spinning him around and ramming his head against the window casing. The pressure against his Adam's apple cut off his air, caught his tongue, clogged his throat.

"Don't screw around, jerk off." Mark held him pinned like that for a few more seconds before he relented and finally pulled back..

Tommy closed his eyes, doing his level best to keep the tears from welling up. They ran down his cheeks anyway. Not since that time at Taft School when they grabbed him in his pajamas and dangled him out the window had he ever been so humiliated, ever let anyone see him cry.

Behind him, he heard a rustle, something flitting close by. Slowly rolling his head to the right, he caught a glimpse of Doreen outside the window; her ridiculous bulging good eye only a yard or two past the bushes. It wasn't possible. She couldn't be there, not at this exact moment. But there she was.

He tried to straighten up, get a hold of himself, but tears kept streaming down his cheeks.

He bent over, dropped his head, hung onto the porcelain basin, prayed he wouldn't vomit and slapped on the faucet. The gushing water cooled his face but did nothing for the bruise and pain inside his throat. He sipped the trickling water, swallowing as gently as possible. When he finally glanced up, Doreen was gone.

"You're a joke," said Mark, his back to Tommy, sopping up the mess on the floor with paper towels, "all of you. Russell. Ole Katie just askin' for it. And you not knowin' a leaf bud from a fruitin' bud. Whacking 'em all off with your dumb trellises. And now blabberin' about a watering system you couldn't begin to understand."

Mark rose up, his snicker growing into a foot-stomping hoot as Tommy shut off the water. "I mean, everybody blows it some time but you three take the prize."

The slap on the back did the trick. Tommy lurched out of the kitchen, stumbled over to his right and yanked open the cellar door.

"Now don't take it so hard, Tommy," Mark called after him. "I've seen 'em come and go. You ain't the first."

Tommy scuffed down the wooden steps, his throat still burning, his Adam's apple still aching and bruised. Tramping around in the half-light, brushing away the cobwebs, he scoured the clammy flagstone walls, shoved aside the wooden crates trying to remember where he saw it. He bent low under the tubular heating ducts, sweeping his arms across the moldy earth. He knew it was here, knew he was within ten feet of it. But where exactly? Where was it hidden?

Pulling back, tripping over some empty liquor boxes, he hurried back to the foot of the steps and started over, making his way to the left this time. Was it on top of the water heater? No. Inside the coal chute? No, again.

Digging under the dusty black chunks with his hands, he finally remembered. He got up, whisked past a brace of supporting posts and came upon the old coal-burning furnace. It was huge, red and round, like a steamship's boiler. He yanked open the burner door. It wasn't there. He scuttled behind the furnace and reached into an open slot. He sucked in his breath as the tip of his fingers grazed the stubby grip and pulled it toward him. It was smaller than he remembered. He flipped open the cylinder. Six cartridges: more than enough. For what? He didn't know. He slapped the cylinder shut and eased his index finger around the trigger. An almost uncontrollable urge came over him to squeeze it, the urge coming at the same time his swallowing became almost impossible.

He reached into the slot again, stretching his fingertips until he touched the tube. Slowly, gingerly, he drew it out. Another slow reach, stretching even further, produced a box of spare cartridges. What was he thinking of? In case, he told himself again. In case of what? He had no idea.

An involuntary shiver ran up his spine, a sensation he'd never felt before; at least not since those days at prep school. There was something at work here, something about the pain that exhilarated him, made the blood race and his heart pump faster.

But this is crazy, he thought. What are you doing?

He stood still and waited for his mind to clear. He waited in vain. The pain in his throat dominated, everything continued to quicken like pulses of electric current.

He flirted with the idea of target practice. After he cleaned himself up and regained a little equilibrium.

"Yes," said Tommy aloud. "I was quite good once. Quite good indeed." He spotted an old burlap sack, tossed in the .32, the silencer and the box of cartridges, folded the sack under his arm and scampered up the cellar steps.

Eleven

It didn't take long for Sarah to shake herself out of it. At first she had just sat there feeling like an idiot. She could just picture Jan on the police beat back in New Haven chiding her: "It's simple, Bucklin -- those who can't deal, edit. They stay off the streets, they keep out of the way."

From that point she continued to put herself down: for overlooking the divining rod and the sawhorses with the red flags--the signs of misdirection; for jotting them down like items on a grocery list and walking off. Then, she switched gears. This was all new to her and she had no way of knowing that some possible culprit, or whatever it was that was going on, was not about to hold still. More to the point, she was only taking soundings. She was an intermediary, a go-between trying to get the police to do their job. In addition, she hadn't yet even completed her rounds.

And there was one more thing. This was her first time up in this neck of the woods. Everything was so oddly secluded: no neighbors as far as she could tell, no traffic on the narrow meandering road. Buffered on all sides by trees, hills and undergrowth. To Katie's mind it was "all so-o-o perfect." In Sarah's view, it was something else.

Still and all, she wished she had taken pictures of the detour signs, wished she'd been a little quicker on the draw.

In any event, she still had her work cut out for her. She would blunder, she would learn; she would get help. She would somehow get the job done.

Now, a few minutes past three on this endless Saturday, Sarah stood at the edge of the back lawn, watching the sunlit shadows flit in and around the main house. While she'd been on her hiatus, circumstances had probably shifted. The games doubtless had entered another phase.

Approaching the spanning back porch, about to pass through the jutting columns, she caught a glimpse of herself through a windowpane. Her face was sweaty, her blouse was wrinkled and her bobbed hair was flopping over her eyes and ears. Somehow in all the trudging around she'd completely lost sight of her appearance and how she must have come across. In her disheveled state, Tommy or Mark might very well roll their eyes, not even give her the time of day.

Skirting back to the drive at the side of the house and her beat-up Honda Accord, she tossed her crumpled linen blazer in the back seat, applied a dab of rouge, brushed her hair, tucked in her blouse, got out her tortoise-shell horn-rimmed glasses from the glove compartment, snatched her Sunday-go-to-meeting blue blazer from the hook above the back door and exchanged her clodhoppers for suede loafers. Heading for the front door this time, adjusting her shoulder bag until it fit smartly, she reminded herself that she was still out in left field and still had nothing to go on.

Knocking produced no response. She heard a buzz deep inside to the right but couldn't identify the source. Slipping through the square-headed doorway, the musty odor caught her attention first; then the peeling paisley wallpaper and the hand-hewn beams of oak running overhead. The wide-planked bare floor squeaked no matter how gingerly she stepped.

Past the front entry hall, she came upon a huge walk-in stone fireplace replete with iron kettles, long-handled frying pans and brass skimmers--all suspended from a trammel. Turning right, she weaved through a cluster of ladderback chairs and gateleg tables, turned right again and came upon the source of the noise. The surfer, whom she assumed was Mark, switched off the juicer, stared at her for a moment and then grinned…

"Well now, what have we here? Got to be the owner of that old clunker on the drive." Mark wiped his hands on his jeans and added, "Hey, darlin', it's okay, I don't bite. Not at first."

Sarah bit her lip. How was she going to pull this one off? The guy had obviously been overcome by some country-western marathon and never recovered.

"Come on, now. You just step right in."

Sarah took a few steps forward through the doorway. Up close, Mark no longer reminded Sarah of a surfer. The whiskey-soaked voice and the hard green eyes that kept looking her up and down were more suited to one of those red-neck characters in that play Katie was fixated on, a supporting player in the cast of *Dark of the Moon*. The full lips permanently set in a cocky leer, scruffy dirty blond hair, juice-stained T-shirt and rippling sunburned muscles completed the picture. The kind of male Sarah had always tried to avoid, the ones with the unknown threat lurking behind the laid-back style. Unconsciously, she patted her bag, checking to make sure the mace was still handy.

Hanging back, Sarah said, "Can you tell me something?"

He didn't respond; just kept grinning and sizing her up.

Trying again, Sarah said, "I'm just checking some things out."

No response again. Still looking her up and down, making things worse.

"You see, Katie's an old childhood friend. And I promised I'd check things out."

"Come again?"

"In her letters, before what happened, she mentioned that--" Sarah stopped herself. Something about the way he was slicing up carrots and beets with the blade of a hunting knife was unnerving her, even more than the steady leer and the grungy look.

"Takin' a survey?" said Mark.

"Not exactly."

"Then what exactly?"

"Sorting things out, like I said. For Katie."

"You got a license?"

"For what?"

"You got any business or experience at this?"

"At what?"

"Nosin' around."

Deflecting, Sarah mentioned writing features for a New Haven paper but Mark wasn't buying it. He squinted at her as though contemplating his next move. Going to work next on a large head of cauliflower he said, "What did Miss Katie say about me in those letters?"

Sarah didn't like the way this was going, sidestepped a bit more and finally said, "Look, so far I've got some bits and pieces. If I could ease her mind when I go back to see her, before the curfew bell, I mean . . ."

The do-si-do was getting more awkward by the second. Sarah kept trying to be offhand about the whole thing and, at the same time, avoid setting this character off, give him any excuse to say or do God knows what.

More slicing of vegetable chunks and then Mark said, "You know, you look awful good. I don't know why. You're not my type. Maybe it's the comin' of spring. And you standin' there, plump and juicy."

"Look, I don't need this right now."

"Uh-huh. And what do you need?"

He was alternating now between nibbling and chopping, smirking and leering. Sensing at last that Sarah wasn't going to play, he said, "Now what is it you think you're doin'? Sarah, right? Yeah, she mentioned you once or twice. Come on, just spit it out."

"What is that supposed to mean?"

"It means you don't really think I'm gonna tell you anything. And you also don't think I'm gonna let you snoop around while things unravel round here. So what the hell's the point?"

It was during this little spiel that Sarah noticed the scar that skirted above his left eye. Caused recently perhaps.

After another pause, Mark said, "Well?"

Sarah said, "I guess you're not amenable."

"But hey, always got an itch to play--football, hide-and-seek, doctor--you name it." Pursing his lips, Mark wiped the blade of his hunting knife on his soiled T-shirt and continued to eye Sarah's body. "I mean, since snoopin' is outta your league, maybe we could find somethin' better for you to do."

The last remark did it. "Look, Jack, why don't you get off the act?"

"At least I got one. You got nothin' going for you so far."

"Right, forget it." Sarah stepped back and framed herself in the doorway. "If it isn't too much trouble, if I'm not putting you out too much, could you just tell me where I can find Tommy?"

Mark shook his head and shoved the hunting knife back in its sheath behind his hip pocket. "Hey, I'm tellin' you to get your butt back in that ol' Honda and quit messin' around."

"Thanks."

As an afterthought, Sarah turned back and said, "I don't suppose you can tell me about a divining rod? One of two with a big W etched on the handle and a barely decipherable W*illy*. One tacked onto a tree embossed in Day-Glo yellow. Not, of course, that it matters."

For a long moment Mark's rugged face went blank, as if his mind had suddenly wandered off. Just as quickly, he was back, the raspy voice minus the drawl. "You know how many quick talkers meander up here? Think they're wise, think they're on to somethin'? But in no time flat they're on the short end of the stick. And then, what do you know? Suddenly, they wake up."

With that final dismissal accomplished, Mark flipped on the juicer and shoved stalks and shards into the open slot.

Padding back past the ladderback chairs in the dining room, Sarah stopped short as Mark hollered, "Kevin is your man."

"Beg your pardon?" Sarah said, glancing back.

"Kevin was Tommy's water boy, hole digger and finder and user of the friggin' divinin' rod; probably on his way back to New Haven or New London or some New-freakin' city. I mean, considering the money he owes fat Benjamin, and the fact there's nothin' holdin' him here. Get it? Okay? You satisfied now?"

"Nothing holding him here?"

"No show, no playhouse. Tommy shut it down. Like I said, it's all peterin' out, goin' back to seed. Like always."

"Why are you telling me this?" Sarah called back.

"Say again?" Mark said for the umpteenth time.

"Why are you being informative all of a sudden?"

After taking a long pull from his veggie cooler, Mark said, "Hey, girl, I'm just sweepin' up. Helpin' things move along." The fake country-western drawl was back.

"Like I said," Mark added, "nothing for you here. 'Cept of course, ol' everlovin' me."

In the dim back lighting of the kitchen she hadn't noticed how striking the scar was above his left eye. But here in the dining hall, with the haze glinting through the windowpanes and off the side of his face, the grooves were clear and clean.

Mark asked her what she was staring at. Mimicking him as she turned left, Sarah called out, "Nothin'. Just considerin' what you said,is all. Takin' it all in."

She stood for a while, leaning against the stone fireplace. She tried to stay objective but the sex scenario kept running through her mind incorporating the scratches above his eye and Russell's innuendos. Still nothing she could corroborate, only more glints and glimmers camouflaging the proverbial what-lies-beneath.

Despite herself, images of the boating accident seventeen years ago crossed her mind. The images came prepackaged from Russell. She shut the images off and added Mark and his parting comments to her list. As before, she was getting somewhere; she was getting everywhere, she was getting nowhere. And the hunger was killing her.

She marched into the kitchen, intercepted Mark, grabbed a bowl full of chopped vegetables, threw some dollar bills on the butcher block slab and said, "That ought to cover it." Just before Mark completed his exit, he cautioned Sarah, advising her again to clear out now. She was alone in a spooky house with wild and crazy Tommy. He also noted her useless car phone and the need for an upgrade in case she got stuck: tri-mode with more frequencies like Tommy's new car, in case Katie was driving, alone, broke down in the dark and had to call home. Sarah disregarded all his cautionary remarks, plunked herself down on a stool and wolfed the veggies down.

Twenty minutes later, around four o'clock, Sarah finished puttering around the kitchen. The sound of water running upstairs had stopped a short time before, signaling—Sarah guessed-- that Tommy had finished his shower and would, at last, be coming downstairs.

On paper, Tommy should have been the first person Sarah had consulted as an ally, confidant and friend. In point of fact, Tommy should have been the first person to prod the police. But from all indications in Katie's letters, Tommy wasn't turning out as advertised. Under that pleasant, genteel veneer, apparently something else was brewing, especially between the two of them. Even before all this, Sarah had wondered about their relationship. Did he have a sense of humor, was he attentive and\or was he a terror in bed? Now, everything was convoluted by Katie's plight and intimations of jealousy. Thinking about all this and her clouded view of Tommy, Sarah was beginning to have second thoughts.

Strolling past the dining room and lingering between the stairwell and the screen door leading to the spanning back porch, Sarah found herself humming under her breath. It was the tune to *Barbara Allen*. The lyrics were "'Twas in the merry month of May, when green buds all were swelling . . ." Sarah's thoughts drifted and turned to Katie's mom. She recalled a willowy form, pale blue eyes, a mellow husky voice and slender fingers strumming a honey-brown old Gibson guitar. If memory served, Sarah and Katie were little kids sitting on a white wicker bench on Katie's back porch, similar to the one Sarah was now eyeing. It was a sunny day in May, just like the opening lyrics to the song. But even though the melody stayed the same, each version got a little darker. At the same time, Barbara Allen's own true love began to change from Sweet William to someone else. When Katie's mom asked what version was the best, Sarah hadn't known what to say. But Katie squealed that she loved them all. "They were all so-o-o-o good."

It was now the merry month of May and green buds all were swelling. But it was not at all clear which version of the ballad would prevail. Nor, despite Katie's recent protests to the contrary, whether Tommy was Sweet William come to life or someone entirely different.

More moments passed until Sarah finally heard the padded sounds of descending footsteps. She swiveled smartly to her left and stood once more by the immense stone fireplace. Presently, Tommy's compact form appeared opposite her at the bottom of the narrow encased stairway. He was wearing an open bush jacket with deep pockets over a fresh blue buttoned-down oxford, and chinos that perfectly matched the jacket. His wispy sandy hair was still damp; salve glistened from his Adam's apple. Clutching a battered old journal, he appeared distracted, off in some other world.

He whisked by so quickly that he was almost through the screen door and onto the colonnaded porch when Sarah called his name. Moving briskly, she called after him again. Tommy turned around and gazed at Sarah's approaching form with a puzzled look.

"Hi," said Sarah, averting the hazy rays of the afternoon sun with the back of her hand. "I know, I know, I should've called first." She left it at that, not wanting to go through a long explanation, especially given the odd way Tommy kept gazing past her.

"It's me, Sarah . . . The maid of honor, remember?" Still receiving no recognition, Sarah added, "Good grief, Tommy, it's only been six weeks. And Russell told you I was around."

"I know. Saw your car." Tommy assumed the familiar nonchalant stance and quietly asked, "What brings you here?"

"Her letters, " said Sarah, peering through her spread fingers.

"Letters? "

"Okay, I'm late. I was incognito. But I'm here now."

"To um . . ?"

"See what I can do. About what happened, I mean."

Tommy kept up the casual pose. But his eyes, which Sarah remembered as sparkling and blue, seemed bloodshot, the sockets lined with gray as if he hadn't slept for days.

"At a loss, I suspect." Tommy said, still tossing things off as if they were discussing what to have with tea.

"Not totally. And I could surely use some help."

"Not what I mean."

"Oh?" said Sarah, wondering where this was going.

Deflecting, looking past her again, Tommy made little innuendoes about how people misjudge other people. The somewhat familiar laconic responses lapsed into a few personal observations. The controlled pose of ease and serenity faltered as he dabbed at his throat. Sarah was glad he was conversing but, for all intents and purposes, he was talking to himself. Every time she mentioned the recent events or inserted some of her findings into their exchange, he merely nodded. Hesitating, then rambling in short quiet bursts, he went on about the possibility that one could become pro-active. No need to remain passive all the time.

"Agreed?" said Tommy, his back still to the sloping lawn, but now looking off to his right in the direction of the woods.

"Sure, Tommy," Sarah said. "No way what happened to Katie has to be accepted."

"Truly."

Tiring of this esoteric banter and the rays of the sun bearing down on her, Sarah said, "We can put it right. We can start now."

"We?" Tommy said, his bloodshot eyes narrowing a bit.

"Absolutely."

Tommy shifted the battered journal behind his back. Sarah asked him what he was hiding, seeking any opening to get back on track. Aside from murmuring, "Old vineyard records," he gently shook Sarah off once again.

"They say it's an inherited pattern," Tommy said, back in his distracted mode. In some apparent attempt at parody, Tommy cast his eyes to the ground, his shock of sandy hair falling across his forehead. "'Don't fret, my boy. Things have a way of working out . . . getting taken care of.'"

"Sometimes," said Sarah, reaching out to him like a friend. "But in this case, it's going to at least take some effort to get a rise out of the police."

Unable to take the glare a moment longer, she pulled her hands away from her eyes and stepped over to his side. Countering, Tommy dropped the journal, turned toward the woodlands and walked away from her. In that instant she caught a glimpse of bulges in the safari pockets but nothing definite registered.

"Come on," Sarah said, speaking to his back. "What would be better than popping into Katie's room together? And bringing her some good news?"

Tommy walked on a few more paces before he paused. His back still toward her, he said, "You haven't been listening."

"Look, let's get off it. You give me your take on all this and I'll give you mine."

Moving on, Tommy said, "The conversation is over."

"What conversation?"

"I'm afraid you'll have to leave."

He uttered something else about private property but Sarah couldn't quite make it out. The words and his form merged with the shimmers of light and the sun-dappled foliage. Sarah wanted to scream out that Katie dies when the world goes rotten on her, wanted to tell him that once she locked herself in her room because some guy in school spread some malicious rumors about her and she refused to eat for days. She wanted to yell lots of things to make him turn around but she realized it was no use.

Shielding her eyes again, Sarah wondered where Tommy was headed. There were no paths as far as she could tell. Just bramble, bits of stone wall and stands of thick oaks and pines. She also wondered why he hid the journal behind his back and then, as if he had more pressing concerns, let it drop out of his hands. Absentmindedly, she walked over to it, plucked it up and began leafing through the creased and wrinkled pages. The jottings meant nothing to her. The W scrawled in the upper right corner of the first two pages told her that the daybook belonged to the ubiquitous Willy who had made random notes about vines, pruning timetables and watering. There were a few scribbled dates, the last entry from sometime seven years back. And there was a memo, ostensibly to himself, about seeing things through.

It was another pointer in some other direction. She longed for Willy's straight arrow with the Day-Glo tip that someone had spirited away. She longed for a rational give-and-take with somebody, anybody at all. On more than a few occasions, her Dad had advised her that once you encounter an irrational person, it can throw off your entire day. The antidote is to limit your dealings thereafter to conservatives, graduates of the Harvard Business School, staunch Republicans and people of that ilk. It didn't take much imagination to picture Dad's response to her last series of exchanges.

Wiping her brow and unbuttoning her blazer, she went back into the main house, slipped into the study, made some more notations and tossed the journal onto the Ottoman. She glanced around for traces of 21st century technology—digital wide screen TVs with Tivo, video cams, lap tops, direct-dial cell phones, etc—knowing full well she would find nothing of the sort in Katie's bucolic domain. The food processor and car phone were Katie's only concessions to contemporary life.

As she ambled back out onto the spanning back porch she sensed something stirring to her left. Sprays of forsythia quivered and then stilled. There was a faint sucking sound as if someone was holding his breath. Then another quiver, the straggly stands of yellow, shaking once again. The intakes of breath and quivering alternated a few more times before the cropped hair and bangs broke through the bushes and the one good eye bulged up at Sarah from the bottom of the porch steps.

"Hey, hon," said Doreen. "Surprise, surprise, right? Well, I says to myself, you draw her a map you're as good as responsible."

"You have got to be kidding."

"No, ma'am."

"Look, Doreen, I don't know what you're doing here but I am in no mood."

"Ah, you see, you see? I should've warned you. But, since you're still in one piece, I'll just do it now and be on my way."

"Oh, puh-lease."

In the haze, with the cakes of makeup on her wrinkled face running and her good eye squinting, Doreen looked as if she was out to play trick or treat. "Listen," said Doreen, "this place is goin' bad by the minute. Tommy called off not just the play but the whole season."

"Well that figures."

"Uh-huh . . . but did you know it sent this Kevin character in a tizzy, ridin' his motorbike in circles, wakin' me up from my afternoon nap? And then Russell buggin' Mark about bulldozing only 'bout an hour ago. Him and Mark about to have at it, then Mark and Tommy actually—"

"Whoa. I know I'm going to regret it, but tell me anyways. How do you know all this?"

"I seen it, I seen it."

"How? What business is it of yours?"

"You're my business, felt responsible like I said. So's I figure I'd best look out for you."

"I'll bet."

"Look, it's not just the bad feelings. It's why--what you'd call background stuff. Like about Mark. Big football star at the high school, then got into a little trouble. But nothin' for the past seven years till these out-of-towners bust in. You add that to his womanizing and nobody in charge, it's like stokin' a fire. Now you get it? I mean, good lord."

"Get what?"

Doreen scuttled higher, fighting the purple Lycra dress that encased her lumpy form with every step. "The danger, hon, the danger."

"Gotcha. So, now that you've done your good deed, you can be on your way."

"Well, if that's the way you feel."

"That's the way I feel."

"Only tried to help."

"Right." Unable to take Doreen's popping eye another second, Sarah bounded past her down the steps. Abruptly turning back, she said, "You really want to make yourself useful?"

"You name it."

"Ask horny Mark how exactly he got the scratches over his eye. Find out who swiped Katie's keys and checkbook; who poisoned the puppy, when where and why. Help me come up with some damn answers."

Sarah didn't know why she blurted all that out. Doreen was doubtless good for nothing besides spreading dirt. Perhaps

Sarah was tired of pussyfooting around; perhaps she was letting off steam. Who knows?

A muted popping noise broke Doreen from her gaping stare. The stillness was followed by two more pops, then silence again. The sounds came possibly from an air rifle somewhere deep in the woods. The next series of pops fused with tinkling of broken glass. A sputtering drone from the same direction cut into the woodland sounds, grew louder, merged with a squeal of brakes. Sarah followed the droning noise as it circled the front of the main house. In a flash, the red motorcycle appeared by the drive to her left, knifed past the lilacs, and zipped down the sloping lawn. If Sarah didn't intercept, Kevin might be long gone. No matter how many ways you cut it, he was the only material witness to Katie's fall. If she couldn't capitalize on his panic, or grab something incriminating he might be setting a match to or tossing away, she would lose this opportunity like she lost the last one; left with the jumble that passed for her notes – doing Katie no good at all. As she hurried toward the apartments over the red barn, she didn't hear Doreen calling behind her; warning her again. She was drawn to the action, like a rambler chasing down a passing train.

Twelve

evin's wild ride had been spurred by Benjamin's ranting, no doubt about it. There Kevin was, straddling the red Harley Sportster, gripping the low handlebars, bothering no one, when Benjamin came bursting out of the garage.

"Off," said Benjamin, closing in fast till his beefy cheeks blocked Kevin's view.

"Just checking," said Kevin as calmly as can be.

"Like hell. You ain't checking, you ain't touching this chopper till you pay up."

Kevin shifted his lanky frame and cast his gaze down and away.

"Well?"

Still keeping his cool, Kevin said, "How do I know it's fixed?"

"You don't."

A long pause. Kevin didn't budge.

"Kevin, I said, get your butt off."

Another long pause: Kevin toyed with the throttle, rotating it back and forth.

"Hey," Benjamin went on, raising his voice another decibel, "don't push it. I'm out time and parts: over eight hours, new clutch, adjusting the carb, not to mention tweaking the spokes so's the rims don't wobble. I'm sayin', goddammit, your bike stays till I see some coin, even if I have to put a lien on the sucker. And you tell Tommy--I don't care what shape his wife's in--that goes for what I done for him too."

Kevin peered across the street at the spindle-railed sag of the inn's porch. Surely somebody would step out and Benjamin would get a grip. Surely something would put an end to this foolery. But no one even peeked through a curtain. The threats kept mounting. And, as if things weren't bad enough, Alice appeared from somewhere around the corner and chimed in.

"No sweat, Benjamin," said Alice, patting Kevin's shoulder, ruffling his denim jacket as if they were intimate. "Back off. It's okay."

"Hey, what is this, your business?" said Benjamin, his sweaty body so close to Kevin now that the smell of grime and perspiration clogged his lungs. "And where you been?"

"Who cares? The subject's Kevin. And he's got some money."

"Since when? And what do you know about nothin'? Why don't you just shut your face and get--"

"I won't and you can't make me, "said Alice sticking her little tongue between her teeth. "He's got some money, I said 'cause I . . . I--never you mind."

"Never mind is right," said Benjamin, his cheeks puffing away. "Stay outta this. I'll deal with you later."

Kevin ran his hand around the sweep of the gas tank and turned the key.

"No, I won't stay out of it," said Alice, still patting Kevin's left shoulder. "I'm tellin' you there's things that can be done if some people would start acting human. Change their tune and quit being the same mean bastard."

At this juncture, Kevin could have backed off and walked away. It was the jolt that did it--Benjamin's knee jarring the rocker cover, nearly throwing Kevin off the bike. The instant Benjamin circled behind him lumbering after Alice, Kevin slammed down on the kick-start, slipped into first, rolled his wrist hard on the throttle and lurched forward. The back end slid out as he popped the clutch and swerved left onto the street. Leaning into the slide, doing his damnedest not to high-side, he eased off the throttle, pulled the clutch lever and peddle-pressed into second. The shouts melted behind him as he gained traction and control, straightened his back, shifted to third and took the steep grade out of town at a steady clip.

With the clutch no longer slipping, he waited for the still point where he evaporated into the flow and hum and the world disappeared. But the still point never came. He couldn't shake off the stiffness of the ride, the hot air pressing on his back, the unforgiving jounce of the front forks as he surged higher. He felt every agitation and change in the ribbon of road as it twisted down, swayed and curved up, dipped and then opened out to the hazy sky. Cranking the throttle, he skirted the deep cuts in the rock face that flanked him on both sides. The exhaust echoed all around him, the torque of the engine out-blasted the exhaust.

Then the view closed for good. The shafts of sunlight flitted through the overarching treetops, hurting his eyes, darting up with the hills each time he downshifted and raced a bit higher.

Where was the release, why wouldn't it come? Like in the rock song. Where was the cool zone between the dawn and the dark of night? Where were the "ripples in still water . . . where there is no pebble tossed, nor wind to blow"? Where was John, his part in the play: the Witch Boy . . . on the wing, sailing easy over Barbara Allen? Blue-eyed Barbara with the light brown hair--blue-eyed Katie and the way she seemed to run toward him . . . between the dawn and dark of night . . . while he waited by the backstage ramp.

Kevin swept down and zipped up yet another rise and then flattened out a bit for the final leg to the estate. He tried to lose himself in the rev of the stroker beneath him. Knowing full well it was no use. Even though he had let go of everything and pulled back. Even though he hadn't returned to the vineyard, hadn't laid eyes on any of it.

He bent low, hugging the bulging gas tank, heedless of the wind swirling the long strands of his hair across his eyes. He force-fed himself happy images: riding in the Adirondacks right after he first bought this bike, heading in this direction . . . painting the set with Katie dancing and twirling below his ladder, reciting her lines . . . the sight of Katie jogging in slow-motion--everything in its place, taking its own sweet time. Before Russell came on the scene . . . and Mark scampered out of the red barn . . . and he, Kevin, was unable to bring Katie back to consciousness, couldn't undo a thing.

Kevin felt the muscles in his gangly arms begin to knot. Up ahead at the bend, he spotted Sarah off by the rear porch, possibly alone, possibly grilling someone, still nosing around. Who did she think she was kidding? Sure, he told her a little about the poisoning of the dog, but that was only because she had bought it. No other reason.

He shot by the main house and veered sharply left, the back end sliding out again as he streaked past the drive.

What was he doing? He'd taken off without paying his bill and thrown his whole rhythm out of whack.

He eased off the throttle as he passed Russell's cottage. But just as he pulled in by the overhang, Mark flashed out in front of him. He twisted sharply right, slammed through the forsythia bushes, squeezed the front brake lever and came to a jarring stop. Flipping the kill switch, he swung off the bike, rocked it onto its stand and sidled behind one end of the hedgerow. As if reading his mind, Mark darted out from the opposite side.

"Hold it. What is this? You couldn't wait? You goddamn couldn't sit tight?"

Kevin glanced around for a way out, tried to fake a smile and then threw up his hands.

"You swiped the bike, didn't you? You damn went and did it."

"It's mine."

"Like hell. You owe money, man."

Kevin slipped his hands in the back pockets of his jeans, pulled them out again and tugged at some hemlock needles.

"Speak, dummy."

"Just testing it out."

"Sure, sure. With Benjamin's blessing?"

Kevin shrugged and kept tugging at the needles. He wasn't about to bandy words with Mark. He wasn't about to bandy words with anyone. All this thinking, misunderstandings, repetitions--what was the point?

Mark moved in on him. "Okay, let's cut the crap. You want Benjamin adding to the mess of characters around here? Do you? Huh? Huh?"

Kevin shook his head and turned the other way. His hands in his back pockets again, he gazed off in the direction of the weathered vine-covered coach-house which sat some twenty yards behind Russell's cottage.

"Well," said Mark, now standing directly behind him, "tell you what we're gonna do, and I mean right this second." Mark pointed over Kevin's shoulder. "That's right, buddy boy. Tommy's shiny little Caddy, windows down, keys dangling, high-frequency car phone just waiting for you."

Kevin shook his head.

"I said, Do it, damn your ass. It's the closest phone, Tommy's off sulking, Russell's gone somewheres. You catch fat Benjamin before he acts, tell him you lost your head, you're getting paid Monday, I'll underwrite it--whatever. That's day after tomorrow, you outta his hair, a million miles away from freaky Alice to boot. How's that?"

"I don't know."

"And you're bringing the goddamn Harley right back. I said, Go! move those feet." Mark came abreast of him, squeezed his shoulder hard, abruptly let go and raised a finger to his lips.

At first Kevin didn't understand. He looked over at Mark who seemed almost transfixed. Following Mark's gaze, Kevin peered forward, well beyond the hedgerow in the direction of the main house until he could almost make out Sarah's sturdy form striding down the lawn heading toward them.

Breaking into that cocky smirk, Mark said, "I'll handle this. You make the call and clear out."

Mark shoved Kevin so hard that he lurched forward a good seven yards before he regained his balance. Glancing back sharply, Kevin wondered what in the devil Mark had in mind. Ordinarily, Mark would have sprung out from the hedge onto the dirt path, palms out mimicking one of his old football moves, like the one he had just employed forcing Kevin into the bushes. But he was edging backwards, nodding to Kevin; pressing his palms straight toward the ground. Like a head counselor during nap time, keeping the peace--all the campers tucked away in their bunks, the playground empty, the canoes docked, the compound shut tight save for one stray girl.

Taking Mark's cue, shrugging off his anger, Kevin drifted off in the opposite direction through the shrubs. He allowed the shadow of Sarah's blazer to brush by the rhododendrons well to his right without so much as a second glance. Moving into his cat-like lope, he felt his mind finally let go: more than willing to erase the incident with Benjamin, this recent encounter with Mark—everything.

Passing the back of the cottage he nodded. No wonder the play upset Russell. Like Kevin himself, when push came to shove, the Witch Boy was the easy rider: no sin, no guilt, no worries, no regrets. A thousand times better than religion, which forced impossible decisions on you that killed the flow.

Almost smiling now, he loped on, lightly, effortlessly. Soon he found himself in the shade of the coach-house behind the wheel of Tommy's twilight-blue Caddy coupe. He turned the ignition key, reached below the padded dash, extracted the hand-set from the floor console, switched to digital and dialed. The first two words--"Mark says"--did the trick. Yes, Benjamin said after a few obligatory curses, the day after tomorrow would do it. No, there would be no consequences, no reprisals. No, Kevin didn't have to return the bike this second. In an hour or so would do fine. And Kevin's decision to leave town was just perfect.

Kevin replaced the handset, flicked off the ignition key and stretched out his legs. Slumping deeper into the plush-ness of the bucket seat, he closed his eyes feeling more and more weightless, as if he was out of his body floating away.

If he could let it ride till Monday, everything would pass. Like the Witch Boy, he could transform back to what he was and leave it all behind.

Thirteen

As Sarah neared the overhang, a garbage can sitting by the barn door caught her eye. It was overflowing with costume pieces and theatrical makeup topped with a crumpled copy of *Dark of the Moon*, the southern Appalachian version of the ancient Scottish ballad that borrowed from *Macbeth*, *Romeo and Juliet* and changed Sweet William into a witch boy who wanted to be human. Only Katie could keep up with the mercurial Barbara Allen and all her transformations. Once when she was thirteen she had said, “Oh, Sarah, to be that desirable and die for love, and do it different times and different ways—sing it, play it--and then take it all back . . . Wouldn’t that be so-o-o cool? Not adopted, not cute and petite but alluring with um . . . you know--stature, like mom.”

Right, thought Sarah slipping on her glasses, just like mom.

The play script was bent back; red slash marks obliterated the lines at the end of Act ll-Scene V. The ragged linen blouse and ripped tights hanging over the edge were doubtless intended for the Kevin's role. From all indications, Mark had called it perfectly. Play production scrapped and Kevin was packing it in.

She squeezed through the sprung door, came upon a flight of rough-hewn wooden steps immediately to her right and started up to the landing. The second she reached the hayloft, Mark was upon her. Spinning to her left, she found herself boxed-in: dried-out bales of hay behind her, Mark on the stairs in front. His denim shirt unbuttoned, almost bare-chested, his hunting knife sheathed by his left hip hugging his jeans.

"Lookee, lookee," said Mark, smirking wildly. "I said to myself if she stays, she's askin' for it."

"Wrong."

"Sure. As if you didn't know where I live."

"Where Kevin lives. So, if you'll get out of the way."

"No no, not the ol' Kevin excuse again."

"You got it. Move."

Mark made a clucking sound inside his cheek and widened his stance. "You know somethin'? You are what I'd call ample."

Sarah slipped off her shoulder bag, measuring the exact location of the slim canister, readying herself to pluck it out with her right hand. "I said, Out of my way. I mean Now."

"Uh-huh," said Mark, his cold green eyes settling on her hips. "First she slips off the shoulder bag. Next it'll be the jacket and dorky glasses. All the time tellin' me she wants out."

"Oh, grow up, will you?"

Sarah's fingertips found the opening of her bag, only about six inches from the canister top. If she could only locate the squirt button at the precise time.

"Come on," said Mark. "I seen you eyein' me in the kitchen."

"In your dreams, Jack."

"Cut the crap. You don't want Kevin. You want—"

"Wake up. You put me on to him. He just pulled in."

Mark stood his ground, smirking less wildly as if conceding the point and contemplating his next move.

"You want me to scream?"

"For Kevin? How about Tommy while you're at it? He'll quit sulkin' and come a-runnin', oh yeah."

"Fine," said Sarah. "I'll yell and we'll see what happens."

"You people kill me, you know that?" Stepping up onto the hayloft, Mark moved closer.

"Kevin," Sarah called. "Kevin!" The air became thicker, the hay scratched her back. Where was the mace? She groped everything in her bag--lipsticks, cell phone, a compact, a penlight, her pocket tape recorder . . . She dug deeper. Mark ripped the bag out of her hand and flung it back over his shoulder. The contents clattered and skewered down the planked steps.

"Okay," said Mark, peeling open her jacket. "You want it this way? What the hell?"

Sarah froze as he pulled the back of her blazer down, pinning her arms. "Wait," she said.

"What for?"

"Aren't you going to finish?" Sarah said, reaching for some way, any way out of this.

"Huh?"

"Taking off my jacket."

The wheels in his brain apparently spinning as if waiting for the right number to come up, Mark began to peel off her jacket ever so slowly. First the right sleeve and then, pivoting slightly, tugging on the left. The second he shifted his glance, Sarah smashed her heel on his instep, shoved him off balance and lunged for the steps. She took the treads two at a time, stomped on her cell phone, lurched and stumbled, banging her knee on a wheelbarrow, then wedged through the sprung door and staggered outside.

"Kevin!"

She glanced left and right into the sunlit glare, opted for the right and skirted around the barn looking for cover. Spotting a flash of yellow, she hunkered down behind a thicket of forsythia bushes, the rough barn wall hard against the small of her back.

She heard the tramp of his boots first, running off in the other direction. Then, a slight panting sound as he returned. The whole time the old familiar childhood sensations came back: the need to hold her breath, the irresistible urge to laugh or squeal, anything to break the tension. She bit her lower lip. This was so dumb. And her thighs were killing her. The need to spring up, to scream, to curse was unbearable.

The tramping sound returned, closer this time, accompanied by the flash of her blue blazer swinging in an arc. Sarah rose, rushing the other way, hoping for a glimpse of the red motorcycle, Russell's lumbering bulk—anything. She no sooner cut back toward the main house when Mark jumped in front of her, whipping her blazer by her eyes, knocking off her glasses. Twisting away, Sarah fell to one knee.

"Playtime's over, Mark. I'm calling the police."

"Like hell," said Mark, still whipping the blazer by her face, lashing at her each time she tried to stand.

Look, creep," said Sarah, guarding her face with her hands, "I am pressing charges."

What are you gonna say? 'Yes, I was trespassin'. But he took off my jacket. Yes, I asked him to. Yes, I stomped down on his ankle. But he chased me. Why? Tryin' to give back my jacket.'"

Mark stepped away for a second, arms outstretched, head flung back. "What do you think, fans? To the throng high up in the imaginary bleachers he pumped his fist up and down. "Let's hear it from the end zone. What do you say?" Spiking an imaginary football on the turf, he spun around and bowed. "Thank you, thank you, thank you."

The sunburned face popped forward again, the jacket lashed out at her eyes. In that same moment, a pair of long skinny arms wrapped around Mark's neck. The murmur that went with the arms said, "Leave her alone."

Without a word, as if playing with a rag doll, Mark flipped Kevin's lanky frame over his shoulder hard to the ground. "Ain't you got business elsewhere?" said Mark leaning over him. "On your horse, stupid."

Sarah scrambled back to the overhang and ducked inside. The sounds of the scuffle behind her, she scoured the wooden steps and dusty cement floor, her eyes darting past the strewn contents of her bag. Finally, she spotted the silver canister under the wheelbarrow. Snatching it up, she rushed back out into the milky glare as Mark punched Kevin in the chest. Kevin doubled over, clutching his upper body. Sarah rushed out, pressed the button and sprayed mace in an arc around Mark's face.

Tearing at his eyes, Mark shuffled backwards. He shook his head in amazement, unable to comprehend what was happening to him. He gasped for air, then swerved around, stumbled and weaved up the grassy slope in slow motion, still shaking his head in disbelief. By and by, he went into spasm, waving his arms in a circle like a wounded animal trying to retaliate against some invisible bird. He kept stumbling, weaving and lurching until he was out of sight.

In the aftermath, Sarah attempted to minister to Kevin but he would have none of it. Each time she touched him or reached over to help him up, he brushed her away. His cheeks flushed like a schoolboy who had never been physically close to a girl.

Kevin kept on rocking and clutching his chest, his features still contorted, his long coarse hair matted with sweat.

"Okay," said Sarah, "this is assault. I'm calling the barracks. We're both pressing charges. Time somebody did something around here."

Kevin shook his head violently.

"What do you mean?"

Closing his eyes, Kevin began to rock back and forth in a steadier rhythm.

"Look, Kevin, one thing for sure, he'll be back."

"No doubt," Kevin murmured. He repeated the words several times, half moaning like some healing incantation.

"So this is where we draw the line, damn you."

Disregarding her, rocking a little slower, Kevin said, "Everything was cool. Why didn't I shut you off . . . pay no attention?" Then he stopped rocking.

The healing ceremony now over, he dropped his arms, rose to his feet and shuffled around aimlessly. "So why don't you do us all a favor? Back off."

At a loss for words, Sarah's eyes strayed in all directions, wondering where his motorcycle was stashed, worried that at any second he'd hop on and take off for good. But Kevin kept shuffling around, in no hurry to do anything. In the steamy white quiet Sarah thought she heard the popping sounds again way off in the distance and the shattering of glass.

Moaning softly, Kevin ambled over to the garbage can under the overhang and fingered the fringes of his costume. Sarah snatched the outfit out of his hands and stuffed it back in the can. "Okay I give. How do we do this? Like Katie? Great.

I appreciate your coming to my rescue. We continue in this vein as we head for the police. Or at least make a stupid phone call."

She immediately dismissed the phone call idea, recalling Mark's advice, recalling how her car phone emitted a weak signal that faded to nil the second she left Lakeville. And she wasn't about to sneak into the main house with Mark lurking around.

Kevin bent over, picked up the mangled play script and whacked it on the rim of the garbage can. "Oh yeah, me and Barbara Allen. Read all about it." With that, he padded through the sprung barn door and started up the rickety plank steps.

"Hang on," said Sarah, retrieving her glasses and blazer and then scooping up her notepad at the foot of the stairway.

"Think I'll wash up," said Kevin as he reached the landing above her.

"What are you, kidding? You responded. What are you telling me?"

"Scene two in the beginning or scene five at the end."

"Wait," Sarah said.

"No time, remember? Mark's gonna be pissed."

Before she could follow, he yelled, "Give me some space, will you?"

"Three minutes tops. And then we leave."

Kevin peered down at her, threw up his hands and disappeared around the corner. A moment later a door unlatched and slapped shut.

Checking her watch, she recalled the drill on the effects of mace: Mark would keep for about another eight minutes. She scurried around retrieving the rest of her stuff, all except the pocket tape recorder and cell phone, which were both smashed.

It was almost five: two hours or so before her self-imposed deadline to report back to Katie. Out of force of habit she hastily jotted down what Kevin may had intimated, knowing full well only one thing was certain. She needed Kevin to both cooperate and corroborate.

At the two-minute mark she called up to him. No response. His remark about Katie only added to her anxiety. Which Barbara Allen was at the center of things? In rehearsal, had Katie begun to inhabit the traits indicated in the play? The notion of rehearsals reminded her of those times when she acted as lookout. Kept one eye out for Russell while Katie went through her paces on the bare high school stage.

She thumbed through Kevin's discarded script, came upon scene two and recalled it almost immediately. A Conjur Woman had told the Witch Boy that he can become human and love Barbara as long as she remains true. Joyful, he then dances with

Barbara, reliving the time they first met, the night the wind came up and the moon went dark. Another quick glance and Sarah came across a latter scene that spins the tale around. The village preacher entices Barbara into forsaking her Witch Boy lover in order to rid the community of demon spirits.

Terrific, thought Sarah. Intimations of lust and jealousy that keep yelling, Buy me! Buy me!

She checked her watch, chucked the script, hurried up the steps and made a sharp left at the upper landing. Assuming the first door was Mark's, she pounded on the second, then lifted the latch and stepped inside. Threading through the clutter of CDs, dirty socks and rock magazines, she glanced into the rustic bathroom, bedroom and tiny kitchenette. Sticking her head out the narrow back window, she eyed the rusty fire escape dwindling down to the ground. She didn't have to wait for the sputter of the motorcycle. It came instantaneously from somewhere nearby and, just as quickly, trailed off.

Something caught her eye. Lying tangled in the weeds in the direction of the pond, an object glinted in the soft sunlight. It could have been the forked tip of a divining rod. It could have been a metal bar, a piece from a trellis, a shiny stick or branch.

Doubling back, hurrying down the steps and out the barn, she decided to call Will Gibble's bluff, bypass him, go to the barracks in Canaan and get some leverage. She made it to her car at the edge of the drive without incident, backed out, braked and paused. In the jumble of pointers, incidents and innuendos, there was only one conceivable option: press charges against Mark. With him out of the way, she could return to the hospital and give Katie something —tell her that, at any rate, she was safe from the caretaker. At any rate, something had been accomplished. Something had been done.

Shifting into gear, she heard popping noises again somewhere off to her right. Taunting her like firecrackers, as if someone was celebrating her departure. Shattering glass joined in the ruckus as she hit third gear and headed back.

Fourteen

For a time Doreen couldn't stop shaking her head and muttering. The image of Mark needling Russell and then throttling Tommy in the kitchen, and the sight of Sarah squirting Mark in the face ending up with Mark half nuts, was just all too much. Things were out of control around here. Helter-skelter. Going berserk.

Now, lingering in the musty foyer trying to calm down her brain, Doreen sensed that even the sedate main house was out of kilter. Facing the huge stone fireplace, she closed her eyes and waited until everything stopped jerking around. She tried an old lullaby, the one to the weary hobo. When she got to the part that went "let your troubles come and go," things got a little better.

"Yes sir, hon," said Doreen out loud, opening her good eye real wide. "Nothing gets past Doreen. Not for long."

She faked it for a minute or two and then, predictably, felt even worse. Brushing by the hearth, she swiveled to her right past the ladder-back chairs, through the kitchen into the pantry. No luck. None of that good French brandy that always sat behind the preserves. No preserves either, for that matter. Just the mildew smell everywhere she turned.

Disoriented, feeling even more discombobulated, she checked out the kitchen cabinets, the cherry-wood cupboard and the entire dining room including the shelves and drawers of the honey-maple hutch. Nothing. Not even a decanter of sherry. But that was ridiculous. There had to be some liquor somewhere. Now what? How could a body fortify itself? Come up with some counter punches without a little pick-me-up? After all, she hadn't had a swig since noon. And if anything called for a stiff one, this bunch of new developments sure as hell did. Without a drink, the ache in her bruised eye got unbearable. Without a drink, her brain got scrambled and things got more and more out of whack.

Catching a reflection of her eye patch and sweat-stained Lycra dress in the oval mirror gave her a twinge. Without a drink, she was a God-awful mess. Her triangle sideburns and neatly trimmed coif looked lopsided. The humidity sure didn't help. It hyped-up her thirst, like a boxed-in animal in a cage. What was going on? The air was never this close, this baking hot early in May. People never behaved this nutty either. Things got a little juicy, sure. But nothing this bad.

It's that Katie, Doreen told herself. You better believe it. Wanting to tear up the road like that . . . bringing in all these extra characters. She had no call, no right. Not after all this.

Doreen was muttering worse than ever, but what else could she do? Who else could she talk to? Who else could she trust? And how much more could she take? All her life at the bottom looking up. Always too plain looking, too man crazy like dumb little Alice. Too clumsy, too uneducated, too trusting, too lower class, and now—if she didn't get a good hold on things—too old. All those years waiting tables for rich idiots at the Red Lion and spots in Lenox next to Tanglewood: then slipping back, tending bar at the White Hart in Salisbury, the Tavern in Pocketknife Square, and then flopping on her butt in God-forsaken Waybury. All those men who had promised her Newport and sailing, Manhattan and a swanky flat, high times in Boston on Beacon and Newberry, and then dumped her just like that. She was well over sixty for chrissake. She had counted every hour for the past six years and three-hundred-and-sixty-three days. If her life didn't pay off, if she didn't have something to show for it, she might as well pack it in.

She scuttled around, her good eye taking in every nook and crevice. It was still no go. No sign of any bracing sauce to pull her out of this tailspin. Nothing to help her get a fix on all the goings-on so's she could nip them in the bud. Come out on top.

Possibly they had hauled away every drop ten weeks ago. That's when the owners in absentia (or whatever it was called) sold out on her. Gave the property away for a song with no warning, no hint whatsoever. Talk about bad luck. This was a doozy.

She cast about in her mind for a logical storage place. They split in such a hurry they must have left at least part of a case behind. Stands to reason. The most obvious spot immediately popped into her brain.

So did thoughts of Willy. Where did Tommy get that crap about gravity fed tanks he was tossing at Mark in the kitchen? And drip irrigation and seepage and all, unless he'd gotten his paws on Willy's log?

She scurried back, past the kitchen and down into the moldy cellar. The half light and cobwebs threw her off. She stumbled over the bottom step and grabbed onto a heating duct, jerking the tube out of its socket, scattering cobwebby dust all over her neck and dress.

"Christ on a crutch," she yelled, brushing herself off. "If it's not asking too much, let's give Doreen a little break here."

Realizing she was losing it again, she counted to ten, pulled back and went over her timeframe. A little over an hour before she was due back to bartend and keep up the front, but only for two more nights. That was all, that was it. But first she still had to plug up the damn holes, keep everything from coming apart. Which was getting more and more impossible with her damn jumpy nerves.

Straining her good eye, she peeked through the splotchy filth, in and around the supporting posts, coal chute and the rest of the ductwork till she finally came upon the scattered mess. Somebody for sure must have been in here. Her own private crate, the one she had carefully covered up with a grain sack was ransacked. And the other liquor boxes were near empty, the few bottles left all mixed-up. Running her tongue across her chapped lips, she tossed aside the rotgut and didn't let up till she laid her shaking hands on a dusty, squat bottle of cognac that didn't look half bad.

A half dozen swigs later and her eyeball ache and that itchy-twitchy feeling was almost gone. The slow burn registered deep in her chest and her mind began to thrum. Straddling an old apple box, she drew a sharp bead on the payoff.

She was at the Plaza Hotel on the posh East Side, no longer wearing the glitzy Lycra crap. No sir. She was sporting a champagne silk charmeuse blouse with padded shoulders over a straight maroon skirt that came below her calves. Complete with fancy ringlets, bracelets, necklaces—the works. The European guys in tails with little mustaches were gliding their bows over the strings of their Italian fiddles, playing Mozart or something anybody with status would appreciate. While she was taking it all in, little tea cakes were served to her by cute young hunks in white jackets with manicured fingernails, and some Swedish thing in braids and a frilly white apron was pouring Danish coffee into a Limoges tea cup and matching saucer. It was her first stop. She'd start with the Plaza and pick and choose her escorts. All the best, all the sharpest, who knew how to handle themselves and speak with a nifty smooth patter. Knew how to help her make up for it all.

"That's right, babe," she said out loud. "Get the peeper fixed by some Park Avenue pro, take it all in and do it up right." Another deep pull from the cognac bottle and she was clicking on all cylinders.

But what to do exactly with these characters running around? What about Willy's log? And what about the combinations of foul-ups that could queer the whole shebang?

The popping noises beyond the broken window caught her attention. At first she didn't know why. Then it hit her.

She hadn't heard the sound in years but with Tommy lunging up from the cellar stairs, his dress shirt wrinkled and stained, clutching something behind his back . . . it could be . . . Yes sir, the way things were going and all, it very well could.

Ducking under the heating vents, groping around past the hot water tank, she located the old coal burner. As if it had been yesterday when Willy had taken her to the spot, told her it was there if she ever needed it. But it wasn't there. No matter how far she reached into the open slot, there was no protection for her. No silencer either that made that neat muffled pop. No spare box of cartridges. And the noises outside were still going on as if giving her the answer.

She made her way up the cellar stairs and out to the back porch. On a left diagonal, she stared beyond the meandering stone fence and deep brush into the stands of maple and oak. She couldn't see the target practice but knew full well that must be what it was. Tommy was going off the deep end; or possibly about to. He, Mark and Kevin--all on the verge of something.

Still clutching the cognac bottle, she sidled back inside and slipped into Tommy's study. Sure enough, there was Willy's log, dog-eared and flopping over the ottoman like some puppy's chew toy. She ripped up the pages with the dates on them and shoved the pieces in her velvet bag. Just in case, and because she was really pissed that people couldn't just leave things alone.

She plopped herself on the ottoman, drained the last of the cognac and leafed through the rest of Willy's scribblings. Smiling to herself, she remembered how he'd jotted everything down during the days when he was the winemaker and lived in the guest cottage. When he used to say, "Let the good times roll." And the plans had looked so good to them both.

Soon she started to croon "Let the Midnight Special shine its light on me. Let the Midnight Special shine its ever-lovin' light on me." Yes indeedy, everything was gonna shine after she cut her losses. If they only knew who they were messin' with. She was a pistol, yes sir. The living end.

After all, that Katie doll started it and she, Doreen, would damn well finish it. Fact is, only a crafty woman can pull the strings and calls the shots. Only a crafty woman truly does herself proud.

In no time, she embraced the musty smells. The odors and Willy's journal made her think of the old-timey books she'd swiped from this study. For the fun of it, she began reciting a favorite passage from one of them: "Nightshade, everything is poisonous including the leaves, stems, flowers and seeds . . .

active ingredients are topane alkaloids, atropine and hyosyamine. The symptoms are . . ."

She let out a low whistle. There was something about secret books, secret information and just plain secrets that gave her a power rush. Secrets and cognac; yes sir.

Padding back out into the gauzy glare that seemed much softer now, she recited some more. "The deadly ingredients in apricots are lodged in the leaves, stems, bark and pits. The twigs of wild cherry branches and certain combinations of potatoes, rhubarb, ivy and mushrooms add to the possibilities. Depending, of course, on the precise recipe and the timing."

Plus, thought Doreen, always keeping your finger on the pulse.

She started whistling again, no tune in particular, walked out onto the slope of the back lawn and then stood still. There was a hush, as if everything was waiting for her to make the next move. She stood there for a while, taking in the silence, breathing in the heady scent of lilac, feeling pretty good about herself.

Fifteen

arah never made it to the barracks in Canaan. She barely made it one mile out of Waybury.

"You're going to have to quit this," Will Gibble said. "You keep it up, you could get yourself arrested."

"Terrific," Sarah said, doing her damnedest to stay calm. "Is that all you have to offer?"

They were standing by the shoulder of the road. The dammed-up Housatonic lay a few hundred yards beyond to Sarah's right. High above, the dry-as-a-bone chute for the Great Falls arched down, as if coaxing the river to spill over and come back to life.

Gibble stood erect opposite Sarah, towering over her by a good six inches. He stiffened his lips and repeated his tired maxim. "Let's keep this on a procedural level, shall we?"

"Oh sure."

"As I said, I am only responding to Tommy Haddam's directives. Don't make me call the barracks. Don't make me--"

"Okay okay." Sarah's gaze swept up and down the arc of the Falls trying to avoid a direct confrontation with Gibble and, at the same time, wanting to pressure him to get off his duff and make something happen. "Look, the mace obviously has worn off. There could be another assault. Conceivably, I mean. At least give me that much."

Gibble tugged on the lapels of his pressed charcoal jacket, glanced at his rectangular watch, set his lantern jaw and continued on the same unmovable tack using the same flat tone. "As I said, if Haddam wants to press charges, it's an infraction. Like a traffic violation. Simple trespass. You go back on the property, it becomes criminal trespass. Is that clear?"

"Crystal," Sarah said, peering into Gibble's eyes. "I get it, I got it. I will stay on the sidelines while you bring Mark in after you see what Tommy's up to."

Gibble shook his head, his flat-cropped brown hair shifting back and forth. His tone still as dry and clipped as ever, he added, "I don't seem to be getting through. I'm not on duty and, as I told you, am no longer on the force. I'm just avoiding unnecessary time and expense. That's it, that's all."

"Wonderful," said Sarah, stepping back and tapping her fingers on the hood of her car. She was sweating again, feeling the mascara running a bit by her eyes.

"And you are a bystander, Miss Bucklin."

When Sarah stopped tapping and cast her gaze back in the direction of the Falls, Gibble said, "Just what did you think you were doing back there?"

"Guess," said Sarah. "You told me what was needed, in case you've forgot."

"I didn't tell you to go looking for trouble."

"That's not what happened," said Sarah, having more and more difficulty keeping her voice down. "Anyways, what's going to be done?"

"About what? Mr. Haddam's complaint, or your version of what may, or may not have occurred, while you were traipsing around where you didn't belong?"

"Fine," said Sarah, digging into her bag, looking him square in the eye again, waving her notebook. "Just turn your back. Take it all under advisement. No worries."

Gibble took a few meandering steps away from her, waited and stepped back smartly. Anxious over any possible missteps, Gibble asked Sarah to repeat her conjectures about the trooper's faulty incident report apropos of Mrs. Haddam's accident. Sighing, Sarah hastily said that neither the trooper's photos nor comments included the arrow of misdirection, or the ruts caused by the dragged saw horses.

"But you've no pictures, only notes."

"That's right. All swept clean along with the diggings, which could also have been Mark's doing, which means that while you're sitting on your hands--"

Before she could complete her thought, Gibble walked away and returned immediately as if having checked yet again with protocol. Once more, he recited the rules of evidence by rote. Then, alluding to "the prior alleged assault and the alleged recent one," he informed Sarah that she had produced "no tangible signs on her person." As for Katie suffering at the hands of an assailant, he demanded the presence of some material on a suspect's hands, talc or grease or sodium nitrate or granular soap powder plus proof that this residue was found around, say, Katie's collarbone along with latent prints. Rubbing his hands as if he had totally covered all the bases, he allowed his thin lips to curl up into a smile.

Sarah stuck her notebook back into her bag, leaned her elbows on the hood of her car. "This isn't happening. You get attacked, you try to prevent more harm and you get waylaid. You get a lecture on forensics. Anything to save the hometown football hero. Do you know how ridiculous this is?"

Gibble's face went blank. A breeze kicked up, rippling the river above them. Below the river the dry-as-a-bone Falls still waited expectantly for the water to flow over. The river didn't budge.

"In the meantime," Sarah added, "there are tangible popping noises which could lead to tangible holes in some tangible person's vital parts."

"Okay," said Gibble, "I'll get Varno on it."

"Who?"

"The trooper on duty."

"You mean it?" said Sarah, standing straight up. "You're serious?"

Easing into his midnight-blue Crown Victoria, Gibble patched his intercom into the barracks. A moment later, he cast his cool gaze up at Sarah who had now positioned herself by his side mirror. "Just for your information, Miss Bucklin, we rank 911 calls. Strokes, heart attacks, accidents and immediate threats of violence are given a one. Indications of burglary are given a two, indications of a prowler a three, et cetera. People who cry wolf are given a ten."

"Meaning, if I can't substantiate anything, I would've been a lot better off doing absolute zilch."

"Exactly."

Sarah checked her watch. Gibble checked his. For a few minutes neither of them spoke.

Hands still firmly on the wheel, casting another glance up at Sarah, Gibble said, “Would you like me to wait?”

“No thank you.”

“Then I’ll leave you with the motto over my desk when I was duty officer.”

“Uh-huh,” said Sarah, looking down the road, hoping he would toss off his words-to-live-by and split before trooper Varno came onto the scene and was immobilized by Gibble’s example.

Ignoring the hint, Gibble said, “‘You get lost in fantasy if you play with theories more complex than the facts justify’.”

“Gotcha,” Sarah said. “Many thanks.”

“For the advice?”

“For doing something. Assuming it’s not too late.”

Gibble’s lips compressed. He gunned his motor and sped off.

Ten minutes later, the pattern broke. Trooper Varno turned out to be almost sympathetic.

"Why didn't you dial 911 or call the dispatcher?" said Varno, raising his baleful eyes as he took down Sarah's statement. "I could have come right over."

"Because Mark was hovering around. Because my car phone is useless. Because Will Gibble pulled me over before I could--look, can we get cracking?"

"Sure." Varno shuffled back to his cruiser, which was parked nose to nose with Sarah's car, made allowance for his potbelly and slid behind the wheel. Noting his drooping eyes and jowls, Sarah felt as if she'd befriended a loveable hound.

"Okay, here's the procedure," said Varno, rolling down his window. "I take a statement from Mark. Then one from each of the witnesses. Then it's all assessed for probable cause. It could be . . . simple assault . . . sexual assault . . . or just breach of the peace. He could claim you were trespassing . . . but you say you've got letters . . . from the owner's wife."

"Right, check, ditto." Unfortunately, Sarah realized, he not only looked like a hound, he had the same rhythm.

"All right," said Varno, speeding up his pace one rpm, "you stay in the background . . . Just in case I need you for directions, additional information . . . that sort of thing."

"Yes, great, sure thing."

Slipping his cruiser in gear, Varno widened his drooping eyes, twitched his brush mustache, backed up and pulled over across the street. Sarah, in turn, climbed into her Accord, and made a U-turn under the dull, shimmering sky. A moment later, she was tailing Varno's cruiser, frustrated over the fact that he was going only five miles over the limit. Feeling as jumpy as ever, she kept tapping her fingers on the wheel until Varno finally began to speed up.

A few minutes later, as they tooled along the winding stretch, back up into the surge of the Southern Berkshires, Sarah relaxed her grip on the wheel. She was, at last, injecting a semblance of law and order on the estate. She had some backup, leverage, aid—words like that. As if to corroborate her thoughts, the wind began to shift. The haze gave way to patches of rosy-tinged blue; the stands of hardwoods and softwoods seemed to ease off a bit and disengage; the humidity dissolved, replaced by a northwest flow. Smiling, Sarah realized she was no longer sweating, mascara no longer smearing her eyelids.

Before she knew it, they were approaching the bramble-covered stone walls. A bright purple twilight washed into the tints of rose and blue, highlighting the chimneys of the main house. She pulled into the drive, got out and waited patiently for Varno by the verge of the overgrown front walk.

When Varno reemerged through the square-headed doorframe, he was shaking his baleful face. "Not there. Nobody around."

"Are you sure?" said Sarah, hurrying over to him.

"Yup."

"Look, it was no more than an hour ago. And where is Tommy? I know for a fact he called Gibble. That's why I was intercepted." In reply, Varno gave Sarah another baleful look.

"Okay, go up to the barn then," said Sarah pointing. "Mark's apartment. Maybe he's sleeping it off."

Shrugging, Varno ambled to the far side of the house. Sarah hung back. The breeze carried the cloying smell of the lilacs and blended it with the pungent aroma of the bridal veils.

Calling back, Varno said, "Past the cottage?"

"Yes. Aren't you going to unsnap that holster or something?"

"Why?"

"Never mind. Just overreacting."

Varno walked on. There was no other sound, just Varno's faint padding through the spongy grass. Again Sarah waited. When she could stand it no longer, she disregarded Varno's instructions and followed in his path.

A trail of tangerine ran across the rim of the horizon. In relief, the barn and hedges formed a tracery of deep shadow. As Sarah let her eyes stray across the back reaches of the compound, the brush of tangerine began to dissolve into a halo of twilight afterglow. Nothing moved. No sounds to speak of.

Presently, past the barn and the tangle of vines, stakes and trellises, something flashed to Sarah's left. At first it was only a flicker. Then it flashed by again and moaned. Varno came into view, rushing after the flitting shadow. Sarah lagged well behind, working her way toward the zigzagging shapes, curious and wary at the same time. It wasn't until she spotted Varno beyond the sawhorses that she was able to make out who he was chasing. For an instant, Mark's darting form was an echo of the mace episode. Only this time he wasn't lurching in slow motion. This time he clutched his stomach and sprinted here and there like some wild wounded creature in search of some unseen refuge. Varno tried to head him but the foot race continued until Mark threw up his hands and staggered into the pond.

By the time Sarah caught up with them, Varno had dragged Mark onto the grassy bank. Though soaking wet, Mark gasped for water and clutched his temples as if his head was about to split. Then it was back to his stomach, begging for something to drink. The brushstroke of tangerine afterglow hung suspended over the pond. The rippling contractions of Mark's bare chest and a glass jar on the bank a few yards away completed the picture. The wide-mouth jar was uncapped, half filled with pureed vegetable juice.

"Damn," said Mark. "Damn it to hell." Twisting and pointing at Sarah, Mark added, "First her. Now somebody goddamn tries to poison me."

As Varno drew out his radio and punched in a few numbers, Sarah glanced at Mark, who, in turn, glanced right back; his cocky leer flashed for a second and then gave way to the pain.

The croaks and ribb-its of a frog chorus started in as if on cue. The afterglow gave up its holding pattern, slipped below the horizon line and disappeared.

Drifting back toward the main house, Sarah looked around for a perpetrator. Some sign of Tommy. Or Russell. Or Kevin. She searched in vain.

Sixteen

arah stood outside in the pitch blackness, finishing the third apple she'd pilfered from the kitchen. It was now a little before seven.

She tossed the core over her shoulder as Varno's rumpled form appeared through the shadowed slot of the front door and wended its way toward her in extreme slow-motion. Sarah was so exhausted and antsy at the same time that everything seemed to be moving at a snail's pace.

The gray uniform huddled next to her. The pen scratched away. The lethargic drone sputtered at first and gradually began to zero in on its mark. "You know something? It must be . . . a good six—no no, make that seven years since anything happened here."

"Ah, so now it comes out."

Giving Sarah a puzzled look, Varno said, "This time all in the space of a week, plus counting you."

"Meaning?"

"It's adding up."

"Go on."

Varno shrugged.

"Talk to me. Speak." When Varno shrugged again, Sarah pressed harder. "Look, I have to report back to my friend. If she's conscious, if she can see a clock, she knows I am way overdue."

"Listen, I only told you to wait because of . . ."

"What? Why can't you just spell it out?"

"There are witnesses. Mark called Will, did you know that? Tommy Haddam called Will . . . we've got trespassing . . . mace. Will also got a call from Doreen . . . from the inn."

"Oh, please."

"Hey, I have to make sure my field report is complete."

"Not like the last one you guys did."

The baleful eyes drooped, the jowls went slack. "What I'm saying is, you're entitled to know. All the ramifications, I mean."

Varno tapped his pen on his pad. "Of course, that stuff in the jar could be nothing. Especially if this guy Mark was in the habit. Of shoving organic things in a blender, that is. They could be spoiled or something." After tapping his pen again, Varno added, "Who knows what the lab report will show?"

"Are we through?" said Sarah.

The baleful eyes widened a notch. “Look, Sarah, using mace isn’t just defensive. It could be offensive. Also, you could be . . . sued. So, on one side of the ledger, we’ve got possible criminal trespassing . . . if a complaint is filed. And assault, when Mark comes around . . . if he decides to press charges. And then we’ve got the alleged witnesses . . .”

Sarah tuned out the rest of Varno’s assessment and ambled over to her car. To her mind, he must have been speaking of someone else. Sarah Bucklin, as anyone could attest, always avoided encounters. She went so far as to avoid Crown Street altogether and bypassed anything south of Church or north of the York Cinema. She even kept clear of each and every Yale quadrangle after dark. What had transpired on the estate was duly noted by Sarah, the reporter and would-be editor, from a remove. This could not be the person Varno was alluding to. And yet again, in this parallel universe, you could never be sure.

Varno rubbed his woebegone eyes and padded over to her. Both leaning against the passenger side now, facing back toward the house. “Now on your side of the ledger,” he said, “we’ve got what you told me. The letters from your friend. And your notes. And maybe Kevin to back you up.”

“Uh-huh.”

"But, then again, this whole thing could be closed as unfounded."

"Which would thrill Gibble no end."

Raising his eyes this time, Varno said, "Give me your number. In case I have to check back."

She scribbled the number of the motel, scooted around to the other side and plopped herself down behind the wheel. "Now, if nobody minds," she called out, "I am going to put a positive spin on all this and see my friend through another night."

The button-eyed nurse held up four fingers. She was standing outside the glass doors delineating the I.C.U. entranceway, about thirty feet to Sarah's left. Sarah nodded, indicating she'd leave in just a sec, and gazed down and away from the broken-doll figure of her friend.

"Not bad, huh? Finally got the state police onto the case. Just like you wanted."

Try as she may, Sarah couldn't come up with a sound bite that said, Good news. She also couldn't help glimpsing at the tubes running into Katie's arms and the dreadful apparatus inserted down her throat. Katie's eyes were still softly closed as if she were in some kind of limbo. Perhaps connected by weak radio frequencies. Perhaps barely connected at all.

"What I'm saying is, gotta give the troopers a little slack. Know what I mean?"

A long pause. Button-eyes held up two fingers behind the whitish glass and pointed to her watch. The bleeps, clicks, hisses and whistles seemed more insistent. The pale green light held steady.

Turning away from the night-duty nurse, Sarah let her gaze stray from the fragile little arms strapped to the side of the bed and focused on the two framed photographs perched on top of the nightstand. Sarah guessed that, for some reason, Tommy must have brought the pictures in earlier during the day.

The picture on the far side closest to Katie's face showed Tommy and Katie holding hands under the green and yellow wedding canopy. The second photo was a blown-up snapshot of Katie and Sarah, taken when they were both thirteen, about to cross a wide lake: Katie nestled in front of the canoe, Sarah stalwartly in the rear primed to navigate, a glinting compass around her neck. In the distance was the faint outline of a wooded ridge. For an instant, it seemed as though Katie's eyes flicked up at the Girl Scout photo and then back at Sarah. It seemed that way. In Sarah's exhausted state, she may have just imagined it.

In that same instant, it crossed Sarah's mind that Katie might actually be better off giving the troopers a little slack, letting things take their course. The way things were going, perhaps Sarah should back off like Kevin said. Like everybody said.

Except for the fact that for Katie, things were either rosy or bleak. She'd looked forward to the spring, to the possibilities of the new theater and the lifting of a seventeen-year-old spell. Her theater and the promise of spring had been scuttled. If Katie was in any way conscious, the spell was doubtless blanketing her mind, clouding out the light.

Sarah could sense Button-eyes calling "time". She could also see her erect shadow on the sterile white wall. Sarah glanced back and signaled for one minute more. It was a silly request. Visiting hours were over fifteen minutes ago. Button-eyes could be pushed not a second more.

"So you might as well come back to life and get with it," Sarah said halfheartedly. But what could Katie truly come back to? Intimations of guilt? A circle of suspects, not one of whom she could trust? Russell and the police still of a mind that she brought this on herself? The state of things in more of a muddle and her erstwhile sidekick of little help?

Sarah glanced back at the second photo. This time she noted another detail. Her left hand was firmly on Katie's back: reassuring her that they could indeed cross over the lake, into the woods and back home.

Just as Button-eyes gripped Sarah's elbow, whispering some veiled threat, Sarah said to Katie, "Like I said, kiddo, not to worry. Got my hand on the tiller." Sarah squeezed one of Katie's fingers a second before Button-eyes firmly steered her out of the I.C.U.

It was twenty after nine. Sarah's body dearly wanted to call it a night. "Got your hand on the tiller, huh?" she muttered to herself. "Right."

She put her body on hold and pressed on.

The stocky supervisor in charge of Mark's floor kept vacillating. At first she was indifferent, then jolly, and now testy.

"And what do you think this is?" she said, her thick arms folded in front of her like a bouncer. "Not only is it way past visiting hours, not only are we up to our ears and understaffed, but your unmitigated cheek surely takes the prize." She spoke with a trace of a music hall parody of an Irish brogue, the lilt in her voice undercut by the hard set of her jaw, the total absence of makeup and a knot of gray hair clamped at the back of her head like a tourniquet.

Sarah fumbled for an excuse. The supervisor crinkled and released her brow. "Are you a relative?"

"Not exactly."

"You mean, 'No'. Do you have some pressing need?"

"Yes."

"The answer is,'No' again. Leave before I—"

"If you give me a chance to speak," Sarah said, feeling her eyelids droop like a Varno clone. "If you give me a second, I'll come up with something."

"Oh, give me a break. Be off with you now. Go."

Sarah's verbal agility failed her, her mind reaching and going nowhere. She wandered over to the elevator as the numbness overtook her. Tomorrow was another day: hopefully much, much shorter. Besides, she had an impending job decision. Her promises to Katie notwithstanding, she had to come to terms with the realities of work.

Just as the down indicator-light flashed, the supervisor called over to her. “Quit moping around, will you? Maybe I’ll have a spare second. Then again, maybe not.”

A ten-minute wait by the flat wooden bench resulted in a return of the stocky figure and a repetition of the maybe/maybe-not shuffle and riff.

Ten more minutes and the supervisor was back with a shake of her plain, open face. “Run it by me quick,” she said. “Is it love that keeps you here, God help you? Is that the story?”

Sarah didn’t correct her.

“Ah, well now,” said the supervisor. “I thought this kind of mooning was dead and gone. Come on, come on, out with it.”

“Did they pump his stomach yet? Did they determine the poison?”

The thick arms unfolded, the red knuckles jammed onto her ample hips. “Poison is it? What have we here, a criminal confession?”

“Whoa,” said Sarah, trying to fake a smile and slough it off. “I just want to know how serious it is. How long he’s going to be laid up.”

“Oh,” said the supervisor, not believing a word.

“Look,” Sarah broke in, “can you just tell me what happened? From the time he hit the emergency room, I mean.”

"You don't want much, do you? Would you like to know exactly when they started the IV? The measurements of the vital signs? How much blood they drew?"

"Blood? What for?"

"'What for?' she says. How do you test, if you don't draw the blood? How do you know what substance it was, how little or how much?"

"When will they find out?"

"After they send it out to some other hospital, maybe Hartford, they'll know. Okay? Goodbye."

"Wait," Sarah heard herself say as the stocky form waddled back to her station. "Did he say anything?" said Sarah, scuffing over to her. "Did he speak? Did he respond at all?"

The plain open face broke into a grin. "That big tease with a line as long as a fishing reel, even in his delirium. Pure bilge, that's all it was."

"Then give me the bilge."

"Take my advice. Forget it, I know the kind."

Just then the phone rang. An orderly flitted by. Then an intern in green scrubs. Next, an elderly woman stumbled out of her room, a restraining strap dangling from her wrist. Two sheets of white cotton barely clung to her spindly naked form as she called for the elevator. A nurse corralled her and led her back to her stall, assuring her that the hotel doorman would return in the morning. The woman returned to her imaginary posh penthouse complaining that it was much too small and the service was terrible and just wouldn't do. Sarah waited during all this by the sliding glass windows at the nurses' station.

The supervisor finally got off the phone, the plain face turning sour once more. "Well, what is it you're waiting for now?"

Sarah leaned over the counter between the partitions. "He said something to you, remember? Tell me what and I'll be out of your hair."

The head nurse swiveled around, rose from her chair, looked in all directions and said, "You'll get out of my hair before I forget myself. You get it?"

"Look, I am so beat, just humor me please? Before I curl up on your carpet. Then I'll leave. I swear."

Another glance around, a pause until two straggling orderlies were well out of earshot, and the supervisor finally pressed her face forward. "'Watch out, I rolled the seven, babe', he said. 'Yes, sir, I am a rolling stone.'"

Pulling back, the supervisor snatched her clipboard. "He was talking rot, clear out of his head. And I only caught the tail end, mind, as I was helping his poor nurse hold him down. So scoot. Any doctor finds me gabbing away and it'll be me, not you, on the carpet."

It wasn't a sharp click. But it stayed with Sarah as she took the elevator down and drove out of the hospital grounds into the darkness. The fog shrouded the drive home, curling around the buckling ribbon of road, washing across her headlight beams like rivulets of steam. As if in her groggy state Kevin's backdrop had taken over, blotting out the light of the moon.

When, at long last, she pulled into her slot at the Lakeville Motel, her mind cleared enough to reach one conclusion. If she was actually going to attempt a third and final pass at this conundrum, she'd have to change her tack one-hundred-and-eighty degrees.

Seventeen

In the dream, the bell clanged as the wind kicked up to eighteen knots. Sarah hunkered down in the little cramped canoe, which turned into a two-mast schooner. The lake became Long Island Sound, the schooner took a starboard tack. The boom swung over her head, the wind slapping and whipping the sails above her, the deck tipping and heeling as Sarah hung on to the binnacle and Katie's cringing shoulders.

Katie yelled, "We're going to tip over. I told you, I told you. I'm going to die!"

Katie kept screaming while Sarah tried to trim the sails. They were both in their Girl Scout uniforms, Sarah stumbling back to the wheel at the rear of the cockpit, her kerchief flying, trying to steer, trying to cut through dead ahead. But the more she took the waves head on, the more the water washed over Katie's body bleaching her uniform white.

"I was bluffing," Sarah said, clutching the binnacle and groping for Katie. "I was never any good at this and you know it." Bracing herself for the inevitable, Sarah peered down at the white caps churning over the hull and Katie's body, rising higher and higher.

Reaching up for something, anything, Sarah found a dice table. The dice were large, the dots faded. She rolled the dice over and over and flung them again and again until they hit the stern and tilted the boat.

On this new steep angle--even though they were far from the breakwater; even though they were in pitch darkness with no light from the moon--holding fast made the water recede, and seemed to calm Katie's twitching form.

"All right, okay," Sarah said, staying on this tack until Katie lay quiet and still, waves no longer splashing on her but no sign of life either.

The sails furled and buckled, the boom jerked so hard in the howl and whistle of the wind that Sarah began to murmur some half-forgotten plea. At that moment, the schooner knifed through the water on an even keel. Turning around, she gazed at the oversized dice. Their dots were as faded as Katie. Each of the dice turned into a buoy. Each buoy spun around, changing the number of dots.

The croupier bellowed, "Seven come eleven." His voice got raspier and raspier, breaking into a fake country and western drawl. "Just like a rollin' stone, babe. Just like a rollin' stone."

Sarah woke up with a start. It was just before daybreak, the fog still swaddling the motel windows. Groping around, she switched on the bedside lamp, fumbled for her shoulder bag and shook out her notepad. Slipping on her reading glasses, she flipped through the pages, grabbed a yellow marker and began highlighting the same number. The jottings were attributed to Mark, Willy's journal, Gibble, Varno, and Doreen. Soon the notes began to merge: "Doreen claims 'nothing for seven years till now' . . . all the entries in the journal date back seven years . . . Gibble and Varno both remark 'it's been a good six or seven years since anything happened' . . . in his delirium Mark moans 'I rolled a seven, babe' . . . "

Sarah tried to stay awake, knowing that she had latched onto the kind of "gut-check" that hard-bitten Jan on the police beat was always crowing about. The red digital numbers on the clock read 4: 48. She propped up her pillow and threw her head back, scanning the pattern on the flickering ceiling. The plaster reminded her of waves, the number seven recalled the buoy leading to the landmarks that led to port.

In no time, the fatigue took over again, drawing her down and under. Images of Katie's fingernails slipped in and clouded her drowsy thoughts. Katie's nails were chipped and broken. Perhaps from the fall. Perhaps from scratching Mark's face.

Perhaps from heaven knew what. And what happens when you roll a seven? Wasn't it craps? Dead in the water? Out of the game?

Back in the dream, she was at the side of the pond as the trace of tangerine afterglow slipped below the horizon. Muffled popping sounds shattered invisible figures made of glass. The figures moaned, then sighed, then grew as still as the pond water. A St. Bernard puppy bayed at Kevin's backdrop of a moon. The moon was dappled in charcoal like a gossamer veil. Drawing closer, Sarah reached into her blazer and pulled out a pair of dice. She rolled a seven that floated onto the dank water. The shattered glass figures began to rise above the pond, disappearing into the darkening night, egged on by the puppy, now nuzzling Sarah's leg and baying at the dappled moon.

Eighteen

y the time she awoke, it was almost eleven, Sunday, May 9th. She had counted on the morning sun breaking through the blinds to revitalize her, heralding a brand new day. But instead, she had overslept and discovered that the sky was totally overcast. Outside her window, the new leaves coated the elms and maples in the near distance like wisps of lace. As a matter of fact everything seemed filmy, even the dandelions poking up along the walks and the churchgoers drifting off toward their places of worship.

She roused herself, washed her face, slipped on a twill split skirt and a white knit top with an open spread collar, slipped on her loafers and reached for the phone by the bed stand. Late as it was, she had two belated calls to make before considering her new tack. The Mother's Day call started out a bit strained. After a few evasions, feints and parries, Sarah made amends, wished her mother well and rang off.

The call to the paper backfired.

“Well aren’t you lucky I happened by here?” said Penelope, her editor back in New Haven. “It’s on the way to my mom’s, had a smidge of unfinished business, and besides, I don’t believe a word. You weren’t really going to leave a voice-mail message. Not the trusty Sarah Bucklin I know.”

Right, thought Sarah. Ask the Canaan state police how trusty I am.

“No sir-eee. Not my Sarah.” Penelope had never gotten over her stint in kiddie-book publishing and her singsong tone only made straightforward communication that much more difficult.

“Well, under the circumstances,” said Sarah, I thought--”

“Now just a sec,” Penelope said, clanking a spoon. The sound doubtless came from stirring Equal into her flowered mug, as she navigated around the chamomile tea bag from the Celestial Seasonings package. “So, your friend’s had a bad accident and you can’t give me a definite? What exactly does that mean?”

Reaching for a quick way out, Sarah said, “As soon as I’ve got her squared away . . . hopefully by uh . . .”

“Yes?”

“. . . Tuesday at noon. At the latest.”

"I still don't get it," said Penelope, clanking the spoon even harder. "I mean, the last time we talked you said, 'It's a given. I'm just taking the few days off I've got coming. Taking a break.' Which I, of course, took to mean you'd be on the job first thing tomorrow." Sarah stifled a sigh when Penelope added, "Bright-eyed and bushy-tailed."

Rambling on, Penelope pointed out all the reasons she had counted on her, beginning with Sarah's steadfast pursuit of her career. In reply, Sarah thanked her for her kind words. There was no way she could begin to explain what she was up to, let alone tell Penelope that some part of her was waffling about the editorial position--a side that felt once she got behind a desk, she would give up on what passed for real life.

"And you did so well coming up with the series on colorful characters," Penelope went on, gently slurping her tea in Sarah's ear.

"Colorful and harmless," Sarah said.

"Indeed, making New Haven seem like a nice enough place for people to frequent. You add that to the fact you're good at spotting holes in stories. I mean, need I go on?"

"I hear you, Penelope," said Sarah, still searching for an exit line. When Penelope shifted out of her flattering mode and started in on deadlines for the *Today's Woman Section*--

assigning stories, selecting art photos, setting the wire stories, etc.--Sarah gave in. Ever since grade school, she couldn't withstand a barrage of appeals to loyalty, honor and duty. In effect, Katie had drawn her out into the world and Penelope was yanking her back inside.

The upshot was that Penelope would cover and do the preliminaries on a retro issue on women's career cycles. The cover story would feature Sarah's latest piece on the socialite who opened a soup kitchen in one of the better sections of town for pleasant, but needy, derelicts. That settled, Penelope clunked her mug on a saucer, mumbled something about her mom being in a tizzy, wished Sarah's friend a speedy recovery, and hung up.

Flustered, Sarah strode off into the overcast mist, brushing by strollers, barging full tilt into the dinette where she wolfed down every no-no on the menu, culminating with a thick wedge of banana cream pie. A brisk walk around Lakeville to work off the calories didn't help. She was at odds with herself, at odds with the enigma surrounding Katie—just plain at odds.

Okay, thought Sarah, enough sputtering around in the dark. Got to see it from the beginning, know where it's going, how Katie fits in or got in the way. Then blow the whistle. Then come to terms with my own stupid life. Get it? Got it. Good.

By the time she returned to her motel parking space, she was fixated on the number seven. Logical or illogical, it was an irresistible key to the whole cockamamie story. She cranked up her Honda and headed back to Waybury.

Pulling over on a side street in back of the Waybury Town Hall, she got out and headed to the rear of Will Gibble's office. The overcast sky glinted here and there with lighter patches of pearl gray. Tramping over the trailing weeds that covered the vacant lot, she felt the palpable silence permeating the village. Even the inn was quiet. Waybury mothers and their kin had apparently deserted their nooks for something more lively.

She tried the back door of the building. It was loose, the hinges rattled, but it was locked, just as she expected. Now what? Who could she call? Gibble? Hardly. His spinster secretary? Probably not. Even if she were home with nothing to do, would she come over and, la-di-da, let Sarah in? Fat chance.

She thought about forcing the door. The answer was no. Stupid idea. Minutes passed as she just stood there at a loss.

Then, seemingly from out of nowhere, a familiar boney form drifted to her side.

"Don't tell me," said Alice, her sliver of a face breaking into a grin. "Breaking and entering, right? Hey, excellent."

The red lettering on her knee-length T-shirt said, "In your dreams, dude." Still grinning, she reached into the back pocket of her shredded jeans and plucked out a bag of red-shelled pistachios.

"Just trying the door, Alice. You never know."

"Sure, man. On Sunday? Yeah, tell me about it."

A gaggle of Canadian geese honked somewhere overhead as Sarah turned the knob again for no reason.

Alice said, "Tell you what," as she pried at a pistachio with the corner of a broken thumbnail. "Gibble says I can check out his new computer whenever I'm footloose. You know, hook up to the Internet, expand my knowledge."

"Oh? And what does your father say?"

"Who cares? Benjamin's probably shackin' up with some sleaze right about now."

"Nice."

"Yeah. Well don't rub it in. Which is the whole point I wanted your dumb advice. I ain't gonna wind up like my old lady, knocked up, splittin' for parts unknown and not much older than me. No way."

She was prying harder at the shells, steaks of red from the vegetable dye leaving little smudges on her chin. "It's Mother's Day, man," she went on. "Some joke." Wiping the tear away from her eye, Alice said, "Anyways, one step at a time. First off, you stop the watchamacallit, the hassling me about the keys and the checkbook and crap, and I'll let you in. Then I'll tell you what I need. Deal?"

"Will Gibble gave you a key?"

"What are you, deaf? Like I said, when I'm on my own, like today. If I get on something like Britannica dot com, learn about the history of rock and stuff, maybe I won't get in trouble."

"Oh sure, Alice," said Sarah shaking her head, "I believe it."

"Who cares? Believe or don't believe. Hey, look at it this way, I got a free pass, you're my guest. What do you know, right?"

To Sarah's mind, it was ridiculous going along with her "free pass ploy." Especially in the light of her alleged dirty tricks and if she was in any way responsible for unnerving Katie. Sarah should have dropped it and gone on to another tack.

Instead, totally against her better judgment, she said, "Okay, kid. You're on."

Alice reached under the mat, inserted the key and opened the door with one quick twist. Sarah shook her head a second time. Once inside, Sarah made a few turns and made her way to the town clerk's office. The door was locked.

Alice drifted in, climbed up on a chair, slid her fingers on top of the doorframe and came up with yet another key. After unlocking the door and replacing the key and chair, Alice said, "Spare-key Betty they call her."

"The town clerk?"

"You got it. She locks herself out of the office, her car, her house, you name it."

"I see."

Move it, Sarah told herself. You're in. Either accomplish something, and get out fast, or leave.

"Fine," said Sarah. "You're going online, learning about the Beatles. That's the excuse, remember?"

"Hard-core rap."

"Whatever. I'll be back in a second."

"Yeah and then we talk. Woman to woman."

"Uh-huh," said Sarah, watching Alice wend her way back toward Gibble's domain.

The room that held the records, the one Gibble alluded to during their first meeting, was paneled. Dark cherry wood soaked up the reflection of the pale afternoon sky making it difficult to see. Putting on her reading glasses, not daring to switch on a light, she searched through the Grand List: the red-leatherette volumes that referenced deeds, assessments and property taxes. Combing through the oversized pages, she came across a conveyance tax received by the town clerk of Waybury from Tommy Haddam. More references to deeds, assessment of acreage and dwellings, and she found a "being the same premises conveyed to Kenneth and Margaret Trumbull recorded in Waybury Land Records, Volume 46, page 544."

The Kenneth and Margaret Trumbull citations only took Sarah back three years. More land record volumes lugged down and flopped on a long wooden table, a lot of "we are well seized of the premises as a good indefeasible estate in fee simple" later, and Sarah finally came upon it. Seven years ago the property was owned and run by one Melanie Landis. Sarah noted the conveyance tax number and land records page.

After hauling and shoving the volumes back in place, she returned to the outer offices and pulled Alice away from the Internet. The graphics Alice had been gaping at were suspect but Sarah had no time to consider Alice's cyber life.

Back at the rear of the building, Alice replaced the key under the mat and said, "Now for the real stuff. About Kevin. How do I handle it? Do I slip him the hundred Russell forked over for filmin' my bod? For repairs to his Harley, I mean. And if so, how does that keep him from splitting?"

"Later."

"What? Hold it, man. I told you I want some woman to woman stuff and I want it now."

"Later, I said."

"Hey, you promised."

Shrugging, striding past the side of the building, heading for the main street, Sarah said, "What can I say?

Alice raced ahead of her, walking backwards, her hands on her hips. "You can't do this. Listen, what you did back there, connin' me so's I would let you in, that's um . . . conspiracy to commit burglary, risk of injury to a minor and other major crime."

"And what you did back there was burglary, larceny and lying."

"Gibble said any time."

"Then why are your eyes darting around? What's the problem?"

"My life, that's what's the problem."

"Not now, Alice. After I see where you fit in, maybe." A quick jog to the left, leaving Alice in a snit, and Sarah was bounding up the creaky steps of the inn.

"Nobody stiffs me, man," Alice hollered behind her. "You hear? You are askin' for it."

No doubt, Sarah said to herself, whisking past the veranda, through the double doors, into the lobby and over to the pay phone at the far wall. While she was pulling out her credit card, she thought she heard whistling. It seemed to come from somewhere beyond the caked-up window to her right. It was high-pitched and intermittent, like a novice birder who couldn't quite remember the calls. Dismissing it, Sarah phoned the paper again. The stringer who was manning the city desk told her that her pal Jan on the Police Beat was around somewhere.

Waiting for Jan to ring her back, Sarah heard the whistling again. This time it was closer. It switched from inept bird calls to jumbled melodies and back again.

The phone rang, the husky tone at the other end of the line cut through the whistle static outside the wall. "Hey, Bucklin, how's your sex life? No no, don't tell me, don't ruin my day."

Sarah waited out the wisecracks and finally succeeded in getting her message across. Yes, she needed a trace for personal reasons. No, she didn't know if Melanie Landis had remarried.

No, she didn't have anything more to go on other than a conveyance tax record and an address Landis hadn't lived at for seven years. No, she had no other sources she could tap and, Yes, she needed it yesterday.

"Look, pal," said Jan, "what do you think I am?"

"A mover and shaker who can access special data bases."

"For a price, sweetie. Especially on Mother's Day."

"Are you a mother?"

"Don't diddle with me, Bucklin. I am in no mood."

"Ditto. I need your pipeline to three-hundred electronic mailboxes plus your contact at the DMV who can run down plates."

"This is gonna cost you, girl, since I am up to my butt and you give me no notice. On a Sunday afternoon, no less, when I've got a hot date blowing in my ear."

"Okay, okay."

"How come?"

"Because, so far I've been getting a lot of grief and just about no help."

"Forget it, if you're going to put it that way."

"That's the way I'm putting it. Do I have to beg?"

"Please, my stomach. Don't make me barf."

Jan put Sarah on hold as some fast-breaking item came in about a North Haven man holding his wife hostage. As Sarah drummed her fingers against the striped wallpaper, she caught a glimpse of Doreen in the alley. Wearing a muslin apron over a high-necked metallic-green dress, she cocked her head twice, waited, and then inched over to a green rusty dumpster and tested the lid. Nodding her head, she retreated out of view.

"No sweat," said Jan, coming back on the line. "The hostage-taker's wife just punched him out and took off. Now where were we?"

"You are going to do me a favor because by the time I trace her using my feeble nonexistent resources, it'll be way too late."

"Too late for what? What for rice cakes is goin' on and where the hell are you anyways?"

"In the boonies. Look, you got the name? Melanie Landis. She owned property in Waybury seven years ago. Where is she now? How can I reach her?"

"I got it, I got it," Jan said. "Give me an hour--provided nothing else comes up and hold your breath for the price. Oh, almost forgot. That hunk of yours: tall, cool, tweedy, short on talk . . ."

"Yes?" said Sarah, waiting for the kicker.

"He sent you some reams of paper wrapped in fat rubber bands. Juicy title: 'Poetry of the Civil War'. Guess he ran out of closet space."

"And?"

"And what?"

"Read me the note."

"Right . . . um . . . yeah," said Jan, accompanied by snapping and crinkling paper sounds. "He says he added some stuff he found in Richmond. Wants to know what you think of the sequence. Found some new references in Charlottesville, too. Be back a little later than planned. In the meantime, yattata-yattaa ba-bing ba-bing."

"Thanks. You read it beautifully."

"Up your nose, Bucklin. Later, huh?"

The dial tone buzzed in Sarah's ear. She replaced the receiver just as Doreen reappeared through the smudged window toting a black plastic trash bag. Blinking her good eye, she glanced around again and warbled something about a train, a "Midnight Special." Whistling as loud as possible, ostensibly trying to cover the squeak of the dumpster lid, she tossed in the bag and scuttled off.

The incident reminded Sarah of one of Jan's axioms: you get more answers from people's garbage than their mouths; they express themselves more directly that way. In the mood Sarah was in, jaded Jan was fast becoming her role model.

Moving outside, Sarah skirted the far edge of the inn and headed straight down the alley. Slipping her hand under the dumpster lid, she snatched out the plastic bag, yanked the yellow drawstring and spilled the contents onto the asphalt. Blatantly tucked inside a large manila envelope marked “Alice” was a stack of letters addressed to Kevin, a set of car keys and checkbooks with a Kathleen Haddam imprint.

Nineteen

arah parked her car in the alley, flipped the trunk latch and deposited the garbage bag. She decided that the wise thing at this point was to put the contents on hold for a while and not overreact or get ahead of the story as she had the day before. The wise thing was to pull back and allow the pieces to fall into place.

The off-key whistling came drifting in again on the breeze, possibly from the veranda. Sarah stepped around to the front of the inn. From somewhere inside the lobby, a grandfather clock chimed three times. But there was no sign of Doreen. And there was still thirty minutes to go before Sarah was due to check back with Jan.

The cloud cover brightened for a second. A swarm of plump little bees dove in and out of the magenta azaleas by the front steps. Aimlessly, Sarah found herself reviewing a montage of experiences including Mark pressing in on her up in the hayloft and the sounds of muffled pops and shattered glass in the woods.

You're at it again, thought Sarah. Let's focus on completing our homework. Let's focus, period.

The sky turned to a chilly gunmetal gray. A car backfired off in the distance. The car reminded her of her own unattended car. She heard something slam and scurried around to the alley. She jerked the latch by the front seat and spun around to the trunk, peeked inside and found the garbage bag still intact. She closed the lid, scuffed back and reflexively glanced behind the wheel. Her keys were gone. Or had she dropped them? Or absentmindedly put them in her purse?

She retraced her steps. She looked under the front seat, flung out the rubber mats, dug her hands into the folds of the velour cushioning. She slapped open the glove compartment, rifled through the registrations, maps and receipts and banged it shut. She shoved the driver's seat forward and back, searched under and around and did the same with the passenger seat. She retraced her steps again, scooting back around to the veranda, walking up and down the worn wooden steps, scouring the magenta azalea clusters, fending off the bees, peering beneath the foliage, raking the loose soil. Then, for the third time, she emptied everything in her shoulder bag onto the porch, sat on the top step and, one by one, replaced each item. It all came to naught.

Was this how it had started with Katie? Then the checkbook and the poisoning of the little St. Bernard?

Putting it all aside, even more determined not to get sidetracked, she moved back into the mahogany reaches of the lobby and dialed the paper.

"Tell me you found it," Sarah said.

"Tell me you'll pay."

"How much?"

"No no no. The question is, What do I have to do, Jan? How do I earn it?"

"Give it to me, will you? I am seven years behind."

Footsteps in the recesses of the nearby bar. Sarah turned her head. It was no filcher of car keys, not Doreen, not Alice either. Just the waitress from the other night, the one with the frazzled hair.

"Hey, Bucklin," Jan barked on the other end, "are you buying into this or not?"

Sarah said, "Okay, shoot."

"After I find out where you're coming from. No deal if you're stuck and have no wheels."

"Talk to me. I thought you were busy?"

"You got it. There's the breaking story on the Yale rape suspect, two stalker incidents and a sidebar about new wrinkles in DNA profiling. Which is where you come in. Tomorrow at four, you interview the medical examiner at Yale New Haven and come up with the skinny: bar codes, negative charges, printing, non-secretor status and the speedier process. You access it to my screen by six. That's two hours before deadline. You copy?"

"Gotcha."

The twinges of guilt registered immediately. Meeting Jan's needs were unlikely; meeting Penelope's time frame for *Today's Woman* was iffy at best. To top it off, as of the moment, Sarah had no means of transportation to anywhere.

"Hey, Bucklin, you still there?"

"Obviously. Where is Melanie Landis?"

"Northrop. Her new name is Northrop. Home address: Stockbridge, Mass."

"As of when?"

"Got remarried a year ago. No, no, no, don't ask how I got this. Put it down to pushiness, uncommon agility and remarkable skill."

"Indeed." If only Sarah could find her keys and if Melanie Landis was home, Stockbridge was only forty minutes away across the Massachusetts line.

Just as Jan was about to hang up, Sarah said, "Just one more thing."

"I don't believe it."

"A few tips on investigative interviewing."

"What are you, serious?"

"One more second of your award-winning time. Please?"

"Why?"

"Because as a guy up here put it to me, I've got no act. I don't know how to play it."

Jan moaned. The clacking on her end of the line grew more insistent, as though a gaggle of stringers were filing in, grabbing any computer terminal in sight and pounding out copy. Two more groans and a sigh and Jan finally said, "You mean dealing with characters who are not champing at the bit like the jokers in your columns. You mean those who've got something to hide."

"Bingo."

"Outta your territory. You mess in the shadows, it's a crapshoot, Bucklin. How many times I have to tell you?"

"I hear you."

"It takes timing. You have to be crafty and, at the same time, seem like you don't give a damn. You'd have to ditch your entire personality."

A baby robin pecked at its reflection in the nearby window, startling itself and Sarah at the same time, and then flew off. Recovering, Sarah said, "So?"

"You're serious."

"Yes. Give me some do-ables, will you?"

Two more groans. "I'm talking pretend, get it? You pretend to know more than you know. You listen. They love a good listener. If they con you, you break the sequence so they can't rethink their story. Like this: 'How long did you live there? Was the weather good? Where did you go that night? What was the neighborhood like? So, why did you stalk her?' You keep them off balance. Like any game."

"And?"

"You catch them while they're doing something. Or get them to do something--putter around, play pool, eat lunch. Someplace where they can't do their number, break into their routine. End of lesson."

"What about notes?"

"What do you want to do, spook 'em? You remember the details. Oh, hey, forget it. Like I said, totally out of your league."

"Sweet."

"In your ear. You better come through for me or you've had it, pal." With that, Jan cut off the connection.

Two more phone calls and Sarah had Melanie's phone number. A ring to Stockbridge and Sarah learned from the housekeeper that Mrs. Northrop would be on the courts warming-up at five. If Sarah didn't know better, her luck was changing and there was something at work here called synchronicity.

A final call to the Red Lion Inn; the pro shop was open till five, they had two overpriced lightweight aluminum rackets left but they didn't sell tennis shoes.

The baby robin was back at the window. But it didn't startle Sarah this time. What did startle her was the sight of Alice's bony form, crossing back from Benjamin's garage diagonally across the street, tools and a hot wire in hand. What was even more surprising was the sight of Alice springing the hood of Sarah's car and then leaning against the front fender, waiting, as if they had an appointment.

"Look," said Alice, "do you want this thing started or not?"

"And how did you know if it wasn't you that swiped my keys? Not to mention other things we won't go into?"

"Oh wow, big mystery, man," said Alice, jerking her scrawny arms up and down; thrusting the hammer, screwdriver and hot-wires toward the gray sky as if doing an incantation. "The woman stands on her head, dumps out her bag seventeen times, curses and kicks the crap out the azaleas for some unknown reason. What can she be doing?"

"And you propose to help me gratis?"

"I decided to forgive. I decided to give you another chance. 'Cause I am confused, man. I don't know myself no more. The guys used to like me 'cause I--"

"Swiped things. And cursed and told dirty jokes."

"Yeah, stuff like that. Anyways, now they want somethin' else. And I don't know what Kevin wants. Hey, you need some help or not? Tit for tat. Countin' lettin' you into Will Gibble's, I figure you owe me rides to hunt up Kevin at the very least. Plus talk so's I can get my head on straight. I mean, I am gonna be thirteen. School's gonna be out. I am at the watchamacallit here."

"Crossroads."

"Yeah. My body's changin' and I got all these feelings to deal with."

Alice twisted around, checked across the street at the garage and twisted back. "Hey look, Benjamin says he's got Kevin by the short hairs. But what if he's nuts? What if Kevin beats it no matter what I do?" Alice's sliver of a face turned crimson, tears welling up in the slits that passed for her eyes.

"Okay okay, we'll work something out. Are you sure you know what you're doing?"

"What, I've been hangin' out at Benjamin's grease pit and learned nothin'? I mean, give me a break."

Alice glanced back one more time. "So, you want the screwdriver banged in the ignition switch? Which won't look so hot but will do the trick. I'm talkin' works like a charm. Or would you rather mess with the wires?"

"The wires will do nicely thanks."

"Watch closely. Notice at no time do my fingers leave my hands."

First, Alice turned the steering wheel until it unlocked. Then she dove under the hood, clipped the black hot wire off the battery to the coil while squirming around, getting her huge T-shirt grimy with grease. Next, she clipped the red wire to the same battery terminal, dove down again and clipped the other end to the starter solenoid. The Honda fired right up.

"You got it?" said Alice. "You wanna turn it off, unclip the coil. No sweat, piece of cake. See?"

"I see," said Sarah as she climbed behind the wheel. "Slow at first, but I'm learning."

"Hold it," Alice screamed as Sarah backed out into the street. "What about me?"

"Tomorrow. After school."

Shifting into second, she saw Alice in the rear-view mirror leaping up and down as if she'd been robbed. Sarah would make it up to her. But, like everything else, it all depended on how things went.

Heading north, crossing the state line past Sheffield, she cruised deeper into the Berkshires. There is causality dammit, she told herself. Things can add up.

A few blocks south of Stockbridge's storybook file of clapboard shops, Sarah located a gap in the endless file of out-of-state vehicles and parked. With the soft hills and darkening sky looming above, she brushed her tousled hair and dabbed her cheeks with Fire-16 powder blush. Smoothing out her white knit top and adjusting her twill split skirt, she mentally went over her ruse. Then, ready as could be, she grabbed her old battered sneakers from the recesses of the trunk, slipped them on and dropped into the Red Lion's pro shop with fifteen minutes to spare. Snapping her fingers, she began to feel a slight edge. Still lost, to be sure, but altered in some way, like a novice who had finally made up her mind to enter the game.

Twenty

Sarah lifted a high lob that sent Melanie Northrop scurrying backwards toward the baseline. Lunging wildly, Melanie tripped and fell. Sarah rushed around the net and offered to help.

"No need," Melanie said in her affected singsong voice. "Don't bother."

Pushing off on the left toe of her white tennis shoes with a pink trim, Melanie attempted to spring up like a schoolgirl. But she couldn't quite pull it off. She had a smooth oval face but the flesh around her thighs was noticeably creased. Her self-conscious movements, coupled with her long blond tinted hair and frilly white silk tennis skirt and blouse, completed the image. It was somewhat a strain for her to appear coquettish instead of acting her forty-something age.

"Well?" said Melanie, striking another affected pose: hands on her hips, knee turned in, hair tossed to one side. "Your serve."

"Oh?" Sarah said, looking for some opening to slip in her questions.

"Your date, remember? In fifteen minutes. You said you needed the practice."

Sarah said, "Absolutely," as she hurried back to her own baseline.

They played on. The courts were nestled inside a grove of spreading oaks. The couples who had been playing doubles in the adjacent court had retired momentarily for cocktails in the clubhouse. Grateful that they were alone, Sarah had made some excuse about her attire, bypassed the fact that she wasn't a member and claimed she was wretched playing on clay and too embarrassed to tell her new beau. On this basis, she had implored Melanie to play a few games so that Sarah could more or less ready herself before he showed up.

As the clouds thickened to an opaque charcoal gray, Sarah plopped a second serve on an angle to Melanie's backhand. Melanie lunged far to her left, chipping the ball with the edge of her racket, sending it meekly into the net. It had been over eight months since Sarah had last played, a time when Katie had run her ragged. Against Melanie, Sarah felt like a pro.

"Love/forty," Melanie said, puffing, moving over to a green wooden bench and dabbing her face with a thick yellow terry-cloth towel.

As Melanie moved back into position, Sarah slammed her first serve into the far corner of Melanie's left service box, jumping on Melanie's weak backhand again. Melanie dinked it over the net. Sarah dinked it back. The feeble volley enabled Sarah to crowd the net, move Melanie back and forth and, at last, try Jan's questioning ploy.

"Hey," said Sarah, blocking another shot, "is it true?"

"What?" Melanie said, lunging for yet another backhand.

"That you had a vineyard?"

"Who told you that?" said Melanie, continuing to pat the ball high and short.

"Someone at the Red Lion. He recognized you somehow and told my boyfriend. Said you really stirred things up."

"Really?"

"Yup."

"After all this time? He actually remembered me?"

"Uh-huh: Quite impressed."

"Even though it failed?"

"Well," said Sarah, puffing a bit, trying to run and talk at the same time, "that's what must've made the great impression. About how it all went wrong, I mean."

"You mean the uh . . ."

"Exactly."

"Ah." Hitting a backhand in amazement, Melanie said, "He actually recalled the details?"

Returning the backhand and remembering Willy's journal, Sarah said, "The whole bit, prunings and all."

Flailing here and there, Melanie said, "Odd. How is it possible we're having this conversation? I don't understand?"

"It's my boyfriend," Sarah said. "Don't want him to make the same mistake."

This time Melanie rushed the net, finally getting a clean forehand shot, and whacked the ball cross-court for a winner.

Panting, hanging onto the post, Melanie said, "Well, tell him not to get his hopes up unless he's got a winemaker with credentials. I never checked, you see. Went in green. Opted for a Seyval Blanc, a true highlands dry white. Couldn't miss."

"A money maker."

"But," Melanie said, still panting, "my man wants to prune the vines very short."

"Imagine," Sarah said, following Jan's lead, trying to sound blasé. "Oh dear."

"'Oh dear,' is right. He claims heavy pruning keeps the quality up. Which I begin to discover leaves you nothing for yields."

"Which led to all the trouble," said Sarah, still without a clue.

"'Low yields bring maximum concentration', he says. 'If the wine shocks the palate, so much the better', he says."

"Oh my."

"Oh catastrophe, you mean. He clips away, indulges in long maceration, no distemming whatsoever, loading the wine up with tannin. And—picture this --he never chaptalized."

"Imagine," Sarah said once again, noting the growing hardness in Melanie's voice.

"No sugar," Melanie went on, batting a ball past Sarah that smacked into the green wooden fence. "A harsh astringent taste. Lost every cent I had."

Suddenly Melanie stiffened and strode right up to the net. "You haven't the foggiest what I'm talking about, do you?"

"Not exactly, but--"

"And why are you yanking me all over the court? What is going on?"

"Nothing. Like I said, I have a personal interest. That's all."

Trotting back to her baseline, Sarah said, "Come on, let's go. Fifteen/forty." Melanie gave Sarah another hard look and returned to her position.

On Sarah's next serve, Melanie crossed Sarah up, rushed the net and sent another winner zinging well to Sarah's right.

"What are you?" said Melanie, planting her creased thighs far apart. "With *The Wine Spectator*? First assignment?"

"Hardly."

Melanie kept glaring at Sarah as if she were some industrial spy. Sarah bounced the ball, waiting for Melanie to move back for return of service. But Melanie didn't budge. "Come on," Melanie said. "Let's have it."

"Have what?"

Skirting the net, Melanie marched straight over to her. "What rag are you with? Out with it."

Standing her ground, Sarah said, "None."

"Oh, freelance, huh? The gutter press." They were standing toe to toe now, Melanie twisting her tennis shoe on the clay, blurring the chalk line. "Don't tell me Benjamin has been opening his filthy mouth. Dredging this up for some extra cash or something."

"Who?" Sarah said, recalling Alice's greasy dad.

"Look, when I said my car was in there for repairs, that's what I meant. When I said Willy was acting on his own, that's what I meant. My God, I can't believe it. What is it, that dumb TV show? *Unsolved Mysteries?* Are you that hard up?"

"Willy?"

Melanie raised her facelift to the darkening sky, her lacquered lips twitching. "You people are the worst. And I actually felt sorry for you, you know that? I looked at your rumpled outfit, your hairdo, your--"

"Save it, okay?"

"No I won't save it. You get on the phone to your publisher or whatever, you even mention my name and you are in for the biggest libel suit you ever saw. How do you people live with yourself, that's what I want to know?"

"I said, save it," Sarah said, slamming down her racket. "As it happens, I am acting for a friend who got shoved down the cistern of your wanna-be vineyard. And as it happens, she is fading and needs some answers. So what am I supposed to do?"

Thrown off guard, Melanie fussed with her white headband, ran her hands through her tinted hair and then carefully put the band back in place. The bank of charcoal clouds loomed closer overhead. A breeze kicked up, sending the temperature even lower.

Adjusting her defensive tone a notch, Melanie asked Sarah who she was, really. Sarah told her flat out.

“Fine,” said Melanie. “Whatever. Perhaps if you had been more forthcoming, I would’ve been more receptive.”

“You would’ve had me tossed on my ear. So let’s forget my feeble ploy and call it a day.”

Sarah snatched up her racket. At the same time, a tall man in his fifties with glistening white hair appeared through the court gate and was instantly upon them.

“Ah, Charles,” Melanie cooed, slipping back into her coquette facade. “At last. It seems this poor thing has been stood up. What a shame.” Blushing, she angled her head and batted her false eyelashes. Charles, in turn, lithe and tan, ran a tapered finger along the perfect crease in his white linen slacks as if readying himself for a photo op and then positioned himself by Melanie’s side.

Shrugging it all off, Sarah made her excuses and turned to leave. Melanie whispered something to Charles and scampered after her.

“Just a second,” Melanie said, fronting Sarah under the girth of a huge Oak limb. “Did that really happen to your friend?

The apocryphal cistern, it actually exists? After the well went dry, I naturally assumed . . . "

Melanie's glossy lips kept pursing, reaching for words. Charles called, Melanie cooed that she'd be right there. Sarah let a long moment pass while Melanie decided what to say.

"Listen," said Melanie, dropping all of her routines, segueing into a soft flat delivery. "Do you know about Willy?"

"The swindler winemaker?" said Sarah, guessing.

"As I remember, he was beside himself when I quashed the whole thing. And right after he went out and . . . I mean, really!"

Charles kept calling and Melanie kept twisting back and waving. "Anyways," Melanie went on, "for what it's worth, he died about six weeks ago from something or other. Which means over six-hundred thou is . . ." Another wave at Charles and then Melanie said, "So you can see why the insurance company keeps harassing me, and why I assumed you were looking for some juicy angle. Thereby screwing up my chances with Charles."

Before Sarah could ask the zillion questions that were popping up in her brain, Charles called so insistently this time that Melanie reverted back to her dulcet tones, waved goodbye to Sarah and sashayed away.

Famished again, Sarah drove around until she spotted another parking space in the vicinity of the Norman-Rockwell-storybook main street of Stockbridge. Threading her way through the clusters of tourists clogging the sidewalks, she settled on the closest and quickest solution. Back to the Red Lion: the 110-room white colonial at the main corner with its fabled broad veranda. Barging straight ahead, she clambered up the broad wooden steps and snatched a rocker from under the nose of a dowdy woman in a rose sun dress and straw hat. Tugging on a frazzled young waitress's elbow, she asked for any kind of sandwich and an ice tea.

As she waited, she jotted down the new findings while they were still fresh in her mind: Willy, the vintner, caused Melanie to go bust . . . in some kind of dire straits himself as a result, did something involving Melanie's car and Benjamin . . . culminating in his leaving this earth as Katie stepped into the picture . . . with over six-hundred thou floating around . . . and Katie possibly, somehow getting in the way.

Sarah shivered as the breeze kicked up again. The wedge of sky visible beyond the white wooden columns was a layer of deep charcoal. A few seconds later, a rumble of thunder sent her scrambling inside through the low-ceilinged obstacle course of antique highboys, couches, cabinets, tables and chairs dating back to the turn of the nineteenth century, strewn about a web of connecting parlors. She worked her way through the swarming guests until she reached a knotty-pine nook at the side of the oaken bar.

The same frazzled waitress said she'd bring her order as soon as she had a chance. Another jostling thrust and parry and a turn to the right and Sarah was at the pay phones crammed at the rear of the lobby. Her back to the bathroom doors tagged with wrought-iron stereotypes of Gay Nineties ladies and gentlemen, she proceeded to wait. The nearest booth was occupied by the same dowdy matron in rose, haggling for season's tickets to Tanglewood. Spewing out some carefully chosen epithets, the matron finally relinquished the space.

After three tries, Sarah managed to make a credit card call to the hospital. It was now six-thirty. Sarah was just about on time.

"I'm sorry," said Button-eyes in that brittle, patronizing tone of hers. "It's pointless. She doesn't respond."

"Just tell her anyway. Just say 'Sarah's on to something.'"

"But she's not aware."

"She hears."

"Not likely."

"Can you prove it? Medically?"

"Doctor says she's in a coma. Sorry, I have to get back to my station."

"Please?"

Trying to cut Sarah off, Button-eyes said, "I could possibly check with my supervisor. Take it under advisement."

"Don't check. Just go over to her and do it."

"I said I would have to check."

"I am counting on you," said Sarah just as Button-eyes hung up.

Elbowing her way back to her knotty-pine corner by the bar, Sarah sat on a spindly cane chair and wolfed down a BLT while the rumble of thunder insinuated itself throughout the inn, like some huge disgruntled guest. One iced tea and two cups of coffee later, and Sarah was headed out of the inn and on her way back to Lakeville, tooling along into the rumbling nightfall, wondering how long could she keep the old Honda going by rubbing two wires together, hoping for the best through the intervals of spattering rain. She also wondered about the timetable, the perpetrator's next move and, above all, what the final upshot would be.

After an interminable amount of driving time, she eased into her parking slot at the motel, got out and resigned herself to the fact that she'd have to leave the car unlocked. The gusts continued, scattering petals of white and pink apple blossoms, dappling the darkened walks and grounds.

By nine-thirty she had sketched-in a vague outline of a beginning and pinpointed the missing pieces of information and where she might possibly obtain them starting first thing tomorrow. By ten, the gusts showed no sign of letting up. The rumbles kept up their mock threat and the rain continued to vacillate between intervals of pitter-patter and spattering release. During one of the quieter intervals, a little before ten-thirty, Varno finally called her back from the barracks.

"Listen," Varno said in that draggy rhythm of his, "just bring it by . . . drop it off."

"And you'll do what with it? Say 'Okay, it's Katie's keys and check book and all, but what does it prove?'"

"It's a matter of seeing the totality. Of the picture, I mean."

"No kidding."

"Look, if it's new information, if it sheds some light, well..."

"Well what?"

"I want to know."

Something scraped outside, like a ladder against a wall. Sarah peered through the blinds and sloughed it off as more machinations of the wind.

"As an officer of the law," Varno added, "I would never let it be said that I overlooked something. Can't afford to overlook things."

"Uh-huh. But you still haven't said what you're going to do with it."

"Secure the contents first and—where, by the way, did you find this trash bag?"

"If I tell you, what would you say to bringing certain people in for questioning?"

"It doesn't work that way. What do you want?"

"What do I want? I want whoever it is stopped and you over Katie's bed, flashing your badge, telling her she was a victim. That's what I want."

"Seriously. I mean, what is it you think you're doing?"

Yawning despite herself, Sarah said, "Shining a ferocious light on this whole muddle. How's that?"

Varno murmured, "Mmm," as if he were rubbing his baleful eyes and nodding off. Another "Mmm" and he said, "If you'd like me to examine whatever you've got . . . just ring the dispatcher tomorrow. That's Monday."

"I know what day it is."

"Ring him after four. In the meantime . . ."

"Stay off the estate."

"And out of trouble." As an afterthought Varno said, "Cross your fingers. No complaint from Mark or Tommy. Not a peep."

"I want you on call, Varno. You hear me?"

"That's my job," said Varno, stifling another yawn.

After hanging up, Sarah prodded herself into calling Tommy. Apparently he had reconsidered citing her for simple trespass. He had looked so vulnerable walking off into the woods and he was still another much needed ally. Sitting upright on the lumpy mattress, she dialed, waiting for the sound of his carefully modulated voice. No one answered. And, naturally, there was no voice mail, no message machine.

She let it ride for now, busying her mind with a profile of the perpetrator. But nothing would wash. It could be one person, it could be two. It could be some random combination. Finding the prime mover, she decided, came down to finding out about Willy. Then drawing a straight plumb line from there. She hoped against hope that Katie would hang tight for another night, and got ready for bed.

Some time before midnight, she dozed off. The first thing that woke her was a rhododendron branch scraping against the windowpane immediately to her right. She fluffed up her two pillows, rolled over to her left side and fell back asleep.

The second time, there was a tearing squawking sound fiom the same direction, as if some creature had just had its throat cut or had fallen into a trap and was helplessly trying to wrench itself free from the metal jaws. The wind whistled faintly. Shadows, like torn fibers, darted across the white stucco ceiling.

Sarah flicked on the bedside lamp and waited till she got her bearings. The rainy night seemed to have all but played itself out. A few birds twittered and chirped outside. Daring herself to peer out through the blinds, she saw nothing but the pitch blackness, the swaying rhododendrons and the outline of the Christopher Wren steeple across the way. She welcomed the signals that daylight was about to break. If only they weren't so persistent, like some defective alarm.

The third time she awoke, she gripped her pillow hard. Whatever it was fluttered against the window a few feet higher than the rhododendrons. By degrees, whatever it was began to flap more slowly. She waited till the flapping stopped. Then, squinting, tugging on the drawstring of the blinds ever so gently--just to know, just to make sure--she saw it. It was black, a raven or hawk silhouetted through the slats hanging upside down, its wings spread wide, its breast gutted and bleeding. She yanked down the window, locked it and pulled the blinds shut. In the next moment, there was a rubbing sound that grew louder and louder.

There was only one thing to do. Call the woman at the desk, rouse her. If nothing else, report the rubbing sounds, tell her about the hideous bird. She lurched out of bed and grabbed the receiver. The rubbing sounds stopped. She took another peek through the blinds. The bleeding bird was gone.

Slipping on her robe and loafers, she drifted outside. Surely there was a trace, bloodstains, drops of gore. With the breeze blowing her hair in her eyes, she peered up and down and all around the rhododendrons. The site was perfectly in order as if some elf had flitted in, cleaned up and polished Sarah's window squeaky clean.

Twenty-One

t the crack of dawn, Monday, May 11th, Sarah swore to herself that this time the pattern would end. She'd suffered the swiping of keys and the torments outside her window. But there would be no poisoning next and none of the rest. Even if she had to race like crazy, she would catch on and catch up. She would blow the whistle today.

By seven o'clock she had showered, given a statement to a pleasant non-descript trooper about the sounds and the gutted bird outside her window. He, in turn, took a look around and promised to canvas the area, talk to neighbors, etc. and file a report.

By eight o'clock, she had consumed another forgettable breakfast at the dinette and, after a series of calls, gotten in touch with the managing editor of the *Lakeville Register*. She was immediately informed that even though the paper had clippings and files that went back seven years, they could not accommodate her. The material she wanted was in the old building, on microfilm and only the publisher had access. Unfortunately, he was presently indisposed and they could not make an exception. No, not even if it was a matter of life and death. When Sarah asked about accessing the information through their databases, the editor scoffed, made some offhand comment about metro reporters and hung up.

A few minutes later she learned that the Lakeville library was closed on Monday. So was the one in Salisbury. The only recourse was the gingerbread house in Waybury. After the first ring, someone picked up. A jolly female voice confided that she and the children's librarian were sorting through old magazines they no longer subscribed to, plus assorted volumes and periodicals for their annual cleanup and book fair. Although the library was normally closed today, they would be happy to make an exception in Sarah's case and nine o'clock would be fine and dandy.

Driving back under the gunmetal sky, Sarah put Willy at the head of her list. If she could find the connection, if she could determine what folly of his had set off this twisted chain of events, she'd let Varno in on the game and force his hand.

The notion of a deadline continued to resonate in Sarah's mind as she moved about in the library basement. She riffled through old Connecticut magazines. She came up empty. None of the discarded periodicals helped. Neither had the distracting chatter of the nearby perky duo. They reminded her of nesting Downy woodpeckers, the way their shaggy gray and white heads kept flicking and bobbing, their narrow beaks poking here and there. Appropriately, they were both short and cuddly, in their mid-forties, bespectacled with identical tinted lenses. Inappropriately, they were preoccupied with the trashiest of the donated piles of fiction.

"Well," said the children's librarian, letting out another cry of exasperation, "get a load of this. A nymphomaniac who rises to the top and becomes a CEO by day and an international jewel thief by night. Who reads this stuff?"

"Beats me," said the cataloguer, dragging a box of books up the stairs, heading to the circulation desk. "Some women around here don't take enough cold showers if you ask me."

The chatter was bad enough, but the slurping of endless cups of decaf coffee and the chomping of assorted crullers and croissants made it even harder for Sarah to concentrate.

"We're willing to share," the children's librarian said, leafing through another bestseller, holding up a chocolate-dipped goody.

"No thanks," said Sarah. "Thanks all the same." Sarah shoved yet another cardboard box back into an empty slot. "Okay, you've only got *The Times* on microfilm but no index or printer. But are you sure about back issues of local papers?"

Draining the contents of her paper cup, the children's librarian said, "Nope. Like we told you, where would we put them all if we went back a whole seven years? "

"Just like we said," chimed in the cataloguer, returning, scurrying down the steps, licking her fingers. "But you need the subject, the exact dates and, besides, who knows if *The Time*s even covered it, whatever it is." Brandishing her digital watch, she added, "Goodness, where does it go? It's almost eleven."

"Fancy that," said her colleague. "Now let's see . . . I make it one box of trashy exposes and another of sleep-your-way-to-the-top."

"And lower your heating bill by half."

They both broke out into guffaws over that one.

"Oh great," said Sarah, half to herself. "No databases, no full text services. I thought everybody was up to speed by now."

The duo paused and frowned at Sarah at the same time, as if she were a naughty little girl who had spoken out of turn.

Brushing the dust off her skirt, Sarah said, "What are the chances you could give me some help?"

This time the double frown went into gridlock. "Well heavens," said the cataloguer, "we let you in here--"

"Indeed," broke in the children's librarian. "Try to be nice as can be . . . "

"Absolutely."

". . . and you're disappointed. Tell us our library services aren't up to par."

"I'm sorry. I'm trying to play catch-up and running into a stone wall."

Recalling another tactic from jaded Jan's grab bag, Sarah affected a poor lost soul look and said, "Look, truth is I really need your knowledge and expertise. But I wouldn't want to impose."

That did it. Sure enough, the gold dust twins perked up, dropped their crullers and smiled. Taking them into her confidence, Sarah revealed she was interested in a crime that may have taken place in this vicinity about seven years ago. The two resumed their chomping and guzzling for a beat or two and then said almost in unison, "The armored car robbery."

"But it didn't happen here," said the cataloguer.

"Although the main criminal was connected to uh . . ."

"Melanie Landis," said Sarah.

"Yes, Melanie Landis," the children's librarian piped in.

"Are you certain?" said the cataloguer.

"Well, the police did ask Benjamin about her car. I definitely remember that," said the children's librarian. "My old station wagon was in for repairs at the time. I still kid Benjamin about that, about my Jeep Cherokee being guilty by association."

"That's right. That is so funny, in a way."

"Yes, I have to admit I still chuckle over it. Though perhaps I shouldn't."

"But, come to think of it, the insurance people are still snooping around," said the cataloguer. "That's what I hear. You'd think by now they'd quit. I mean, it is such old news."

"The details," said Sarah, unable to humor them any longer. "Where can I get my hands on the details?"

"Head librarian's the best bet," said the cataloguer. "But she's visiting her nieces, not due in till tomorrow. Still, she would know. She saves every clipping about Waybury. Like old people save string."

"Where?" said Sarah. "In a folder? In a drawer?"

Before they had a chance to stop her, Sarah bounded up the steps. Like everything else in town, Sarah found the main reading room cluttered, neglected and slipping into decay.

Making her way through the debris, the only thing she found that distinguished the chief's bailiwick was a mound of mail strewn across a table next to the main entrance, addressed to the head of library services. By the time the duo caught up, Sarah was shuffling through a wooden bookcase that ran from the floor about twenty feet straight up to the rafters.

"Shouldn't be doing this," said the twosome again in unison.

Already in motion as if caught up in Sarah's rhythm, the cataloguer said, "Oh well, what's the harm?" In no time, both of them weaved in and out of the adjacent stacks and returned with a rolling ladder. Soon all three were rifling through the shelves: Sarah working the bottom portion, the cataloguer standing on the middle rungs, the children's librarian high above, stretching left and right and edging her way down.

Moments later, the cataloguer waved a yellow file folder over her head. "I've got it."

The two cleared a swath in the middle of the head librarian's table and began sorting through a pile of articles and pictures until they came upon a dozen or so articles held together by a metal clip. They arranged the shards and pieces in chronological order and fanned them out clockwise from left to right. Out of the dozen, Sarah selected three from the *Torrington Enquirer* and scanned the facts:

ARMED ROBBERY LEAVES ONE MAN KILLED

Winsted--An armed robbery resulted in a shootout behind the National Iron Bank on Route 44 yesterday, leaving one of the guards dead. Police have pieced together much of the day's events. At about noon, Norman Stone, 49, of Lakeville parked his Dunbar armored truck in the rear of the bank where he was scheduled to make a routine pick-up. He left the vehicle, opened the back doors and proceeded to load the bags from a handcar up to his partner, 50-year-old Brian Ayers of Salisbury. A moment after securing the money inside the armored vehicle, two men in hooded masks sprang out of an alley and accosted the guards with drawn handguns. During the ensuing melee, Brian Ayers was killed and Norman Stone was forced at gunpoint to drive off to some undisclosed location. Six-hundred-and-seventy thousand dollars was reported to have been stolen. The investigation has been taken over by the FBI and the state police Western District Major Crimes. Both of the alleged felons are still at large.

GUARD: HE HELD ME AT GUNPOINT

Winsted--Norman Stone, an armored car driver who was forced to drive to a designated drop two miles from the scene of yesterday's robbery, said, "I didn't have a chance. The guy scrambled into the back of the truck, I headed for the front. The guy fired. I could feel the muzzle blast on the right side of my face. I drove wherever he wanted. If it weren't for the older guy talking him out of it, the second guy would've done to me like he did Brian."

SUSPECT WILLY STARK CAPTURED

Winsted--Norman Stone, 49, the driver of the hijacked armored car gave state troopers all the information they needed. According to Stone, the leader had a hitch in his knee. Moreover, he shouted to the second man, telling him there was to have been no shooting. He was supposed to have remained in the rear of the armored van covering Stone and the other guard. The killing and the kidnapping of Stone should have never taken place. After unloading the money, the two alleged felons bound and gagged Stone but not before Stone got a glimpse of a car "stripped-down with rental plates," and heard another pull away--"a deep throated foreign job with dual carbs, like a Jag."

The last article went on to disclose that a Jag was reported missing from Benjamin's Garage in Waybury by its owner, Melanie Landis. A rented car found abandoned at a commuter parking lot in Winsted was traced back to Willy Stark, 68. Willy was employed as Landis' vintner and was heavily in debt. In addition, Willy walked with a limp. The amount still missing was well over six-hundred thousand and Stark's accomplice was still at large.

Noting the date of the armed robbery, Sarah deduced that by midnight tonight, exactly seven years will have passed.

"So?" said the duo.

"What's the upshot?" said the cataloguer.

"We assume you're not just a book writer," said the children's librarian, "doing some kind of research or something."

"More like someone from that insurance agency, I'll bet," the other chimed in. "Stands to reason."

"Well, what can I say?" said Sarah, asking for a copy of the Connecticut General Statutes. In response, the two eyed each other and arched their brows. "Please," said Sarah, glancing at the clock.

While she waited for them to sort through the reference section, the newsprint underscoring the "muzzle blast" and the popping sounds heard on the fringes of the estate merged in Sarah's mind. These thoughts were quickly eclipsed by the thick paperback the cataloguer slapped down next to the clippings.

Skimming through the sections, Sarah came across 53-A, Penal Code. Under the code she found Limitations. Under Sections 54-193 she located Class A Felony. Robbery, 1st degree was listed under 53A-134. The key words were "7 years . . . not to be prosecuted after offence."

Right, Sarah thought. It's buried, stashed away. You can dig it up tonight, kiddo, and you're home free.

"Found something?" said the children's librarian, waiting patiently by her cohort's side. "What is it?"

"Tell you later," Sarah said. "Right now, got to check with good ol' Benjamin."

"About the car, you mean," said the cataloguer calling behind Sarah's back as she began scurrying out. "Then the case is still open and your company has a new lead."

Pivoting around, Sarah said, "You guys were great. Better than a data base. I mean it."

As she vacated the premises, another thought crossed Sarah's mind. Why wasn't Katie's misfortune provocative local news? Did only sensational items merit a special folder? She wanted to ask the dynamic duo but she let it go.

"I don't give one goddamn what Melanie Landis told you," said Benjamin. His bloated face turned a splotchy red as he leaned under the hood of an old Buick, catching the dripping gas in a rusty tin can. "And I sure as hell am not gonna hassle with no whacko female."

"Hold it," said Sarah. "Are you by any chance referring to me?"

"Who else?"

"And where did you get this information?"

"Mark called right after you gassed him. Said you and that Katie are cut from the same cloth. Better keep Alice away before she gets infected."

"Oh, that's cute. That's real cute. What else did he offer?"

Grunting as his belly jounced against the intake manifold, Benjamin attempted to attach a hose to the inlet on the carburetor. "Mentioned about Kevin too." Pointing at the red Harley in the corner of the third bay, Benjamin said, "Seems he's the only one of your bunch who's finally got the goddamn message."

"What's his motorcycle doing here? Is he still--?

"Forget it. Whatever you got in mind, he's as good as gone. You get the picture?"

When Sarah didn't reply, Benjamin added, "Nobody diddles with me. I ain't as frisky as Mark. No way I'm gonna wind up groanin' over some hospital phone 'cause of some fruitcake female. So take a hike."

Part of her would've liked nothing better. Benjamin reeked of sweat and oil. Even the overhead fluorescent lights were smeared with grime. There was no inch of space to rest your eyes, no sight or smell that wasn't repellent. But she wasn't about to leave until she made the final link.

"You hear me?" said Benjamin, swatting a darting insect away from his splotchy cheeks. "Damn. You warm weather people are the worst."

It was yet another Mexican standoff. Sarah reached for one of Jan's tactical ploys. At the same time, she recalled that Jan expected her to do some leg work in New Haven by four, an obligation Sarah couldn't possibly meet.

"Okay, Benjamin, let's break the routine. I slip you the stuff with Alice's fingerprints over it in return for a little information."

Benjamin's dull eyeballs locked, a vein in his thick neck pulsed. He stood and rubbed his oil-soaked bald spot. Then he clamped one end of a hose to a can of solvent and suspended it from the underside of the pale green hood.

"Okay," said Sarah, trying ploy number nine. "I gave you a chance."

Still ignoring her, Benjamin reached behind the wheel, switched on the ignition, moved back under the hood and raced the engine at different speeds. Lingering, shouting over the noise, Sarah added, "Let Alice aid and abet. Let her go to juvenile hall. I mean, what the hell?"

Within seconds, the chugging motor cut off and Benjamin called back, "Ain't no point in bluffing me, girl. I just told you. I goddamn spelled it out. Don't try to jerk me around."

He sprayed the linkages around the carburetor with an aerosol solvent and said, "Show me you got somethin' on that brat of mine. Come on, come on, I wanna see it."

"Why don't you glance across the street? I will gingerly hold up the envelope containing the keys and check book belonging to Katie Haddam plus Alice's incriminating love letters. Okay? Will that do it for you?"

Benjamin sidled over to the wall and hit a button. The overhead door grinded on its track and reluctantly rose. Sarah walked across the road, reached under the driver's seat and flipped the trunk latch. Using some Kleenexes from her bag to keep from smudging the prints, she extracted the items in order, waved them, slipped the contents back into the envelope and deposited the envelope back in the trash bag. A moment later she was back beside the rusty green Plymouth.

"One other thing," said Sarah. "I'm sure Doreen will corroborate." Scrunching up his face, Benjamin dove back down under the hood. "It just gets worse and worse, doesn't it?" Sarah added.

After disconnecting the fuel line, vacuum lines and the linkages, Benjamin said, "Okay okay. If you tell that wimp Tommy he still owes 'cause she still owes me."

"Meaning?"

"That is my damn dozer sittin' on the estate. I was supposed to clear away for a new parking lot, concession stand and—never mind. You tell him I want what's comin'. You tell him like I said."

Sarah hastily made a note about the bulldozer and said, "Deal. So tell me about Willy and the Jag. I know the insurance company recently jogged your memory."

Benjamin screwed up his eyes. "How many times, how many times? It's the same as I told 'em and goddamn keep telling 'em over and over. Mark drops off the Jag and early the next morning it's gone. It turns up later, dusty as hell with the trunk sprung and the cops—somehow, who knows how?--trace it back to Willy."

"And what about his partner?"

"Christ, it's like some broken record: 'Who's his partner? who was in cahoots? could it've been a she?' I don't freakin' have a clue!"

Benjamin emerged from under the hood, shook the carburetor next to his ear till it sloshed and plunked it down on his workbench. Disassembling the parts, he said, "You satisfied' We through?"

"How did Willy die?"

"Jesus!" said Benjamin, slamming down the air horn on a crumpled frozen dinner tray, catapulting the needle and float onto the grimy floor. Dropping to one knee and combing the area, he said, "Whudduyou want from me?"

"I want to know what I'm up against. One slacker? Two weirdos? Four ruptured ducks?"

Retrieving the carburetor parts and slapping them back in the tray, Benjamin suddenly relaxed and threw up his arms. "Hey look, all I know is Willy was flat busted and wanted somethin' to come to somethin'. A wine you could leave open and come back to, I don't know. The guy was at the end of his string. Give him a break, huh? Give us all a break."

"Right, all you poor ol' local boys. Talk to me. Who was close to him? Who visited his cell?"

"Who else?" Benjamin grabbed an accelerator pump and was about to dunk it in a coffee can when Sarah grabbed the can and shoved it to one side.

"Just say the name."

With a grin spreading across his porky face, Benjamin said, "What would a rat-face over-the-hill gimp settle for? Who would make a perfect match?"

Sarah knew who he meant but couldn't bring herself down to his level. She thought of asking if Doreen could have also dispatched the armored guard, but she let it ride.

Holding onto the grin, Benjamin said, "Pitiful, huh?," slid the coffee can back and plopped in the pump.

Settling for what she had, Sarah hurried out of Benjamin's grunge pit. Before she had time to react, Benjamin shambled past her, snatched the trash bag out of her trunk and barged back across the street.

"That wasn't the deal, Benjamin," said Sarah yelling at him. "I said I would stash it someplace."

"Yeah, in a pig's eye."

"You're a welsher and a lousy father."

"And what are you? Rate you're going, you're gonna wind up like your little friend."

"What is that, a threat?"

For an answer, Benjamin hit the switch. The bay door ratcheted down and slammed shut. It occurred to her that the bag was of no use. It had lots of fingerprints on it now, Benjamin would doubtless ditch it and, besides, what did it prove? It was a dodge, a deflection from Doreen to Alice.

At the inn, Sarah left a hurried apology on Jan's voice mail. Then, following a waitress's directions, she padded up to the top of the dark landing, got her bearings and made her way down the dingy corridor to the black lacquered door with the brass knocker. She knocked. She tried the knob. She felt something give, the latch slipped and the door eased open.

She stood there raking in the contents. It was a sad room, filled with overstuffed mismatched chairs from some bygone era. Travel brochures lay in a pile on a rumpled daybed. On a shelf jutting over the bed sat a wooden radio shaped like a cathedral with an oval green dial and a half dozen little leather-bound books. A calendar displaying dried floral arrangements hung by the radio's side. Opposite, in a far corner, a hotplate and assorted crockery rested on top of a dwarf-sized refrigerator. Dead ahead, a torn shade covered a single window overlooking the alley. Here and there, half-empty bottles of Jack Daniels and John Jameson Irish whiskey careened on the rippled carpet.

Sarah stepped partway into the room. The only items of note were two empty tartan-colored suitcases concealed behind the door to Sarah's left—their lids hanging open, the luggage begging to be filled. There was also a black and white grade-school composition book leaned against the smaller suitcase like a sandwich sign.

Sarah plucked up the notebook. It was filled with handwritten recipes . Certain roots, leaves and barks were highlighted in yellow. The latest entry--a hasty scrawl under the heading of foxglove--noted that it was the natural form of the heart stimulant digitalis (Dr. Dudley's highly touted swift killer of dogs).

There was one thing more. Hidden behind the luggage was a neatly packaged box of sundries: lotions, oils, bath bursts and the like. Resting in the center of the clear plastic cover, like some religious icon, was a glistening cake of handmade soap, tied with a ribbon, delicately embossed with the words "Lilac Moon."

Sarah stood there, unsure of her next move. Hang around for the rest of the afternoon hoping to catch Doreen? Catch her doing what? Packing? Then what? Accuse her of making notes about foxglove? And how did Sarah discover the tablet? By breaking and entering of course. Brilliant. What had happened, happened on the estate. What Doreen wanted was, doubtless, waiting for her on the estate. Even with a hundred holes still left in the story, sometime between now and the witching hour, Doreen would dig up the well-over-six-hundred thou and head for parts unknown. Otherwise, why work on Katie to drive her off? And, when that failed, do something drastic to get her out of the way?

To Sarah's mind, the only way to nail Doreen was to catch her in the act of digging and snap her picture holding the proverbial "smoking gun."

Sarah stepped out, closed the door quietly and hurried back down the dingy stairway. Before she could turn the corner into the lobby, Alice's skinny form shot in front of her and blocked her way.

"Gotcha. You are a rat, you know that? Big time scum."

"Is school out already?"

"Don't change the subject. I saw what you pulled out there with my old man. That's right, I was watchin' from right here. And after all I did for you. It wasn't bad enough leavin' me holdin' the bag yesterday. Oh no. You had to go and stiff me."

"Hold it," said Sarah, staring down at her. "As it happens, you are still on my list."

"That's a crock."

Alice shuffled over a few steps, twisted a lock of her lifeless mousy hair, then stepped right back shoving her face up at Sarah. "You mean that Katie stuff, right? The keys and all."

"You got it. Now, if you don't mind."

"I mind, I mind. None of that's got anything to do with me 'cept the letters."

"Then why was it all together?"

"'Cause that sleaze Doreen wants it to look that way. 'Cause I was dumb enough to listen to her. She says, 'Write to him if he won't talk to you.' She says, 'Leave 'em right here by my letter drop, that way Benjamin won't be the wiser.' She didn't even mail 'em. And where does that leave me? You trust a woman 'cause you figure they know about the cramps and the feelings and all. Or will talk to you so's you know where you stand. Then look what she does."

Her beady little eyes welled up with tears. "I don't know what's happenin' to me, man."

It was all Sarah could do to keep from patting her bony shoulder. Instead she brushed by her. Alice kept pace down the stairs all the way up to the double front doors.

"Okay," yelled Alice, "I didn't suffer no grief when your pal bought it. But I didn't do nothin' except what I said. That's all, that's it."

On the veranda, they both stopped short. Fronting them at the bottom of the buckling steps was the stiff frame belonging to Will Gibble. "Is there some problem?" said Gibble.

"No problem," said Sarah as Alice jerked on the hem of her latest raunchy T-shirt, shifted to Sarah's side and dug into her jean pockets for the last of her pistachios.

"I heard from Officer Varno. Something about a bag of incriminating items. Is that so or just more conjecture?"

Alice shuffled her feet waiting for the axe to fall.

"My mistake," said Sarah.

"Oh?" Gibble set his jaw and tried again. "I don't suppose you'd know anything about my spare key? And who was at my computer yesterday? Sometime in the early afternoon according to the 'time-used' log on the network server."

The tumbling graymetal clouds folded in, around and over each other, still seeking some release. Alice bit into the corner of a pistachio nut.

"Sorry," said Sarah, waiting Gibble out.

"I see. Tell me, when are you due back to work?"

"Tomorrow at noon."

"Good. If no charges are pressed and you stay put, that will be just fine."

Sarah didn't answer. Yesterday by the Great Falls she had sensed a touch of compassion. Gibble had, in fact, given her the benefit of the doubt and sent Varno in. Now it seemed to be back at the same old stand, keeping a lid on things, giving his all for the status quo.

Still fishing, Gibble said, "Because if Mark and Tommy hold pat, yesterday's little incident will be forgotten. The file will be closed as unfounded and we'll all be none the worse."

"Yup," said Sarah as Alice stepped behind her, making sure that Benjamin couldn't spot her through the greasy bay doors across the way.

"By the way, Alice," said Gibble, "how did you get from school to here? I thought you had soccer practice till Benjamin came by?"

"Don't sweat it," Alice said. "What are you, my mother?"

"I picked her up," Sarah said. "Owed her a favor."

"Oh really? Would this have anything to do with--?"

"Can this wait? Can somebody give her a break for a change?"

Gibble stared at her, his cropped hair glinting like metal filings under the flickering shafts of sunlight. "Let me assure you, Miss Bucklin, that's what we're here for. And, if you possess anything that points to criminal mischief--provided you obtained it without committing some infraction—we're interested."

"That's what I keep hoping for."

"Well?"

"I'll let you know."

"So," said Gibble reaching for some kind of closure, "Alice is keeping out of trouble and you're leaving tomorrow?"

"If all goes well."

"And you have nothing to report about the use of my computer?"

"Not a thing."

"Very well. We'll leave it at that." Gibble turned on his heels and walked briskly back up the street.

Sarah waited till he was out of view, steered Alice into her car, hot-wired the ignition and took off toward Katie's estate.

After a few minutes, Alice pulled out of her funk and said, "Okay, maybe you're not a total scum bag."

"Thanks."

"Hey, hold it, what if I miss Kevin? What if he pays my old man off and shoots over the covered bridge?" When Sarah didn't respond, Alice turned her sliver of a face and hollered in

Sarah's ear. "You hear me? I'm talking about the one we just passed."

"Pays him off with what money?"

Alice thought it over and said, "Right. He's still broke and needs Tommy to pay him off. Which Tommy won't do 'cause Kevin is Katie's business. Yeah. That's the ticket. Which means my money is still a factor, right? So he's got to stick around."

Alice held still for a moment and then, as the road twisted higher and higher, got antsy again. "So, what's the plan? And what's this about givin' me a break?"

"In a minute."

With every turn and buckle in the road, something in the trunk rolled and jounced.

"Okay, wait, I see, I get it," said Alice. "We collar Kevin at the barn and lay it on him. Make him reveal his intentions. Good move."

Another series of rolls and jounces and Alice said, "So, you believe me now, right? You trust me."

"Hardly."

"How come?"

"Where would you like to start? The passkey to Gibble's office or your feelings about Katie?"

"Oh, that's swift. When are you gonna give it a rest?"

A few seconds later, Alice said, "Why me? What is it? You got characters like Russell who says he's gonna bulldoze to whatchamacallit."

"Glory?"

"Yeah. He's hooked up with some holy-baloney TV station. He's gonna show his flick of me and runaways from New Haven and I don't what-all. And guess where. Guess where he's gonna do his live whatchamacallit."

"Telecast?"

"The playhouse, man. This weekend, I hear. So how does that grab you? If your buddy wasn't wracked up, where would freaky Russell be? Which to my way of thinkin' makes him prime bozo number one."

Sarah's mind couldn't deal with thoughts of Russell or Kevin's motorcycle or anything else. One likely suspect was all she could handle. The heavy-laden clouds rolled closer, the thunks inside the car trunk grew louder.

"Hey, man, you listenin' to me? What is it? What are you so jumpy about?"

"Nothing."

"Yeah, sure. She's squeezin' the crap outta the steering wheel but she's cool. Everything's fine."

Sarah slammed on the brakes, unlatched the trunk and got out. There, jammed against the spare tire was a glass jar, exactly like the one that did Mark in. She grabbed it and hurled it against the trunk of a massive oak hovering by the road.

"What's happening?" said Alice, leaning out the car window.

"Not a thing," Sarah answered. "It's all going according to plan."

"Right. Tell me another one."

Driving on, Sarah finally faced what was eating at her. In a sense, all that had happened recently--including Doreen's tricks with the keys, fruit jar and maybe even the gutted bird—were jabs at Sarah's hapless character. The framed snapshot closest to Katie's nightstand told the story. It was a joke. Sarah standing stalwartly behind Katie in the boat was a trick shot. The rowboat was moored to the landing. Just when they were supposed to switch places, cast off and head across the lake, Sarah had almost tipped over the boat clambering to get back to shore. She wasn't about to get into trouble, not Sarah, no sir. Her hands were cupped over her ears when Katie screamed that a person who never stuck her neck out was a lousy friend and a zombie to boot.

Katie's escapade had been cut short by the Scout leader's motorboat, intercepting her before she got halfway across. After being tossed out of camp and grounded for three weeks, Katie barely spoke to Sarah. A month later, all was forgiven. But Sarah never quite got over it. And the same feelings of guilt, anger, frustration and concern for Katie's safety were with Sarah now, multiplied a hundred fold. When it came to certain childhood hang-ups about boats and things, Sarah and Katie were worlds apart. When it came to certain childhood hang-ups, they were one and the same.

Twenty-Two

hat does it, man," said Alice, racing back across the bend in the road on the approach to the estate. Catching her breath, she leaned on the hood of Sarah's car. "I have had it. Your ideas are lame. Kevin ain't here. Nobody is here."

"Maybe. Maybe not."

"Oh sure, right, right. You sit here real cushy while I do all the leg work 'cause you don't wanna trespass. No way, Jose`. Take me back to the covered bridge. Come on, come on, start the car."

"What for?"

"'What for?' she says. 'Cause what else can I do? Unless Kevin somehow paid Benjamin off and has already split. Then I'm gonna gut you, man, and . . . and I'm gonna . . . "

The tears welled up and the bony frame twitched as she wiped her eyes with her towel of a T-shirt. "Hey, what are you lookin' at? What time is it anyways?"

"Going on six."

"You see, you see?" Reaching down by Sarah's seat, Alice yanked the latch, scooted out, hot-wired the ignition, slammed the hood and scrambled back in. "Move it, move it. You do owe me, man."

"Look, kid--"

"No, you look." Alice grabbed the sleeve of Sarah's rumpled blazer. Her red-rimmed little eyes were wide open. "Come on, I'm beggin' you. I can't go home, Benjamin'll kill me. This is my last shot. I gotta know where I stand."

It was silly. Alice didn't stand anywhere. Kevin had probably never even given her a second thought. But what else did the kid have going for her? Besides, the bridge was only a few miles back. Sarah turned the car around and, without a word, took Alice to the verge of the gurgling Housatonic.

Five minutes later, Alice got out and peered through the narrow covered shaft to the other side. No sounds. No sign of any traffic. She wheeled around. "Don't give me that look, man."

Sarah shrugged.

"Whadduyou know about it? Nothin'. All day all I hear is, 'Just do it, just say no, just get yourself some protection.' And Benjamin says if I do anything he'll break my neck. Don't you see, don't you get it? Kevin's my ticket outta this pit. A whatchamacallit."

"Answer to a prayer?"

"Yeah. What do you think?"

Sarah shook her head.

"Oh, forget it. Like I said, whadduyou know? All the pressure you get and everything goin' by so fast. Life sucks. But you're so old, you probably don't remember."

Sarah thought of saying something to her, something that might help. Nothing came to mind.

"Nobody listens to me," said Alice. "Why is that? Why?"

Sarah spun the car around, Alice ran to her side. "Okay, Sarah, here's the deal. If nothin' happens on this end, we go to plan B."

"Which is?"

"I catch up with you. Maybe he is hidin' out, afraid of Mark, don't know Mark's wracked up. Or maybe he's waitin' for Tommy somewheres to pay up. Later."

"Yup. I'll see you," said Sarah, reaching out her window and touching Alice's arm.

"What was that for?"

"Nothing."

"Don't get cheesy on me, okay?"

Sarah pressed on the gas, crossed over the covered bridge and wended her way back. Climbing higher into the tree-lined surge, she compared her own girlhood with Alice's. Hadn't puberty always been a hassle? Yes. Boys? The specter of sex? Yes. Then why was this so different? Because it was Alice. And the fact that she didn't have a chance.

A moment later, the blue and gray cruiser overtook her. Grudgingly, she pulled over to the side of the road as Varno brushed his Smokey the Bear hat back from his receding hairline and shuffled toward her. Sarah rolled down her window. Varno leaned in and lowered his hound dog eyes.

"Well?" said Sarah.

"You didn't deliver the so-called evidence. Then there's this prank last night outside your window you reported. Plus Will Gibble just told me you brushed him off."

"So?"

"Will also said you were with this Alice kid. And I just passed a skinny girl by the covered bridge. And it looks like you're headed back to you-know-where."

Sarah reached into the glove compartment and flashed her camera by Varno's brush mustache. "No problem. I'm going to hang back, use the zoom."

"Oh, come on, Sarah, use your head. We're waiting for the lab test on Mark."

"Only one problem," said Sarah, putting the camera back. "That would leave Doreen home free."

"Doreen? From the inn?" Varno rolled his sleepy eyes.

"So if you'll give me a little slack . . . "

Bracing his left hand against the windshield, blocking her view, Varno said, "Think about all this. You are doing nothing but spinning your wheels."

"Except that it's coming down to the wire. And I'm going to hand it over to you."

"Hand what over?"

"That hard evidence you guys live for."

"The bag?"

"No. Some photos. The kicker."

Varno ran his forefinger back and forth across the rim of his hat and did a slow double take. Then, leaning on the roof of her car, peering down on her he said, "Forget about it, okay? Please tell me you're not going to do something dumb."

Something squawked over Varno's radio. Varno turned his head. "I am saying, before you think of taking even one tiny step . . ."

"You'll be the first to know."

The squawk would not let up.

"Give me your word," said Varno, looking over to his cruiser and back at Sarah. "Because even if you come upon something . . . . anything . . . "

Sarah reached out and grabbed his sleeve. "You'll be on call. The dispatcher can radio you on open air, right?"

"Look, you listen to me. You--"

As an afterthought, Sarah reached out and grabbed his sleeve again. "What would you think of coming with me? Taking over, so to speak?"

"Don't do anything," Varno said, raising his voice, totally distracted by the static under his dashboard. "Not one thing." He released his palms from the roof of her car and shuffled away. Soon he was spinning around, the squeal of his tires joining the yawp of the radio. He sped off in the opposite direction into the fading billows of gray.

By seven-thirty, Sarah couldn't take waiting a second longer. She had bided her time in vain. And the scent of lilac kept reassuring her somehow, kept reminding her of Doreen Gunning the motor, she had driven her car across the street onto the estate, and then tramped into the main house, past the wall-high brick fireplace, through the dining room to the butcher-block kitchen counter and a phone. Now, chomping on another apple, she was modifying her plea to Button-eyes.

"Just humor me, that's all I ask."

"Listen," replied Button-eyes, in that unwavering condescending tone of hers, "I've already told you Doctor reports that from all external signs--"

"What about internally, in her mind?"

Just then, Sarah caught a glimpse of Tommy's blue Eldorado through one of the crosshatched windows. It glided onto the gravel driveway and came to an abrupt stop. But it wasn't Tommy who emerged. It was Russell. His lumbering form barged past the cross-hatched kitchen window and headed toward the cottage.

Back to the phone, Sarah said. "Look, there's a difference between deep and light, right?"

"That's correct."

"Okay then. What I'm saying is, Katie's choosing not to respond. She's now in such a depressed state, it only appears she's gone in deep."

Another minute of bantering until Button eyes cut Sarah off. "I'm sorry. I have other pressing duties. As I've told you and told you, I am not authorized to whisper messages your friend can't possibly hear." Button eyes excused herself and hung up just as Russell reappeared in the shadows. He was clutching a briefcase and buttoning a jacket that was as opaque as the darkening sky.

Hurrying outside, Sarah managed to step between Russell's bulk and the Caddy. After a few pointless thrusts and parries, Sarah said, "I don't care what you're up to. I don't even care that this is Tommy's car. I really could use your help."

Russell reached into his jacket pocket and jangled his keys. Sarah, in turn, took the briefcase out of his hand and set it down on the drive. "To fix Katie," Sarah said. "Time is telescoped, remember that one?"

Russell nodded in recognition of one of his catch phrases. It meant that for Katie there was no future and no present. Only an endless past, the result of a deed from which she could not extricate herself except through grace .

"Locked," Sarah continued. "Hearing those stupid lines from that ballad: 'She heard the death-bells knelling . . . ' Locked in some dark hole because of the crap you put into her head. Because she's such an airhead she bought it."

Russell shifted his gaze past Sarah into the gathering darkness. "Did you know I asked my mother to stop teaching her those lyrics? That I told her not to take her to Macbeth? To stop encouraging her?"

Pulling on his jacket, trying to regain his attention, Sarah said, "Russell, all you have to do is wait with me. Corroborate, exonerate Katie. That's all, that's it."

Gripping the briefcase in his burly hands, Russell said, "And nothing will change. Let me tell you something. Only yesterday I heard on the news that some twisted person lured a girl Alice's age through the Internet. That's right, another online predator who targets girls age 13 because they're old enough to travel alone but totally innocent of the dangers. So there you have it. A 13-year-old cheerleader from New Milford who meets a 25-year-old married, grocery clerk on a chat room who called himself "Hot es300". These girls need guidance, they need . . ."

He stopped in mid-sentence, reached in and inserted the ignition key as if it were the solution to the problem.

Pressing him back, Sarah said, "What are you good for, Russell? Besides your ramblings, besides your mouth?"

Russell brushed her aside and opened the car door. Sarah slammed it shut. Russell threw his briefcase so hard that the latches popped open and the papers flew across the gravel. On his knees, picking up the strewn material, Russell said, "This is such a waste."

Sarah snatched the keys from under the dash and hurled them in his face. "She's fading. She's not a possible news item or fodder for your loopy crusade. She's going under, you sanctimonious creep!"

Russell snatched up the keys, tossed the briefcase in the back seat and climbed behind the wheel. Talking to himself, Russell said, "I received a call in the main house. A meeting has been arranged. A promise of support at last." A firm nod of his head as he hit the ignition and edged out of the drive.

Sarah strode over to her Honda, hidden from view about twenty yards away on the rutted road to the playhouse. She unlatched the trunk, checked her canister of mace, snatched up her camera bag, attached the zoom lens to her SLR and grabbed a flashlight. For all intents and purposes she was alone and could only do what she could do: keep her distance, take snapshots of Doreen in the act, turn them in. She repeated this litany several times as she made her way down the scraggly slope into the recesses of the estate. As if she weren't exacerbating the act of trespassing and knew exactly what she was doing.

At length, Sarah was still alone. There was only the croaking frog chorus, the rasping of crickets, and an occasional glint from the moon peeking through the blackened sky. She had waited by the guest cottage, by the overhang of the barn, and had even hunkered down among the sweet spikes of lilacs. Nothing had stirred, nothing had broken the monotony.

Now, killing time, Sarah switched on a light in the study of the main house and moved from room to room. Willy hadn't necessarily stashed the loot outside. He could have shoved it under the floor boards, behind a false panel, somewhere in the eaves.

She shuffled past the hearth, doubled back around the ladderback chairs in the dining room, took a right into the kitchen, peered into the pantry, turned around and lingered at the unhinged cellar door.

Why not? Then again, why not anywhere? Why not nowhere, someplace else--under the covered bridge, well back of the meandering stone fence where the glass shattered? Why not some trysting spot where Doreen had already come and gone?

She flicked on the cellar light anyway, padded down the dusty steps and combed through the cobwebs and examined the moldy supporting posts, duct-work and the boiler. She poked around the coal chute with a rusty crowbar. Coming across a half-empty crate of liquor bottles, she thought of Doreen and the possibility she was half-drunk somewhere biding her time. After all, she still had a few hours before the witching hour when the statute ran out.

Another notion crossed Sarah's mind. She hurried back upstairs, shut off all the lights and waited. Perhaps if the compound were totally dark and quiet, Doreen might feel the coast was clear, traipse down to the cellar, have her snort and then proceed.

Sarah made her way in the darkness, reached the hearth and sat motionless against the cool brick wall. She could just picture Dad in his pin-stripe suit, behind his vice-presidential banker's desk responding to all this. "You're telling me that not only did you trespass on two different occasions, you wound up sitting in the dark, alone, holding your breath?" And Mother would doubtless pipe in, "Unbelievable. You think you know them and now this. Please, please, give me strength." Sarah had been brought up to avoid risk and spontaneity at all cost, to be the perfect bystander, to make her way in this world by following the sensible path. No matter. She had come this far and would have to at least take one more step.

Another stretch of useless waiting. She went over the available communication links immediately after the Doreen sighting: one phone here, two in the playhouse; get in touch with the dispatcher, stay on the line till the dispatcher contacted Varno and then sit tight.

But what if Doreen still didn't show? What if this all came to nothing?

Unbidden, the old Appalachian spiritual *Lonesome Valley,* another from Katie's mom's repertoire: ". . . nobody else can walk it for you. You got to walk it by yourself." A recollection of the circus poster in Katie's old attic came next. High above the crowd, the montage depicted the Flying Wallendas walking a tightrope, juggling chairs and performing other feats of derring-do. The caption read: "Life is on the wire. The rest is just waiting."

The circus poster did the trick. Sarah went down into the cellar, grabbed the crow bar, returned to the hearth and retrieved her shoulder bag and camera. Hurrying out the back porch, she scurried down the grassy slope, passing the cottage and the barn, her only thoughts the utter futility of her whole plan.

Striding by the shoots, briars, and spikes of lilac, she snatched out her flashlight. If nothing else, she'd do what she should have done two days ago. She'd open the cistern, find the coveted retaining rod lying at the bottom of the well, dislodged, stowed away from prying eyes. The reason why the plywood sheet and boulders were probably placed there in the first place. Intercepting Doreen wasn't the only option. At this point anything that cast a shadow on the trooper's report would do.

To her right, a faint rustle. She flashed her light. A baby rabbit scampered by and burrowed under a clump of gray-green tendrils. "That's cute," Sarah muttered, gripping the crow bar tighter. "Even the rabbits are playing games."

Another rustle, this time behind her. The rustle faded as the rasping crickets and the frogs down at the pond took over the soundtrack. Ahead, through the tracery of leaves and branches, the moon peeked out again like some curious extraterrestrial craft.

She approached the stakes, trellises and tangle of vines. There were brand new mounds of dirt. She flashed her light to her left, just off the beaten path. Gone were the boulders and the thick sheet of plywood. In their place was a weathered cylinder of wood, reinforced by strips of rusted metal, dappled with patches of mold and soil.

Obvious move, she thought. Put everything back the way it was. Replace the cover. Sweep it all clean.

She rammed the flared end of the crow bar under the moldy cover. One of the rusted metal collars snapped. Cautiously, she pried up the cover, gingerly propped it on its edge using the crow bar as a brace, and aimed her light directly down into the yawning shaft. The beams glinted off a pitted extension ladder and followed the rungs down until they touched bottom.

There, in repose between two detached retaining rods, lay the slight compact form, dressed in the same bush jacket and blue oxford button-down shirt. The shock of sandy hair flowed across the forehead as usual; the features still soft, perfect and fine. In his right hand was a revolver fitted with a six-inch barrel which lay gracefully across his chest. Only a small gaping hole in his left temple marred the symmetry.

Sarah tried to scream and bolt away but no part of her would move. Still clutching the flashlight, she lowered her eyes to her watch, telling herself to mark the time, add what and where to the equation, run off and report.

The watch disappeared under a blur of red cloth, covering her face, snapping her head back. She reached up to free her eyes and mouth but a knot of cloth at the base of her skull tightened. She tore at the material pressing against her forehead but her arms were jerked and twisted away. She lurched forward. The counterforce spun her around and rammed her into the trellises, her ribcage striking something jagged and hard. As she crumpled onto the moist ground, she longed to clutch her side, to knead and sooth her burning ribs. But the counterforce kept yanking at her hands and tied her wrists behind her back.

This time the hour and the minute didn't matter. Neither did what and where. The only thing that existed was the searing pain. The only recourse was to hold perfectly still.

Twenty-Three

or a long time she worked on her breathing. Each full breath tore at her ribs. Slow little gasps eased the pangs. She turned ever so carefully onto her left side and worked on the blindfold, rubbing her forehead against the stubbly ground until the cloth slipped down a smidgen, just enough so she could perceive shadows and shapes.

Something rifled through her shoulder bag. She twisted her head and stared. It was no good, still like peering through a streaked veil. And the twisting motion intensified the sharpness of the pain.

Then, at last, the snicker gave it away. Dim at first but soon breaking from a chuckle to a howl.

More labored effort. Sarah propped herself up to a sitting position, her wrists and forearms straining behind her back. This time, when the ache in her right side eased a bit, she held still and tried only to focus.

Suddenly the sinewy form seized what must have been the mace and hurled it down the cistern, spinning so fast that he smacked into the rotted cover, toppling it over, sending the crow-bar brace clanging after the canister.

Clutching his stomach and doubling over, Mark shouted, “Goddamn. Scratch my eyes, stomp on my ankle, gas me, poke a revolver in my face and then poison my drink. I mean, what the hell?”

Reeling back, he smashed what sounded like the flashlight, then ripped up the notepad and flung the pages in the well as if tossing things in Tommy’s face. About to add the blur of the camera to the mix, he switched gears and chuckled again. “Now I ask you, fans. It was a struggle, right? the gun goes off, what can you do?”

Carrying on his mock trial, Mark continued to make his case: claiming that Tommy had a screw loose and was insanely jealous; claiming that, as rumor had it, Tommy was a crack shot; claiming that Tommy tried to force him off the estate at gunpoint. All these claims ostensibly aimed at getting Sarah’s vote.

But Sarah barely heard him. A clammy cold sweat exacerbated the metallic taste in her mouth and the all-consuming ache. She kept envisioning Tommy’s body lying in the rancid water only a few yards away. It was all she could do to keep her body from shuddering.

No movement for a few seconds. Then shoveling sounds, biting into the earth, the mock trial apparently over.

"Willy, what did you do? I've dug everywhere." Another long silence and then, "But, hey, there's one shot left, damn your ass."

Another blurry image. Mark doubtless looking through the viewfinder of Sarah's camera, twisting the focusing band of the zoom lens. "Yes sir, fans, not to worry. There 's always the option play." Warming to the subject, Mark's voice became more animated. "Get this. No sooner does ol' Tommy go kerplunk when here comes Varno."

Facing Sarah now, Mark said, "So I take another deep swig of veggie juice and then it hits me. But—and this is the good part—while I'm grabbing my guts, I realize a guy who's gassed and poisoned is above suspicion."

Terrific, thought Sarah. Rub it in. Sharp, quick as they come Bucklin fell for it like a simp.

Stomping the ground, Mark shuffled around the cistern as his stomach got to him again. Then, recovering, playing once more with the zoom lens, he turned back toward Sarah. "Got to keep in practice, you know. Else a prime-time player could go to seed."

Another grope of his stomach, another long pause. Mark cocked his head, whirled around and peeped once more through the lens. “Hey, lookee lookee. He bought it. Yes sir.” Ambling over to Sarah, he jerked her to her feet. Sarah’s squeal was muffled by the cloth gag as Mark shoved her into a tangle of vines. Snatching something out of its sheath, he whispered, “Maybe your ribs are cracked. Maybe they’re not. But either way you are stayin’ put. ‘Cause even if the bones don’t splinter or pierce a lung, they’ll still do a job on you.”

Sarah’s eyes flickered, seeking the outline of the well. If someone was coming, they could come this far. And if they came this far, there were the diggings, the open cistern and Sarah springing out somehow.

“Well now,” Mark said, scampering away. Struggling with the rotted cover, he shoved and scraped it over the mouth of the cistern. A moment later he was back.

“There. We don’t want to queer this thing. After all, swipin’ your car keys didn’t stop you, or the gutted bird or the jar. And you lookin’ so juicy lyin’ there on that queen size bed. Don’t want this all to go to waste.”

Shifting back to his imaginary audience, Mark paced off a few yards and said, “But, still and all, let’s consider her counter play. She don’t take my warning, she frees her hands. She dumps over the lid, scoots down the ladder and comes up with Tommy's pistol. Then, even though she's riskin' a punctured lung and even though she don't know squat about guns, she sees me comin' back and aims the thing."

Mark's hand slapped his side, something flashed and skewered past Sarah's ear, striking the stake just past her head. The blade was still quivering as Mark worked the steel back and forth and yanked it out of the wood. Holstering the knife, Mark continued his address to the phantom bleachers. "A guy bet me once. Said a bullet was faster than a blade. I said, It depends. Anyways, he kept poking me in the gut till we settled it. The payoff is, I stuck him like a pig." Raising his hand high, Mark added, "True story." Then, slapping his side, whirling here and there, he shouted, "Pow, there's goes the armed guard. I mean, knife or gun—whatever. You play it as it lays."

Abandoning the spectators, he plucked up the blur of a camera and peered in the direction of the barn. "Damn. Not there, dum-dum."

Moving to Sarah's side, Mark whispered, "Take my warnin', huh? Don't cut the party short." Jangling what must have been her motel keys by her ear, he added. "After the final whistle, there's the victory party. Now that's a tradition."

Pointing the lens once more toward the barn, he said, "Hey, what are you doin'? Get the hell back." With that, he scurried off.

She eased herself forward. If she could free her hands, she could pull off the blindfold and signal whoever had just come upon the scene. Even under the folds of cloth she could make out the gap by the splintered well cover. Mark, in his cocksure haste hadn't bothered to totally cover the hole. Better still, one of the metal straps was loose. She hunkered down, grateful that she'd at least had the brains to wear a split skirt. Gasping, trying to ignore the tearing sensation in her side, she reached behind her and pried up the end of the rusty strap. She worked on the cloth, rubbing it back and forth behind her until the fabric began to tear between her hands.

Then she stopped. If the visitor was someone Mark was the least bit wary of, he wouldn't have left her there to rove about no matter how battered her ribs were. His warning notwithstanding, if she weren't under his remote control, like a puppy bounded by an invisible fence, he would have, at the very least, tied her feet.

A glint of moonlight played inside the recess of the well. Even under the streaked bandanna, she could sense the milky dead eyes of Tommy's corpse. Bobbing and weaving, she wrenched herself up, swiveled around and straggled back toward the estate.

Pulling at the frayed cloth that bound her hands behind her, she edged past the stakes and latticework, trying to put the image of Tommy's body aside for the moment, straining to keep up with events.

At the verge of the overgrown garden, she peered over the bandanna but still could barely see. A vague imprint of clouds scudded across the sky, fogging the slice of moonlight. She heard voices up ahead. The words were scrambled, fading in and out amid the croaks and cricket sounds.

Kneeling down, arching her back, she rubbed the fabric against some brambles, pricking her fingers; then against the hasp of a rotted wooden gate; then against a protruding nail and the shards of some plaster garden statue; then back to the protruding nail. All the while knowing she was playing into Mark's plan. That the more she tried the more frustrated she would get, breathing deeper, tearing at the muscles and tendons, forced to stop. He could then simply amble back, gaze down at her crumpled bod and do whatever the hell he pleased.

The image caused her to yank harder at the fabric until she worked her way down to one loose strand. The strand shredded with a jerk and a yelp. Fumbling at the blindfold, she tugged it off, half-expecting the lights to come on so that she and the rest of the patrons could exit the multiplex and go home.

Letting her eyes take in the embroidery of shapes, she zeroed in on the two moving forms up ahead. The first figure obviously was Mark. It took only an instant to identify the second. It was gangly and lean. It had shoulder-length hair. It belonged to Kevin.

When the voices rose again, she drew closer. When the shapes were about fifty yards ahead, separating in front of the overhang of the barn, she pulled back behind a thicket of shrubbery. Here the scent of lilacs was overpowering, drawing her in like the beginnings of some arcane ceremony.

She clutched her side, stifling a whimper, straining to make out the words that filtered in and out. At first, they made no sense. The laconic tones of Kevin's voice were chopped off by Mark's howls and jeers. Little by little, a few snippets reached her ear.

"Your fingerprints."

"Your divinin' rod."

"Willy's. You set up the fake detour."

Mark's reply seemed to add to Kevin's complicity. But Sarah couldn't be sure exactly when and how. The voices kept drifting and receding like a short wave radio running low on batteries. Then, as she edged beyond the shrubs, Kevin's voice broke through the muddle.

"If Tommy hadn't laid me off . . . if Katie would wake up . . ."

Whirling around, arms reaching for the scudding clouds, Mark yelled," Hey, man, you just sat back and watched!"

Mark mumbled something about the money Kevin had in his pocket. "I'll tell Gibble you stole it," said Mark, raising his voice again. "To get your chopper outta hock. So split, jerkoff. Move that skinny butt."

"If you hadn't hit on her," Kevin said as Mark shifted to the other side. Kevin muttered something else, Mark threw up his arms again.

"She scratched my eyes, pal. She goddamn clawed me."

There it ended. Mark ambled away. For a while there was no sound at all. Then a few minutes later someone cried, "Hey, Kevin!" It was Alice, somewhere beyond the main house and the road. Mark yelled, "Get her the hell outta here." Kevin's beanpole frame hesitated for a moment and then drifted off.

Sarah remained immobile. She was incapable of going near the well again, let alone wrenching the gun out of Tommy's dead hands and calling Mark's bluff. Gradually, she let her eyes stray behind her, back in the direction of the playhouse.

Since entry to the phone in the main house was blocked by the roving presence of Mark and Kevin—not to mention access to her car--that left either the phone by the stage manager's booth or the lobby. It was too far. But she had an understanding with the dispatcher in place--as it turns out, the only sensible thing she had done. In minutes Varno could be on his way. Besides, she couldn't just there, and she couldn't come up with another ploy.

As she hobbled back toward the vineyard, she heard Alice's high-pitched whine again, still somewhere beyond the main house and the rutted playhouse road. She kept on, stumbling forward, clutching her side with both hands, threading her way past the tangle of vines. To distract herself, she thought of Alice's prospects, dragging herself back to daddy Benjamin's tar pit, grounded for good. She thought of Kevin, tooling around other byways and backwaters on his red Harley, still brooding over Katie: wrong about Katie's lust; wrong for standing by and watching; right in digging her out; wrong again for expecting gratitude and love.

"Right, Jan," Sarah said under her breath, lurching a half dozen steps, sucking in her breath and moving on. "It is a crapshoot."

She kept the pattern up: lurching, pausing and pressing herself onward. At the rate she was going, Mark would catch up with her in the open, yards short of her goal. She pushed on anyway, wincing and crying out in pain, finally reaching the swath of saw grass.

About a hundred yards from the back of the scene shop, she stopped short, gasping for air. She bent over, waiting for the sound of Mark's sprinting footfalls. She stayed like that for a long time.

What was he waiting for? Didn't he see her? Possibility one: there was a glitch, some kind of snag. Possibility two: everything was still going according to plan.

A motor kicked over somewhere in the distance. The clicking lifters told her it was her car. No doubt Mark was moving it deeper under cover in case anyone drove by.

Up ahead far to the right, where the rutted road met the grass swale fronting the box office, sat a yellow bulldozer laying in wait. The huge excavating blade rested on the turf as if poised to dig some massive hole.

Sarah straggled and weaved, her ankles twisting, her legs feeling like dead weights as she zigzagged forward. She clenched her teeth, hoping her lungs wouldn't collapse, leaving her prone in the weeds coughing up blood.

Somehow she reached the back of the theater. A pale tint of lavender moonglow streamed across the clapboards. She scuffed by the costume shop and the scene shop. Pausing till the pain eased just a jot, she watched the cloud-swirl above her mask the tinted wedge. Russell had called it perfectly. The shadow-play was taking over. Too bad he was spineless. Too bad about everything.

She clambered up the ramp to the rear entrance of the stage, still focusing on her single tactic. Working her way across the backstage area, she glanced around for a place to hide after the call. Was there a trap door? No. A cat walk above the fly loft, a grid? No. And even if there were, she could never reach it, never climb a solitary step.

Slipping into the stage manager's booth offstage in the wings, she snatched up the receiver. The dial tone was live, the numbers clicked, the dispatcher answered after the second ring. Taking a breath, Sarah said, "Hey, it's me. Tell Varno I'm trespassing. I'm--"

The dry, methodical voice abruptly cut her off. "Okay, now slow it down."

"Don't talk. Just listen."

The work lights snapped on. The sinewy arm shot past her face and shoved her out of the way. Totally spent, she slumped to the wooden floor. The phone wire snapped out of the jack-plate in the wall. Sarah rested her head against the edge of the partition and gave in.

"They'll rate that a six," said Mark, shuffling over to her. "No, on this kinda night, better make that a ten."

Plopping down next to her, Mark reached into his jeans and displayed a handful of tablets as if he and Sarah were buddies on the same hospital ward. "Oh, man, never mind the stomach pumpin', the slurry, activated charcoal and all the rest of the freakin' agony. This scopolamine really does a job. You run off at the mouth, don't know where you are half the time . . . "

Receiving no answer, Mark added, "But hey, you didn't buy the punctured lung crap, did ya? "

Mark shook his head violently, like a swimmer suffering from too much water in his ears. Then he stretched out his arms, rolled up his denim sleeves a bit higher and flexed his muscles. "But at first you did, right? Asked yourself, Are the ribs bruised or really broken? Is Mark still poisoned or just out of his head? Where is it goin' down and how can I get close to a phone so's I can let somebody know?'"

"Oh yeah," Mark went on, pulling himself up, flexing his forearms and deltoids. "The second you started back toward the cistern, I knew I was still clickin', knew I had you down.

'She's got no style maybe, but she's got the scent,' I said. 'Give her a little slack, play a couple of head games. She's bound to lead you to it. Right smack to the freakin' X that marks the spot.'"

Having no clue what he was babbling about, she gave in to the heaviness in her eyes, keeping the cold clammy feeling at bay, reaching for pure nothingness.

Another interval and Mark leaned over her, resuming his confidential tone. "Know what? Lately I keep remembering something. It was a while back . . . Katie was some kinda junior apprentice or somethin' . . . her mom standin' there all willowy and slim, in a bright yellow sun dress teaching her some guitar chords . . . The point is, I was trimming hedges-- my first job, you see—and they wouldn't give me the time of day. Know what I mean?"

Sarah kept ignoring him, but Mark wouldn't let up. "A year or so later, I showed 'em. You know anything about football? What it takes to be a middle linebacker?" Not waiting for an answer this time, he let his thoughts roll on. "You size up the whole playing field at once, know where every play is going as it happens. Even before. Damn!"

He was shaking his head again, ostensibly fighting off the after effects of the drug. "Okay okay, I got beat a couple of times this past week. Misjudged a few plays. But I am gettin' it back, I tell ya. Like that thing with Tommy, I was damn quick. And now, if I can pull myself together, watch out."

Disoriented again, Mark ambled through the black velvet wings onto the stage, crouched low, peddled backwards, then shot ahead letting out a howl as he crushed some imaginary ball carrier.

Sarah turned away. The stage reminded her of those old lyrics Katie once sung: "Oh mother o mother, go dig my grave . . ." The stage reminded her that the witching hour was approaching like a fait accompli.

Minutes went by, Mark kept going through his paces, faltering, egging himself on. Sarah remained immobile. She let go of all the pieces of the puzzle save one. When Mark held up both his arms, striding across the spanning stage, proclaiming that it wasn't Katie or Tommy who was cleaning house, it was him, Sarah turned back.

Encouraged, rushing toward her, Mark added, "Ain't it a wonder? I search high and low, my brain all clogged from the scopolamine, when you second the motion and confirm my hunch. Oh yeah."

"Why did you do it to her?" Sarah said, looking directly at him.

"Oh, are we talkin' now?"

"In the rain, setting up a fake detour. What went on in your sick brain?"

Holding up two fingers, Mark hollered, "You are this far, bitch. You thank your stars I still am not in one piece."

In the silence, he puffed himself up, rushed back and strutted around the stage. The strut grew more pronounced until the imaginary fans in the front row applauded. He bowed, checked his watch and then looked out across the empty rows. "Okay, we are on schedule. We got Tommy on ice . . . Russell on a wild goose . . . Kevin and Alice cleared off. Which leaves? You got it, I'd say any minute. I mean, it's gotta come down to this."

He uttered the last line as if pleading for reassurance. When he received no reply, he darted over to her, grabbed the lapels of her jacket, jerked her straight up and pulled her across the stage. Paying no heed to her cries and whimpers, he steered her past the apron, down the steps and up the carpeted aisle. The wooden rafters above her swirled until he shoved her into the lobby and pressed her against the box office door. "You'd best think about what use I can put you to. You'd best think hard."

Pivoting around, Mark reached inside the box office and ripped the phone off the wall. Then he stepped back and pressed one of the levers fastening the brace of front doors. He eased the door open a jot, gazed out into the darkness and lingered there motionless like some dazed peeping Tom.

Sarah leaned against the ticket window feeling hapless; having no function, no means to help or hinder. She wasn't even sure she could watch.

After a while, she managed somehow to sidle over behind Mark. Through the narrow slot separating the double doors she was able to make out the outline of the grass swale and the looming bulldozer at the verge of the rutted road. Glancing up, she could also make out the far edge of the steel-framed marquee hovering over the entrance, tilted toward the skimming clouds. For the first time she noticed that the marquee was lit.

"Know what it says?" said Mark, winking, again treating her like a buddy. "'Revival'. Ain't that a kick in the head?" The snicker was back now. The cold green eyes more steady, the lithe muscle-toned body returning to form. "Russell figures I've had it, bulldozes just enough so's his lighting crew can make it through and puts up his flashin' sign. So then I do him one better."

The snicker turned into a leer as Mark went on. "Now get this. I call the main house disguising my voice, catch Russell helpin' himself in the kitchen. I send him on a wild goose way outta town while I position the dozer, you know, in case shovels wouldn't do. Knowing in my gut I just gotta be right. Later, I leave a message at the first meeting place requestin' facts and details, changing the time and place. I got that bozo turnin' every way but loose. I tell you, even poisoned and drugged, I am a goddamn whiz. "

The leer turned into a wide grin. Finger to his lips, he made a shushing sound. No longer a dazed peeping Tom now. More like a loopy bandit about to ply his trade.

A moment later, it began. It started as a squeak at the rear of the playhouse, first from the costume shop, then the scene shop, then it skittered forward on the right, passing alongside the clapboard slats and shingles.

Mark whispered in Sarah's ear. "This is the best. I've got it nailed!"

Sarah strained her eyes, squinting hard as Doreen came into view. She was pulling a child's red wagon, wearing white painter's overalls about two sizes too big spattered with sludge. She also sported yellow gardener's gloves, a train conductor's striped hat and high-top basketball shoes. Something shiny was tucked into one of the deep pockets that flanked her hips and another object bulged out of her back hip.

Her back to the bulldozer all the while, Doreen suddenly halted, swiveled and stared at the massive blade that rose high up over her shoulders. Whipping out the pistol with the attached silencer, she jerked sharply in all directions, paused and held the gun steady in the direction of the lit marquee.

Then, pocketing the weapon, she cocked her head left and right. Still leery, she shuffled straight ahead in Mark and Sarah's direction, paused again, looked up directly at the marquee, scanned the area all the way around and adjusted her black eye patch. Doing an about face, she walked back to the dozer, stared at it once more, returned to her little red wagon, removed her cap and scratched the side of her head.

Tossing the cap aside, she plucked out a pint bottle, took a few swigs and wiped her lips. She scuttled to her right across the rutted road, pitched the bottle into the woods, returned, drew out the pistol again and waited.

Pocketing the gun a second time, she grabbed a long-handled spade out of the wagon, paced off ten yards and planted herself directly in line with the entrance doors. She paused yet again and then commenced to dig.

"Jesus," said Mark confiding to Sarah. "Exactly where Willy was gonna set up a wine tent. I will be goddamned."

Exactly where Katie was about to excavate for a concession stand and parking lot, thought Sarah. Mark couldn't let her boot him off the estate and queer his chance to find the loot, oh no. Or, even worse, let her beat him to it.

Mark snapped his fingers as Doreen's spade struck something hard. Grinning, running his fingers slowly down the nape of Sarah's neck, he muttered, "You led me here, babe. Mine was just a wild guess but you goddamn endorsed it."

Sarah shoved his hand away. Mark kept grinning.

Ever so carefully, Doreen dug out a rectangular border over a foot deep. When she finished, she flung the shovel aside, fell to her knees, bent over and began tugging like mad. She kept at it, yanking at the thick wedge of grass with all her might till, at last, she managed to rip it off in ragged sections.

She reached down, clawing at the dirt, hurling clumps of soil here and there, halted and let out a squeal. In no time she had her arms wrapped around a mucky strongbox less than two feet square. She clutched it to her bosom and squatted in the furrow rocking to and fro.

Mark shifted his weight from one foot to another, champing at the bit, once again the cocky middle linebacker waiting for the snap of the ball. As soon as Doreen sprang to her knees, pried open the lid and drew out the first dusty sack, Mark grabbed Sarah's arm and shoved her against the doorframe. "Later, you read me?" For emphasis, he rubbed his knuckles across her breasts.

Sarah twisted away. Mark pushed the unlatched door wide open and drifted out past the marquee. Reflexively, Doreen fumbled around, drew out the pistol and sprang to her feet.

"Oh Lord," said Mark, raising his hands in mock surrender. "I do think I've been betrayed."

"Out! you get outta here," said Doreen, drawing a bead between Mark's shoulders. "This is my time. Mine."

"Now now, ol' Willy lied when he pulled that amnesia crap. And you lied when you said he never let on."

"That's right. He let on to me. ME."

Sarah eased out into the charade. Another tint of moonglow, another shift of consciousness from sense to senselessness and somewhere in between, the only constant the shivers of pain.

All the while, Mark and Doreen continued to spar, shifting positions until Sarah was no longer able to see past Mark's back. Presently, Sarah, the invisible spectator, gave way to Sarah the bystander. The bystander, in turn, recalled Tommy's body lying in the dank water at the bottom of the well.

The bitter taste in her mouth returned along with a rush of adrenalin. She shuffled over to the right and forward, moving beyond the marquee into the night shadows. Staring back at the altering shapes, she wondered when the hunting knife by Mark's twitching right hand would flash. It all came down to increments: how far Mark would go, how Doreen would counter each thrust and parry.

"Fool, you killed Tommy," Doreen hollered, firmly planted in front of the spoils, Mark now fronting her about twelve yards away. "You better hightail it."

"And you slipped me poison and are threatening my life. Better run for it."

"No, sirree," Doreen screeched. "It's on your head. On you."

Mark rolled his shoulders around as if he had all the time in the world and, stretched his arms straight up and let his left arm drop to his side, his right hand poised over the sheath. "You don't want to do this. And I don't want to waste the energy. Don't want to explain you were crazy drunk and what else could I do?"

Mark edged forward. "Hold it," said Doreen. "Willy taught me how to use this. Taught me good. And I found the extra box of shells. Ha! Thought you had me, you dumb jock."

Mark moved his right hand just a notch closer to the sheath. Sarah kept still, too insubstantial to matter to either Mark or Doreen although she was only a scant twenty yards away.

Giggling, Mark said, "Goddamn, Doreen, you are gonna force my hand. But if that's you way you want it, if you really wanna play . . . "

He looked back over his left shoulder and positioned himself directly between Doreen and the glinting "Revival" sign as if posing for a movie still, spreading his legs hip-width apart. "This is so lame, but hell, you called it."

An involuntary shudder ran up Sarah's spine as she realized Mark knew damn well she was standing there. He was staging this final play of the game for her benefit. As if she truly was rooting for him. As if, when it was all over, she would burst into applause.

"Signals on three," said Mark. "My knife against as many bullets you can squeeze off. Can't say fairer than that."

"You bastard," said Doreen, her hand shaking so badly she had to grip her wrist to keep the gun steady. "You botched everything from the get-go. Killed the damn guard."

"Heads up, here we go. Ready . . . set . . . one . . ."

On the count of "two" Sarah scuffed forward, peering into the distance, half-expecting Varno to appear. Surely by now the dispatcher had relayed the aborted message. Surely by now he was close at hand.

In that instant, oddly enough, a figure did appear, headed this way. But it wasn't Varno. It was Alice. Her scrawny frame raced across the rutted road, masked by the dozer, still looking high and low. In that same moment, Sarah pictured a squeeze of the trigger, a stray bullet, a hurtling knife. Mindlessly she lurched forward, throwing her hands up just as Mark yelled, "Three!" Alice stopped dead in her tracks, Doreen scampered to her left. Mark backhanded Sarah across the face, the force of the blow sending her sprawling to the ground.

Sarah clawed at the moist earth trying to pry out a rock but the pain immobilized her. Glancing back at the muddle of curses and shifting shapes, she screamed at Alice and pleaded with her to clear out.

The second Alice ran off, as if from out of nowhere, the dozer started up with a roar. Mark wrenched the gun out of Doreen's hands. On a diagonal, Mark backpedaled until he reestablished his movie-still position. In response, the dozer rumbled toward him—the crawler tractors chewing up the turf, the motor revving violently. Mark pointed and jeered at the hulking figure in the cab. The torque revved higher, the dozer kept coming. Mark bobbed and weaved and backed up a few yards more, his shoulders fully highlighted now by the flickering neon sign.

Making a cross-draw like a Hollywood gunslinger, he whipped the gun from his left hip and fired. The bullets struck metal, ringing out as the massive flanged blade picked up speed. As he fired away, the pings glanced off every part of the dozer, up and down and all around, mixing with the growl of the motor and the grinding of the cogged wheels like some crazed Caribbean steel band. Mark shuffled his feet just as the turf from the churning roller belt flew up in his face.

He dove to his left. But the surging blade caught him, hauled him up and pinned his upper body against the marquee. Sparks flared and metal crumpled as the crawler tractors continued to spew rock and earth in their wake. The sparks kept blazing, then sputtered intermittently, then crackled once or twice and then ceased. The grinding noises faded, the surging blade relinquished its grip. The dozer reluctantly went into reverse and came to a halt. Russell clambered down like some giant storybook bear, hurried over, lifted Sarah up and slipped her into the open dozer cab.

Shifting into low gear, taking the ruts as slowly as possible, he headed back to the main house. Through the circuits of pain, holding on as best she could, Sarah dimly caught a glimpse of two scuttling figures to her right. One was pulling a child's wagon through the moonlit fields toward the tangle of vines. The other was trailing far behind, darting to and fro, hopelessly waving her spidery arms.

Twenty-Four

t the hospital, after the examination, shots and taping, Sarah began to regain some sense of equilibrium. Seated in a metal chair in one of the cubicle-like recovery rooms, she noticed Russell peering in on her from the outside corridor. His ruddy cheeks appeared sallow, his bulky form sagged as if some burden had been lifted and he'd been stripped of a role he no longer wanted to play.

Sarah half-whispered, "Did you notify them? About Tommy?"

Russell nodded. And, for some reason, kept staring at her.

"Oh," said Sarah. "Right. Thanks again for . . . "

Before she could complete her sentence, Russell waved her off, stepped inside the room and continued to gaze at her.

At length, she finally remembered what he was after. Soon after he had trundled her to the parked Caddy at the edge of the drive, he had begun to unravel. Despite her dazed protests, he warded off the subject of Tommy's body; and Mark's physical condition was also of no consequence. Neither was Sarah's mental or physical state. In point of fact, Russell seemed to have forgotten that she had been part of the episode at all. In the darkness, sitting in the plush driver's seat waiting for the ambulance to arrive, he had one sole concern: justifying his actions.

At first, he grappled with his agency in the scheme of things. "One can not play with the Lord's plans," he muttered. He recounted previous insults and incidents. He cited the fake calls as a case in point--the last one allegedly from a second benefactor, a guest at the White Hart Inn in Salisbury. Slapping his hand on the steering wheel, he said, "You don't fool around with God's plan. There is blame. There is punishment."

He said the word "punishment" without much conviction.

He tried harder. The last straw was the sight of the bulldozer poised in front of "God's revival tent," obviously placed there by Mark. The last straw was exacerbated by Doreen's drunken body clutching sacks of loot, twelve-year-old Alice's tawdry cries for Kevin, and Mark's gyrations, "butcher knife" in hand. Not to act was tantamount to admitting that his parents' drowning was no more or less meaningful than the degradations of the past few weeks or the sight in front of his eyes. The universe was indifferent. He could start the bulldozer or not. Let Mark strike down the "tabernacle" or continue to do heaven knows what. Russell crushed Mark as Mark was crushing Russell's faith.

At this point, the logic of it all escaped him. Now and then he would say, "Did I enjoy it? Did I really?" The notion of enjoyment confused him even more. After all, it was he, not Mark, who had smashed the marquee. It was he, Russell, who had crippled the revival tent. He told himself, "There are no accidents, nothing happens at random." But he said it almost inaudibly. Then he fell silent, not once responding to Sarah's whimpers or asking what had happened to her. He just sat behind the wheel until the agitated sirens and whirling lights were upon them and, even then, remained in a stupor.

Now, glancing up at Russell again, Sarah said, "Just tell them it was a search and rescue." Amazed at how hoarse her voice was, she added, "That's your excuse."

"Not true."

"True enough."

Russell's face went blank as he grappled with this notion. Shaking it off, he moved closer to her and said, "The scratches over Mark's eye--did you ever find out?"

Sarah nodded.

"Did Katie lead him on?"

Sarah shook her head.

"Ah." Russell lowered his eyes and shuffled his feet. He walked over to the doorway and turned back. Finally he said, "I did come by, you know. Those photos by Katie's night stand . . . I put them there."

"Why?"

More hesitation and lowering and raising of eyes. "The one of Tommy," he went on, "was to remind her of her marriage vows. The one of the two of you in the boat . . ."

"The drowning of your parents," said Sarah, the hoarseness still there, the words still caught in her throat.

"I should go back . . . "

"Yes."

". . . and remove the photos."

"And talk to her."

Another puzzled look and another long pause. Searching his memory bank, Russell came up with, "Do not go gentle into that good night . . . Silently, he searched for the rest and then shook his head and said, " Not scripture. It's Dylan Thomas." With that, he turned away and shambled off.

Sarah called out, "But it's good stuff," assuming he was headed for the I.C.U. "Do the poem for her. It might help." Her voice had a bit more resonance but she wasn't sure he heard.

A few minutes later, Varno popped in for a second time. During his initial stint he had gotten more and more frustrated. Exasperated, he had repeated over and over, "You promised to sit tight." In reply, she had murmured, "You promised you'd be on standby." Trying to get a statement, Varno had elicited a few cryptic phrases from Sarah like, "get out Willy's old file" and "what can you charge her with now—conspiracy?" Sloughing off her vague tips, he went on with his set of queries: Why was the estate deserted when he answered her aborted call? and what was everyone doing by the playhouse, a spot that was almost impassable? He also wanted to know how the marquee, freshly dug trench, spade, bulldozer, bullet holes, pistol, and so on and so forth, fit in to the hodgepodge of circumstances. He had asked dozens of questions but Sarah was in no condition to respond except to ask him over and over to look in on Katie.

This time Varno started slowly. "Feel up to it now?" He tapped gently on the same clipboard which now held a dozen more forms. "Can we start over? Give me something. What can you tell us? What exactly did you see? What did you hear? What did you witness?"

"First things first." Sarah attempted to rise and steady herself.

"Hold on," said Varno. "Look, we are talking major crime. When you factor in Tommy Haddam's body in the bottom of that cistern--"

"Did you do what I said?" said Sarah, holding on to the back of a chair, her voice beginning to resonate at last. "Somebody has got to exonerate her."

Varno just stood there gaping. The fact that her face was swollen perhaps starting to register; along with the fact that her cracked ribs were bound tightly and she was still woozy from the codeine and the spiraling fatigue. And perhaps he also realized that she was in dead earnest.

He started in once again with the same old weary hound-dog tone but a tad less insistent this time. "Look, I know I'm pestering you but . . ."

"Answer me."

Rubbing his sleepy eyes, Varno spoke as gently as he could. "Listen, in addition to everything else, Mark just came out of the O.R. in critical condition. Shattered pelvis, broken bones in his back and . . . This is a god-awful mess. Can you help me out here?"

"I gave you a lead."

"Right—Willy's file . . . statute of limitations has run out . . . possible charges, possible conspiracy. Who are we talking about? What is going on?"

"Either you get on your horse, Varno, or I will cite you. You will get a big fat reprimand and nothing further from me."

Varno ran his fingers over his brush mustache and said, "I don't know . . . maybe . . . because of what you've been through and all. And if you finally give me some tangibles!"

"Just do it," said Sarah making her way slowly to the doorway.

Varno slipped past her into the hallway and glanced back. "Wait a minute. Hold it. This is foolish. What about her husband?"

"Not now, for heaven sake."

"Don't mention him and say twelve words?"

"Eleven: 'This is the police. The assailant's been apprehended. You are blameless.'"

"I walk in, lean over and say those words? Just like that?"

"Just like that."

Varno sucked in his little paunch, tapped his clipboard a few more times and said, "Don't let it get around . . . that I did this, okay? You swear?" Sarah held her ground. Shoving the clipboard under his arm, he trudged off, down the antiseptic-white corridor in the direction of the I.C.U.

Disregarding the directive to sit tight till she heard from the admitting office, Sarah began her long trek in Varno's wake. Dragging her way past two elderly men circling aimlessly in their wheelchairs, she opened her eyes wide. It didn't help. She was still too groggy to walk, let alone think straight, and kept losing her balance, brushing against the cool stucco walls.

The walk was endless, the dull aches and pains coursing through her body, reminding her at one point of Marlon Brando's ordeal careening up the gangplank in *On The Waterfront*. Battered and bruised, on the verge of passing out till he reached the loading docks and signaled the end of corrupt union rule.

Get off it, Sarah told herself. Focus. Do what you came for. Finish what you started.

When she finally reached the I.C.U., she held on to the counter at the nurses' station. Button-eyes stopped pecking at her keyboard, looked up and perused Sarah's face and body as if searching for a concealed weapon. At about the same time, Varno appeared out of nowhere at the opposite end, shaking his head.

"Like the nurse said, it's no use."

"The nurse is wrong."

"Now about your statement . . ."

This time Button-eyes gave both of them one of her patented looks.

"Later," said Sarah, trying to shoo Varno off.

Button-eyes settled her gaze on Sarah, apparently ready to issue a statement of her own.

"I need something now," said Varno lowering his voice.

Grabbing Varno's clipboard, snatching a pen from his pocket, she scribbled three directives: *Track down Doreen. Recover the money. Take it from there.* Slapping down the clipboard and pen, Sarah pushed off from the countertop.

"Can I get you a wheelchair?" said Button-eyes, employing the requisite half-whisper colored by her customary chilly but benign tone.

"No thanks," said Sarah disregarding both the nurse and Varno's retreating form.

Before Sarah could take another step forward, Button-eyes stood up and pressed her face through the glass partition. "I don't mind telling you how bizarre this is. I still have only one patient in the I.C.U. I never have just one. Then, at this ungodly hour, I have to deal with a stepbrother who pops in and out and a state trooper who follows suit and tells me to humor you. Need I remind you . . . "

"Excuse me," said Sarah moving past her.

". . . that just because we are short of staff," Button-eyes went on behind Sarah's back, "doesn't mean I won't take the necessary steps. Doctor will be by in less than—"

Apparently aware that she had been steadily raising her voice, Button-eyes cut off her soliloquy. Sarah walked on, starting to loose her nerve. What Varno had intimated was true. There was no way she could gloss this all over.

Regardless, Sarah kept moving, through the tinted glass doors, skirting past the empty bays on her left, straight to Katie's bed. Reflexively, she reached out for Katie's hand and held it. The hideous tube had been removed from her throat but she was still attached to the two monitors gauging her vital signs. Her eyes were closed, her impish face lifeless, her perky little body broken and spent.

"It's all resolved, kid," said Sarah, lying in her teeth. "You heard it from the horse's mouth. Just a hideous mistake."

No response. No other sound in the eerie greenish-white space save for the hissing of the air-conditioning and the drip of the i.v. bag dangling overhead.

"I know, I know, I'm late. But I kept in touch, right? Kept you posted."

Squeezing Katie's hand, Sarah said, "Okay, you want more facts? You got it. It seems Mark had to stop you from digging up some loot. Long story, some other time, huh?"

What now? She mustn't panic, that's the last thing Katie needed. Mustn't keep grasping at straws. At the same time, she couldn't really believe it had been for nothing. Even without any rhyme or reason to the world, it couldn't all come down to zero. Zippo. Zilch.

"So, you are absolved. Scout's honor, cross my heart."

Just then, a fidgety, balding M.D. with wire-rimmed glasses slipped through the glass doors and whisked to Sarah's side. Gesturing with both index fingers, he indicated that Sarah would have to leave immediately or else. Sarah nudged him away. The doctor glared at her in disbelief and hurried off.

"Okay," said Sarah, releasing Katie's hand. "It's not good, it's really awful. But I can't do it alone anymore. I can't make it, Katie. I never could."

The tears streamed down her cheeks, her sobbing echoed across the room. She wept for Katie, she wept for Tommy. She wept for the little St. Bernard. She cried for everything lost, forsaken and gone. She patted Katie's wrist, stuttering incoherently, begging for a signal, pleading for one tiny little sign that Katie would somehow pull through.

Desperate now, she looked directly up at the sterile white ceiling. "You know it's not fair. She's a believer. You have to give a believer a break. It's a rule."

Nothing. The same hollow emptiness prevailed. She cast about in her mind for another ploy, something she'd overlooked, something that could be postponed till tomorrow or another day. Anything to put off the fact that Katie was slipping away and Sarah's presence was beside the point.

When all the spirit drained out of her, Sarah slid down to the polished green tiles and laid her head by Katie's side under the slow drip of the i.v. In so doing, Sarah may have done more damage to her ribs, made it impossible to raise herself up from the floor. No matter. There was nothing left. It was over.

After a time, there was an imperceptible stir. Sarah held on to the side of the bed and pulled and tugged herself up. With a jolt, the sharp pains returned. There was no point in wishing any more, no point in hoping. But she pulled herself up anyway.

For an instant, Katie's eyelids seemed to flutter. Her lips pursed into the old familiar Cupid's-bow. Then all movement ceased.

"Oh no you don't, kiddo. You don't flicker like that and shut off. No way."

In that same moment, as some lethargic orderly came traipsing in, Katie's fingers began to twitch. As if she were a time traveler locating a switch that would return her in time to help a friend. She may have also been reaching for sunlight as she passed the chilly orbit of the moon.

About the

Author

Shelly Frome

Lilac Moon is by a seasoned veteran of the stage. As Associate Professor of Dramatic Arts at The University of Connecticut, Shelly Frome is certainly no stranger to the world of theater. Among his publications are *The Actors Studio* (2001), *Sun Dance for Andy Horn* (a novel) 1990, and *Playwriting* (1990). Mr. Frome is author of four plays: *Death in the Stacks*, *Last of the Good Guys*, *Sun Dance for Andy Horn*, and *Harlequin Jones*. In addition, he has written thirteen articles on acting and playwriting, and composed twenty-one plays, and nine dance/theatre pieces.